LP ROD *ME*
Roderus, Frank
The Keystone kid

*cc*

| DATE DUE | | | |
|---|---|---|---|
| 9/2015 | | | |
| | | | |
| | | | |
| | | | |
| | | | |
| | | | |
| | | | |
| | | | |
| | | | |
| | | | |
| | | | |

# THE KEYSTONE KID

## FRANK RODERUS

**WHEELER PUBLISHING**
*A part of Gale, Cengage Learning*

GALE
CENGAGE Learning·

Farmington Hills, Mich • San Francisco • New York • Waterville, Maine
Meriden, Conn • Mason, Ohio • Chicago

GALE
CENGAGE Learning

LIBRARY OF CONGRESS CATALOGING-IN-PUBLICATION DATA

Roderus, Frank, 1942–
    The Keystone Kid / by Frank Roderus. — Large print edition.
      pages ; cm. — (Wheeler Publishing large print western)
    ISBN-13: 978-1-4104-6791-1 (softcover)
    ISBN-10: 1-4104-6791-0 (softcover)
    1. Large type books. I. Title.
PS3568.O346K49 2014
813'.54—dc23                                          2014002870

Published in 2014 by arrangement with Hartline Literary Agency

Printed in the United States of America
1 2 3 4 5        18 17 16 15 14

*For my grandfathers*

# CHAPTER 1

I guess I'm the only one in the valley, or anyplace else for that matter, who knows all of it because, you see, I was right there from the very first moment the kid stepped off of that train. Now don't get me wrong here. I'm not trying to say I was smarter than anyone else or knew any of it ahead of time or planned on being there at that depot for any special reason. You see, at that time the TC&W spur had only been laid and in operation for six months or so and it was still a big enough novelty that most anyone in town just naturally headed for the depot when the courthouse clock showed 10 A.M. Jess had sent me in the day before for the month's supplies, which is why I happened to be on that platform when the short freight with its lone passenger car backed hissing and clanging to its daily stop at War-cry, which I personally have always thought is a silly name for a town where grown-up men and women make their homes.

Anyway, the kid was the last one off the passenger coach that day. Two drummers had gotten off ahead of him, smiling and nodding and bobbing their heads, their Adam's apples bouncing in and out of view thirstily behind the screen of high, hard, but not really fresh collars. They had been here before or maybe they hadn't, but in their own way they belonged, here or in any other town where they happened to be spending the night.

The kid, now. He would have stood out in any crowd. Tall and gawky, thin as a lodgepole. But not the rawhide kind of thin like you think of a bronc peeler being. This was a downright puny kind of thin. And pale. He was about the same shade as a fish's belly, with not even a freckle to give him color. The truth is, he had a soft, smooth complexion that any girl alive would have envied. No one was going to peg him as an outdoorsman of any sort. The color he lacked in his face he made up, in spades, with his hair. It was a dark, deep red. Auburn I think they call that color. Not a bit carroty but as red as anything ever could be.

It was his clothes, though, that really reached out and grabbed the attention. He couldn't have done a better job of that if he had personally gone to each and every man on that platform, grabbed him by the shirt front, and shook him like a terrier with a rat.

I don't expect anyone to believe what he was wearing, but here it is: Button-up, ankle-high shoes. Brass-riveted jeans so shiny new they must have been about as flexible as wearing stovepipe sections. These mostly hidden by Angora chaps so woolly they must have weighed more than he did. A glaringly yellow shirt of the flap-front variety with twin rows of buttons running up the front — and no pockets to mar all that loveliness. The buttons were Chinese red and matched the pattern of curly stitching at the front of the shoulders. They also matched the red silk kerchief knotted in a thin band around his neck. Crowning this gorgeous outfit was a hat. An especially lovely hat. Five-inch brim that was as flat as if it was freshly ironed and with a tall, four-dented Montana peak crown. It looked sort of like an overgrown cavalry compaign hat but bigger and altogether grander. It had a dainty little two-cord band around the crown in a matching fawn color.

He stepped out of the coach and stood for a moment at the head of the fold-down steps with a battered valise clutched in long, thin fingers. It was hard to tell with him being so pale anyway, but I believe his knuckles were white from holding the grip of that valise so tight.

He came into view and paused there and all conversation on the platform quit. Just like that. Quit cold, and all eyes were on that boy. He swallowed hard and his shoulders dipped a little. Not much. I would have been willing right then and there to wager that he was wanting to duck back inside that railroad coach and was keeping himself out there on public inspection only by a powerful force of will. His Adam's apple bobbed, too, but I didn't think it was with a drummer's thirst.

The kid squared his shoulders and hiked his chin into the air and drew himself up to all six-two or so of his frame and stepped down to the platform level. The loafers and the sightseers and the curious who were gathered there, me among them, remembered their manners and turned to whoever was nearest and began talking again, sneaking sideways glances at the kid but trying not to stare. But I'll bet an awful lot of fellows suffered eye strain that night from trying to peer out the corners of their eyes. And to give credit where it was due, there

10

was not a single outright, out-loud snicker or laugh heard on that platform. Not right off there wasn't, anyway, not while he was still there.

The youngster — I guessed his age at something like eighteen or nineteen — looked around him and seemed a bit confused. I don't know what he expected, but what he saw was an ordinary small town and a bunch of men in ordinary clothes, most wearing suits and vests and ties and a few of the loafers being so lazy and shiftless they left off their ties and collars. I don't know what else anyone could have expected. Unless, of course, this boy came from a farming community, which Warcry is not. They tell me farmers will go into town wearing their coveralls and work boots, which I would think would be a mighty slovenly way to be. Of course that is just what I have been told, and I guess even a cowman is prone to exaggeration from time to time. Anyway, the kid looked kind of confused in addition to looking so out of place. He turned to the nearest fellow — I disremember who — and asked something of him and got some finger-pointing directions toward the center of town. He clumped away, having to sort of bow his legs so he could walk with all that wool

11

between his knees, his valise bumping against the snowy slopes of those chaps. We all stood in an amazed and respectful silence and watched him out of sight.

"Now there goes a boy of rare and glorious courage," I told Handy Cauthorn, who was standing near me at the time.

"Do you think he could be a front man for some circus group or traveling show?"

"I haven't heard of any coming here. You?" Handy swung his head from side to side. "And he didn't have much baggage. You'd think a front man would be loaded down with posters and stuff." I shrugged and put the kid out of mind. "It doesn't concern me anyhow," I said, which just goes to show how wrong a fellow can be at times, "and I have work to do. I'll see you tonight at the Bull Shooter."

"Most likely."

I made my way back to Wiggins's store, where our heavy wagon was parked at the loading dock. Nothing had been added since I left, but then I hadn't expected anything to be. Wiggins and both his helpers had been on the platform too. And there was no big hurry about the loading. We had all day to do it as I wouldn't hitch the team to start home until morning. That way I could stay another night in town instead of stopping at the Barton place where the folks are friendly enough. I'm not complaining about that, mind. But any more the babble and yammer of all those kids just sort of gets to me and makes me nervous and irritable so that food doesn't sit right in my stomach.

I sat and smoked my pipe and watched while they loaded the hogsheads of wheat flour and kegs of sugar and molasses and hundred-pound sacks of dried beans and potatoes and onions and the crates of canned milk and canned fruits and sacked-up sides of smoked bacon and the five-gallon tin of coal oil and all the little things we would need. It was all checked off the list and the tarp lashed in place by the middle of the afternoon, which left me with some free time; so I sat on the dock and smoked and soaked up some sunshine, as it was still early enough in the spring for that warmth to feel good in my bones. And I don't believe I once thought about that kid the whole of the afternoon.

I had a light supper at Elsie's and went back to the hotel so I could change to a clean shirt and shave, which I prefer to do in the evening when my work is done and the time is my own. I dried the lather from under my ears and slicked my hair back and took a brush to my coat and hat and figured I was ready for whatever came.

The Bull Shooter is on the north end of town near where the depot is now and the new shipping pens, empty this time of year but close enough to hear the bawling of the young steers when the cattle cars are running. There is a big picture on the front of the place instead of a name sign. It shows a chunky shorthorn bull with a pistol aimed at him and flame drawn around the muzzle of the gun. What makes the picture so remarkable is the way that bull is hung.

They say that back when Dodge City, Kansas, was wild and woolly and just starting to clean itself up so decent folk could live there, a bunch of do-gooding women objected to the picture of a bull on one of the saloons and made the owner turn that bull into a steer so the ladies would not be offended. Some of the men in Warcry got to talking about that one night and decided they sure would never be trompled by the opinion of their womenfolk, by God, and to prove it they dragged out a ladder and some paint and gave our bull a pair of seeds like watermelons. If they'd been real, you could have cut him and held a Rocky Mountain oyster fry for the whole volunteer fire company off that one bull alone. Which came to mind, I guess, because the Warcry fire company's annual oyster fry would be coming up in a few more weeks. Our spring branding was almost finished and would be all done soon, and the oysters were packed into buckets in the icehouse ready for the big date.

It wasn't quite dark yet but the Bull Shooter was beginning to fill up with men from the town and some from the close-in places, people who could take a fresh horse and make it to town and back in the one evening, which none of us from the south end of the valley could do. Jules Sidlow made room for me at a table near the bar and dragged a chair over, and I made myself comfortable and got my pipe stoked amid the good-natured grumbling of the younger fellows. I never have understood where that joke comes from. That old pipe of mine doesn't smell at all bad that I can tell.

Hiram brought a tray of foaming mugs to the table and we shot the bull awhile. Nothing important. Just slow, comfortable, quiet talk of the kind that relaxes and enriches a man. Bill Dean's mare Flame had a colt on the ground that looked like it might make a stallion prospect. Jule's boy Tommy had written home to say his grades were all right and, no, he was doing fine and didn't need

15

more money. One of the Barton kids had had a flux of some kind and Doc'd had to drive out there but it didn't seem to be anything serious.

We passed a couple hours that way and the place was pretty full, seeming almost to have a life of its own, the low hum of many conversations washing through a body like the purring of a contented old barn cat.

About nine o'clock that kid came in. He stood in the doorway for a moment as if he couldn't decide if he was welcome or not. Whatever he was thinking, he came the rest of the way in and found a place for himself at the wall end of the long bar. There was no way he could keep himself from being conspicuous, but that was about as close to it as he could get. All the tables had someone at them.

The kid was dressed the way he had been when he arrived, but he had taken off the Angora chaps. He was carrying them draped over the valise, which he set next to the wall by his feet.

Hiram went to take his order and the kid dug into his pocket for change before he made his request. He got a beer and paid for it right away and when a spot opened next to him sidled closer to the free-lunch stuff spread along that end of the bar.

I guess most everyone had already done their talking about the kid — I know our table had — for he didn't cause near so much quiet disruption as at the train station. And aside from what he was wearing the kid was not doing anything to cause a fuss. He wasn't trying to butt into anyone's conversations and seemed to be giving most of his attention to the cold ham and hard-boiled eggs and soda crackers on the counter.

Wayne Tynell came in a half hour or so later. By then the kid was on maybe his second beer and his second platter of ham. It was no trick to see that Wayne had been hitting someone's jug before he ever set foot in the Bull Shooter that night.

I suppose if I were a respectable and proper sort of gentleman I would refrain from making any comments about Wayne Tynell. But I am not, and it is my personal and totally biased opinion that Wayne is a spoiled, cantankerous, sulky, miserable, overprotected, wet-eared, sorry little son of a bitch. Which I say with apologies to Mrs. Tynell, who is a very nice lady. It is her husband and her son that I can't abide.

Perhaps I should say right now, too, that this is not a brand-new opinion. I haven't had any use for Warren Tynell for nearly twenty years, since the first time I saw him working roundup and watched him bring his horse in dripping blood at the mouth and shoulders day after day. Once in a while that sort of thing might be necessary, but not every day. And the boy grew into the image of his pappy. Hard-handed and big-mouthed and never a thought for any living thing but themselves, dumb animal or human being either one. It did not make things any better that they were neighbors, their place lying just to the east of ours at the southern end of the valley. At least for the years recently past I hadn't been out where I would run into them while doing line riding or something. That was one good thing, at least.

So, yes, I am prejudiced against the Tynells and will admit to it before anyone accuses me of it. It is naturally so, that's all.

Anyhow, Wayne walked in swinging his shoulders and puffing his chest and took one look at this odd kid at the bar, and the idiot stopped short and started pointing his finger and honking with laughter, practically in the kid's face. I guess he had not been in town long enough to get any forewarning, but I thought it a damned cruel thing to do.

Wayne grinned like a possum eating and

18

hooked his thumbs behind his belt and swaggered over to the bar. He took the space between the kid and the wall and called for a whiskey in a voice loud enough for everyone in the place to hear. The kid was already so embarrassed I thought his red silk neckerchief was going to be lost to view.

Wayne knocked his drink back in a hurry and called for another. He pretended to stumble and gave the kid's valise a solid kick. He turned to face the room — I guess most everybody was watching him anyway as we all knew how unpredictable he is — and registered great shock and surprise on that square-jawed, handsome face of his.

"What have we here?" he cried. He stooped and picked up the kid's Angora chaps. "Is there a lamb rustler in the place?"

He held the chaps before him and did a little pirouette on his toes and recited the Mary-had-a-little-lamb children's rhyme in a falsetto voice. He got a few laughs from some of the younger and maybe drunker fools in the place, and that seemed to encourage him. If he had shut up then, things might have been different. But not Wayne. He had to push it some more.

He wadded the woollies into one big hand — no mean feat, that — and jammed them hard into the kid's belly. The impact nearly doubled the skinny kid over on himself. "Yours?" Wayne asked in a superior tone.

"They are mine," the kid said. His voice was far from loud but it could be heard clearly. There wasn't another sound in the Bull Shooter just then. The kid's voice was calm and mild. If he was scared, and he should have been, for Wayne Tynell was twice his size, it did not show there.

Wayne took a half step backward and made a big show of staring at the kid from his toes to the crown of his hat. Wayne bent close to examine the chaps again. "Whoowee!" he said. "You sure must ride the range hard, podner, in awful cold country, yes sir. Where you from, podner?" His drawl was like a stage parody of a cowman's speech.

The kid stood clutching his chaps to his belly. He still had half a soda cracker in his other hand. He popped the cracker into his mouth and chewed on it, his eyes — a dark, dark shade of blue, I noticed — fixed on Tynell.

"I asked you where you *from,* podner," Wayne demanded. His tone had turned sullen and ugly. I glanced around the room and I think that even those few who were his buddies were not so ready to laugh now.

"Pennsylvania," the kid said. He wiped cracker crumbs from his lips and gave his attention to the chaps. He shook them out, straightened them and carefully folded them across his left forearm. He stepped around Tynell and bent to lay the fuzzy chaps on his valise.

Wayne grabbed him roughly by the arm. You could see the power Tynell put in it. His plate-sized hand wrapped around the kid's upper arm and he was squeezing hard when he jerked the kid erect. "I wasn't through talking to you," he snarled.

"I answered your question," the kid said. He must have been hurting but he didn't let it show. This was a boy who had a whole lot of control over himself, and I had to admire him. No matter how funny he dressed he was entitled to that much.

Wayne began to shake him. "You tryin' to insult me, Keystone State boy? Huh?"

"No."

Tynell was shaking him so hard the kid's hat tumbled to the floor.

"You figure you're so tough you can insult me and get away with it? You think you're bad, huh? What do they call you, huh? The Keystone Kid? Yeah, I bet that's your handle. The Keystone Kid." Tynell flung him against the wall. The kid's head cracked against the wall and he looked a bit rubber-legged. He was trembling now, glancing at the men nearest him although he did not ask them for help.

Wayne moved closer and poked him in the chest and again in the stomach with stiffened fingers. The kid's face went as white as a piece of carved chalk. Tynell poked him again, a short, vicious little stab of the knuckles into the kid's stomach. The kid gasped and doubled over.

He straightened and fish-mouthed for air. He looked at Wayne and shook his head. "I won't fight you, mister," he said. "Everyone here knows you could beat me. You don't have to prove it."

"What's this? The Keystone Kid is yellow? I don't believe it." Wayne reached forward and began methodically slapping him in the face, back and forth, one side and then the other, the slaps coming slowly and with plenty of time between them.

The kid made no attempt to fight back. He closed his eyes and stood trembling with his back braced against the wall. Most of the older men in the room turned their eyes away rather than watch this humiliation.

Me, well, I don't like Wayne Tynell anyway. And he'd already proved the kid a coward if that was what he wanted. I figured that was more than enough. I levered myself to my feet and made my way over to them.

Wayne was still slapping at the kid and of all the silly things, *he* was the one who was getting madder and madder as the blows continued and still the kid didn't do anything except stand there, stiff, with his eyes closed.

I grabbed Wayne's wrist and told him, "Enough," and he shook his hand free and slapped the kid again. I grabbed at Wayne again and he lashed out backhanded and sent me sprawling onto the plank floor.

Well, I have been blessed with some pretty good friends, and I don't think I'd more than hit the floor before a bunch of them were there, half of them helping me up and the other half squaring their shoulders and giving Wayne some ugly looks. To give the devil his due, I don't believe Tynell had realized what he was doing there before his hand had been moving, for when he saw me on the floor he sort of blanched and began mumbling explanations that no one was interested in hearing. When he saw the kind of looks he was getting, he ducked his head and hurried out of the place, forgetting to pay Hiram before he went.

The kid was still against the wall, the only change in him being that his eyes were open now. There were bright red blotches on the pale white of his cheeks and there was more, brighter red at the corners of his mouth where some blood was seeping out. He swallowed, and I well remembered the salt-copper taste he would be knowing right then. He looked, though, more curious than shamed, and I regarded that as an odd thing. No one else seemed to be paying him any mind, I noticed, and I could understand how they would feel embarrassed for him since he did not seem to have sense enough to feel it for himself.

As for what I did next, I would like to take credit for being overcome by humanitarian impulses, but the truth is that I didn't much feel like having people fussing over me and being solicitous and trying to be helpful, so I gave my friends a hurried thank-you and gave the kid a follow-me sign to get him out of their hair too and left the Bull Shooter for the cool air and the darkness outside.

# CHAPTER 2

I went back to the hotel, the kid trailing along behind with his valise and his chaps, and took a seat in one of the rockers on the front porch. It was pleasant there, the air smelling fresh and clean and a spill of yellow light making bold diagonal patterns on the flooring. The kid piled his stuff on one of the empty chairs and pulled another next to mine. There was no one else on the porch; at this hour everyone would either be abed or cozied up in one of the few saloons in town, the others being one right inside at the hotel — which catered to commercial travelers and those who fancied themselves as belonging in the upper crust of the Warcry pie — and a coupla low type dives frequented by the rowdier elements and some railroaders and transients and such. The Bull Shooter was pretty much the property of stockmen and cowhands and the like.

"Thank you," the kid said when he was seated. "It was awfully good of you to try to help."

"Sure," I grunted, and I guess I was a bit short with him, but the way he'd put that kind of got my dander up. After all, I hadn't just *tried* to help him. I'd done it. More than he had done for himself.

But I regretted it almost as soon as the grunt was out of my throat. If I was going to feel peevish now, there was no point in taking it out on the kid. And whatever purpose he had in coming here, it was certain he was not visiting friends. He didn't have a friend in the town and little likelihood of making any. I sighed to myself and prepared to do my duty as an elder statesman as a way of trying to make amends, though to him or to myself I was not certain.

I stuck out a hand for him to shake and told him my name and waited for his.

The kid opened his mouth to speak and hesitated and all of a sudden flashed me a smile. He made a soft, bubbling sound and in a moment I realized he was kind of chuckling, though for his own benefit, not mine. "The Keystone Kid," he said. I noticed that he said it with amusement, without a hint of bitterness of tone or expression. If he hadn't just made such a fool of himself, showing himself as a coward, I would have really liked that.

Either way though, bitterly or gaily, if he wanted the name to stick it was all right by me. I have known a number of men who would turn their heads from old habit when someone else's name was called, and I never knew it to make any difference to me nor to anyone else around here. It was what happened here that counted and not what a man — or a woman — had been somewhere else, not the good or the bad of it. The kid might have been a saint or a circus strongman somewhere else. But now he had already begun to build himself a reputation in Warcry. It was not one I would have envied, but he was entitled to it.

I grunted again and nodded and commented on the weather and he said yes, it was awful nice all right. Which pretty well wrapped up all we had in common. We walked under the same sky, breathing the same air, and that was just about that. Logically I suppose I should have said good night and gone in to bed but I've always been one to save scraps for stray dogs and carry orphaned calves in for bottle feeding, and I guess I am past being able to change my ways.

I cleared my throat and nodded toward

his valise and chaps and said, "There's probably rooms available inside yet. If you were looking for one, that is."

He gave me a quick, embarrassed little look and shook his head. "I'm not looking for a room. Thanks anyway."

I cocked an eyebrow at him and kept remembering that the Easterners I had met before didn't seem to think a thing wrong with asking or answering all sorts of questions that here a man might consider personal and private and worth fighting over should anyone pry where he had no business. "Where're you staying the night, Kid?"

He didn't seem to take any offense at all. He shrugged and smiled and said, "I thought I'd just wander around some and see what the town is like at night. I slept a lot on the train." Which had to be a lie. I'd taken a joy ride on that spur when they opened it, and they had done a lousy job of preparing that roadbed. No sober man was likely to be sleeping along that stretch.

"Oh?" I asked skeptically. I put my best, beady-eyed stare on him and waited. In a moment he smiled again and gave in to the truth.

"I'm looking for a job," he said. "Until then I can't afford a room."

"Uh-huh." That sounded more like it,

28

especially when I considered how he had set about making holes in Hiram's free-lunch offerings. He couldn't even afford the price of a meal. I pushed myself to my feet, feeling the effects of the hour and of that tumble I'd taken in the Bull Shooter. At least the kid had sense enough to leave me alone while I was doing it and not jump in unasked with help I didn't want. "Come on then," I told him. "You can bunk in my room for tonight."

He wasn't stiff-necked with pride, which I guess he had proven earlier anyhow. He jumped to his feet and grabbed up his things and said, "Yes, sir."

I was awake at four as usual and sat on the side of the bed in the unfamiliar surroundings of the dark hotel room. I took a minute to get my bearings on where I was and fumbled cautiously on the bedside stand to find the box of matches and scratched one alight. I turned the wick back on the tiny little room-for-hire lamp until I got an almost adequate butterfly of flame and could see somewhat in the dim light.

The kid was breathing deep and regular from a far place down in his sleep. Until I saw him there, I had forgotten about him. He looked awfully young and nearly as white as the sheet with only that bright patch of red hair showing any real color. I thought about letting him sleep and decided I better not. But I almost had to. He did not give up his sleep easily. Not that he was grumpy about it. Just hard to reach away down there. I finally had to shake him awake.

"Huh?" He was bleary-eyed and blinking.

"Come on, Kid. Time to roll out."

"Whazit? G'way." He tried to burrow back into his pillow. I stripped the blanket back and yanked the pillow away quick enough that his head bounced a few times. He sat up then and seemed more aware of what was going on. "Yes, sir." He blinked a few more times and looked around. "Hey, it's still dark out."

"Of course. Happens this way every morning until the sun comes up. Check it as often as you like. You'll see that I'm right." I put my hat on and shirt and pants and began the struggle to get into my boots. "Are you coming?"

"Yes, sir." He got dressed, shirt and pants and shoes, and his hat last. "All set," he said when he was done.

"Uh-huh." I picked up my war bag and waved toward his valise. "Get your stuff then."

"Yes, sir." He picked it up. He looked right curious, but he didn't ask where we were going.

I opened the door to the hall and made sure there was a lamp burning out there before I blew out the light in the room. "Come on."

I showed him the way out back and we made a stop there and then went over to Wiggins's store, where the big wagon was parked. There were no town people on the streets at this hour. I put my war bag on the floor of the driving box and told him he could leave his stuff there if he liked.

He looked around the dark, deserted town as if he expected to find someone peering at us from in hiding. I shivered a little in the morning chill and wished I had brought a heavier coat.

"Do you think anyone . . . I mean, do you think it will be all right here?"

"Sure am glad I'm not from Pennsylvania, Kid. It must be awful to have neighbors you can't trust." The kid looked properly chagrined. He put his stuff on the floor of the box beside mine.

We went over to Elsie's and even though it was coming on four-thirty by then, there was no light showing in the front window. I rapped on the glass and rattled the door

31

and pretty soon there was a glow of light from the back room. Elsie's voice reached us through the closed door. "Okay, okay!" I opened the door and we went inside.

Elsie stuck her head through the doorway from her living quarters at the back. She gave us a cheerful wave and said, "Hidee. I shoulda guessed it was you. Get the fire and the lights going while you wait. I'll be out in a sec." She popped back out of sight but left the door open so we would have enough light to find her lamps. I handed the kid a box of matches and told him to get the lamps while I got the big cooking range to heating.

Elsie had her wood laid and ready so all I had to do was touch it off and feed in some bigger pieces as they were needed. I checked to see that the hot-water reservoir was filled — it was — and pumped fresh water into the big coffeepot so it could start heating. By the time Elsie was dressed and out front, her range was about ready for use. She inspected it carefully and used a poker to rearrange some of the burning chunks to her liking before she turned to us.

"Sit down, boys; sit down. What'll it be this morning?"

I am more comfortable in a chair than on a stool and so took a table near the end of the counter where she could reach us easily. "Beef, lovely lady," I said. She is fat and homely and friendly and very dear and knows good and well that I like her and would not make fun of her for anything in this world. "And as many fried eggs as you can carry, and some fried potatoes since the oven won't be ready for biscuits for a while yet."

"There's peach pie if you don't mind leftover from yesterday's baking."

"And some peach pie, by all means."

She got busy and soon produced several loaded platters, which I did my share to empty while the kid did more than his share, and we topped it off with pie and coffee. By the time we were finished, Handy Cauthorn and Billy Kaye had come in, and Elsie was busy with their orders. I was in no particular hurry, so I leaned back in my chair and let the kid fetch refills on the coffee.

"With an appetite like that," I told him, "you'd best find a job soon. What kind of work are you looking for?"

He ducked his eyes at first but brought them back up to meet mine before he answered. "I want to be a cowboy," he said. I could not say that I was paralyzed by the shock and surprise of it, considering the way he was dressed.

"Uh-huh. Could you use a piece of advice then?" He nodded. "All right. Don't go asking anybody for a job as a cowboy, then. There isn't any such job."

"Sir?"

"Kid, there's no such thing as a cowboy this side of the Mississippi River." He looked like I had just stolen his favorite toy, so I hastened to explain. "There's lots of cow*hands,* who do the working with beeves. And there are cow*men,* who own those beeves and hire the cowhands. Or the waddies, which you don't hear much any more. Or the cowpunchers, which you do hear nowadays, though when I was a kid, a cowpuncher was someone who rode the cattle cars and used prods to keep the beasts on their feet and might not know a thing about how to work cattle outside of a closed little pen. But, Kid, there just ain't any such thing as a cow*boy.* Do you ask for a cowboying job, you will just be telling the boss that you don't know a thing about it."

"Oh," he said in a very small voice.

"I suppose it's a silly question, but I don't suppose you've ever worked around beeves before?"

"No sir, not exactly, but the . . . the place where I came from had some milk cows,

34

and I liked them just fine."

"Uh-huh." That was about what I'd expected. I buried my nose in my coffee cup and did some thinking. But hell, what else could I do? If somebody didn't take this kid in — and that was surely unlikely after the performance he'd put on the night before — he would starve to death or something. And if he couldn't pay for a meal, he sure couldn't take a train for home. So what choice did I have?

"Look, Kid, you aren't likely to get a riding job until you learn a little something about it. As a matter of fact, once you do learn about it, you might not *want* a riding job. In the meantime, I can take you on as a cook's helper out at our place. The boss has been looking for one, and if I say so they'll hire you. Twenty-five a month and keep. What do you say?"

He didn't need any time at all to say, "I'll take it." He thought for a moment and added, "What about the cook? Do you think I'll be able to get along with him?"

"I sure hope so, Kid. I'm him."

"Oh." He didn't say anything more but I could see his estimation of me going down, just like that. I don't know what he had taken me for, but I guess that wasn't it. And it was easy to see that an apprenticeship to

a cook was not his idea of glowing opportunity. Well, I can't say that cooking was
my fondest dream either, but it has its com-
pensations.

"Come on, Kid," I told him. "Now that
you're on the payroll, let's put you to work
and see if you can hitch a four-horse team.
We have lots to do today."

He grinned. "That much I can do, boss."

He could, and did, and we were rolling by
daylight. We had a heavy load and thirty-
five miles to go, and I was expected home
in time to fix the evening meal before the
crew got spoiled from having too many of
Mrs. Senn's and Katy's meals and threw
me out of the job.

# CHAPTER 3

I stopped five miles out of town at Ransom Creek, named for Leroy Ransom who had taken up land upstream and not from any sort of criminal activity the way most strangers seem to assume, so I could let the horses blow and have some more talk with the kid.

"Would you mind a few questions and maybe some suggestions, Kid?"

"No, sir. I'd appreciate any advice you could give me."

"In that case, would you mind telling me where you got those clothes you're wearing?"

He got a hangdog and rather painful look about him.

"You don't have to tell me if you don't want."

"I guess I don't mind all that much. I was . . . well . . . I got them from a fella, a cowboy he said he was, working in a Wild

West show in Philadelphia. He told me . . . well . . . that all the cowboys dressed like this. And I'd need a proper outfit if I was to get a job out West." He shrugged and grinned. "From all the cowboys I'd ever seen and from the covers of the dime novels, I just figured he was telling me the truth."

"He set you back pretty hard for those duds, did he?"

His boyish grin got even bigger. "Twenty dollars. He said they were worth more but he had others. And he wanted me to be able to land a job right off and not look out of place when I got here."

"If you learned anything from that, I guess the lesson was cheap at the price, Kid. But I think you'll find that most folks are just folks, wherever you go. Actors and costumes belong on stages or under tents."

"Yes sir," he said dispiritedly. He got a stricken look to him. "Surely though . . . the Wild Indians . . ."

I shook my head. This sure wasn't his day for seeing dreams come true, and I really felt sorry for him. "There aren't any wild Indians, Kid. Haven't been for years. Why, you probably saw hundreds of Indians, dozens anyway, around the train stations on your way out here. Nowadays they mostly live on their reservations, but they don't have to if they'd rather go into business or something somewhere else. And they dress, eat, laugh, scratch, get married, and tickle their babies' bellies the same as the rest of us."

"Oh." Again that weak, sad voice.

"How'd you come to be here anyway, Kid? This never was much for being wild and woolly or Indian-infested country, even back when the Indians were loose and hostile."

"Well, you see, this was as far as my savings would take me. And with a name like Warcry . . ." His voice trailed away.

I slapped him on the back. "Cheer up, Kid. At least you got into the real, live, cattle country. That's what this valley is, you know. One big old beef-making machine, powered by grass and water and the sweat of men and horses. If you want to learn about the business of being a cowhand, this is a good place to do it."

He did look cheered then. "Do you think I could learn?"

"Don't know why not. Even fellows born to the job had to learn it sometime, and you needn't feel too bad. I've never known a cowman yet who had time to learn it all before he died. You just have some catching up to do. That's all."

He was smiling again, if only tentatively.

"This place where we'll be working. Is it near any ranches? Real ones, I mean? With cowhands and everything?"

"Hell, Kid, it *is* a ranch. The biggest and the best in the south of the valley, which is to say it's the best in the whole valley. Didn't I tell you that, Kid? This is cow country around here."

He was grinning broadly now. "A real ranch, then. And cowboys . . . cowhands, that is. And a bunkhouse?" I nodded. "And horses?"

"Lots of horses," I assured him.

He was practically jumping up and down on the seat he was so eager. "I can't hardly wait to get there," he said.

"I think you're going to have to," I told him. "We've got thirty miles to go yet. All the way down to the right of that notch you can see in the mountains down there. Right at the foot of them. See it?" He nodded obediently when I pointed. "But that will take a while. Besides, I've asked my questions, but I still have those suggestions to make. If you'd like to make life a little easier for yourself when you meet the boys, that is."

"Yes sir, I would. I was . . . sort of embarrassed when I got off that train yesterday."

"All right. First thing then is for you to

take off your clothes. Right down to your drawers."

"But . . ." He hesitated. Looked around.

"Aw, there's no one around here to see. That's why I picked this place."

"Okay," he said, but he didn't sound at all certain. He climbed down to the ground and took them off.

"Empty your pants pockets." He did. He had a few coins in one pocket. A broken stub of comb in another. Nothing else. "No pocketknife?" He shook his head. "You'll have to get one out of your first pay. A man can't work stock without a good knife. Use it twenty times a day probably and never realize how much you need it until someday you lose it or forget it somewhere. Remember that and get one the first chance you have." He nodded, just as serious as he could be.

"Now throw your shirt and pants in that creek and tromple them some underfoot." He gave me a look that plainly said I had lost my mind. But he did what he was told. When he was done, I told him, "Good. Now throw the pants down in the road in front of the team."

He did, and I drove the team forward, backed them, eased them forward again and backed them to where they had been. "You

41

can put your pants back on now. It won't hurt you to let them dry in place, and you gotta be decent in case we pass any women-folk." He shuddered a bit, but he did it.

"Fine. Now wallow your shirt in the dirt a little. You can spread it on the tarp to dry." I hoped it wouldn't be quite so glaringly yellow when it was dry and dirty.

"Now for the most important part, Kid. Take that pretty hat of yours and hold it under water until I holler whoa."

This time I'm sure he thought I was completely round the old bend. But he did it. I gave it plenty of time while he stood in the middle of Ransom Creek. "If it's any easier you can stand on the brim," I sug-gested. I'll bet his feet felt like blocks of solid ice by the time I let him out of that snow-melt water. "Now bring it to me. And hand me that scarf, too, please."

I punched that peaked cavalry crease out and gave the crown a slash of the hand on top and a pinch of the fingers on the sides so it would have a more normal shape to it. The silk scarf I spread across my lap and set the hat onto it. I pulled up the corners of the neckerchief to draw the hat brim into a curl, narrowing toward the front, and tied the scarf like that.

"There. When that soggy mess dries out it

will hold its shape as good as if it'd been done at the factory." I laid the hat on the seat beside me. "Put your shoes on, Kid, and let's go. We're wasting time."

"Are you . . . ?"

"I'm sure. Don't worry about it."

"If you say so."

"I do. Oh, yeah. One more thing. When we get home, everyone will be out working. Hide those Angora chaps. Hang on to them if you want. You might need them one of these days. But I'd suggest you shave them or shear them or something before they're seen in public again."

"Yes, sir." It was a very subdued kid who rode the rest of the way home with me.

It was a coupla hours and ten miles further down the road — with his shirt back on and some of his dignity restored — before he said much of anything. When he did he was again hesitant. But curious. I guess really I had been expecting the question. Not looking forward to it. But expecting it. For a while before he spoke he had been giving me side-angle glances and working up the nerve for it.

"Would you mind if I asked you something? Something personal, I mean?"

Hell, he was going to hear it anyway. It might as well be from me as from anyone else. And I knew for certain sure what this eastern boy was going to barge in and ask right out loud. The only surprise was that the kid had the nerve to ask it.

"It's about . . . well . . . I was wondering what happened to you. I mean . . . have you always been that way?"

I guess I was feeling a bit bitter and grumpy about it myself by then, remembering it anew as if I didn't already get reminders each and every day. So I was more blunt about it than I might have been and set the kid somewhat aback. "What you are asking is, have I always been a gimped-up old cripple?" I stared down at my twisted left leg and withered arm. "The answer is no. I haven't always been this way."

"Look, I'm sorry. I didn't . . ."

"It's all right," I interrupted. "You answered my questions. You're entitled to an answer for yours." I loaded my pipe and was conscious for the first time in quite a long while of how awkward the procedure might look to a stranger, though really I have gotten so used to it that I no longer notice it myself. I still have the use of my left hand and all that. It just isn't real strong, and I can't straighten the arm or move it much so I have to place things down to the hand instead of reaching for them.

"What happened was that I used to be a cowhand," I told the kid. A top hand, though he wouldn't have known what I meant by that if I told him. "And a bronc peeler. I topped off the rough string before the spring and fall roundups and worked cows the rest of the time." I shrugged. "Seven years ago I still thought I was salty enough for the broncs. I was wrong. Stayed on one of them one jump too many, and he fell on me. Rolled and wallered around some. And since then I've learned how to cook. More or less."

Which was it in a nutshell. Nearly forty-five years in the saddle, ever since I was a button of a kid, and now fit for nothing better than stoking a stove or holding down the seat of a wagon.

Yet I was plenty lucky at that. If that blockheaded Appaloosa stag had gotten me with the saddle horn that day, I'd have had grass roots in my hair all this time. And George Senn. If he hadn't been the kind of good-hearted man he was, I would've been limping around some town looking for handouts and odd chores instead of staying on at a place where I could earn my keep. A lot of fellows end their days stove-up and useless. I had a job. So I really didn't have a thing to complain about and a power of things to be thankful for.

And I sure had a lot of good memories. Most of them from right here in this valley, from the day almost twenty-five years ago when old Fred Resnick and us in his crew trailed a herd of stock cows in the hard way, through Arawan Pass, and took up land at the south of the valley. I chuckled to myself. Nowadays everyone tells of how smart Fred was to take the pass rather than go around and get the herd caught in the unseasonal floods that year. The ones that took more than two hundred head from a herd being brought into the north of the valley. The truth is that we were totally green about this country. We just didn't know any other way in.

Fred died, good Lord, sixteen years now it had been, and George Senn bought the FR-Connected Bar from his estate. Range, buildings, cows, and the whole caboodle, including most of the crew, including me, and George had been as square a man to deal with as Fred, and no man can say better than that. And I do ramble on at times, which is exactly what I was doing just then.

The kid was sitting quiet and polite, maybe thinking I was mad at him or maybe just not wanting to intrude any deeper into my memories. But hell, that shouldn't often be an unwelcome intrusion for there are so many more that are joyous than are painful. Even the thought of that liver-colored Appaloosa isn't so much painful as it is a reminder that I was just stupid and slow that day. If I didn't know enough to know when I should turn loose of him and swallow some dust, I had no business being on him in the first place. And that day I didn't, though I certainly should have known better.

Anyway, I gave the kid a smile and said, "So I'm not completely ignorant when I tell you about cowhands and how to work a cow critter. Pay attention, Kid, and you might learn something."

He said, "Yes, sir," and seemed a little cheered, but he still was mostly quiet the rest of the way home.

I stopped to rest the horses a mile or so from headquarters and then took that lumbering team of big-hoofed drafters up the shortcut the boys use when they are hurrying toward town to do some helling or are hurrying home to get there in time for breakfast. There is a proper road up to the cluster of buildings at the headquarters place. It follows a year-round stream that comes right down through the place, providing us with a steady supply of live water in

47

the corrals and irrigation for the big garden. But I wanted the kid to see the place all at once and so took him over top of the last little foothill rise.

The big horses made it to the top with their shoes a-popping into the dirt and their nostrils flaring, and the FR-Connected Bar was laid out below us a few hundred yards away.

Lordy, but that is one pretty place. The big old main house two stories high, built of logs by Fred and his missus but now long since added to with wings to each side, sheathed with planking and painted white and a long porch added across the front with white supports spaced every so often. And the fast-running stream bubbling behind the house.

Upstream is the long, low bunkhouse built of logs also and with white chinking. The cookhouse with the long dining room and kitchen and the lean-to summer kitchen behind it — and my bedroom, separate and private in that building. Also a storehouse, ice house, and root cellar behind my cook building.

Right behind the main house, across a footbridge, are the laundry and some storage buildings. Downstream from those the blacksmith and tool shed, and below those the huge hay barns and low machine and wagon shed. Further down are the horse corrals and, away from the creek, the breaking pens. That put the horses too far from the bunkhouse for easy handling, but George had moved the corrals downstream from the big house first thing after he bought the place. They had been above the house, across the creek from the bunkhouse. Some of the boys insisted they could taste a difference in the water after those corrals were moved, but I think that was all in their heads. That water was clean. And fast moving.

All of this was set in what was left of a cottonwood grove. Much of the timber had been cut down to make room for the buildings, but the oldest and grandest trees had been left, along with a good many younger and shapelier trees, to insure against the place being bare when those old-timers turned silver and died.

Like I said, it is some beautiful sight.

"There it is, Kid. The FR-Connected Bar. Home."

He wasn't talking just then, though. Or maybe even hearing. His eyes were wide and there was pure delight in them, glowing out from somewhere deep inside. From the place where he kept his dreams, I would've

49

bet, for that's the way the place has always struck me, too.

The kid raised his eyes along the flow of the stream, to the towering, awesome weight of the mountain beyond. It hangs there in green and blue and gray jagged beauty, so near it is a part of the place even though there are seventeen miles of rising hills between the headquarters and the near flank of the mountain proper. This time of year there were still broad fields of white near the top, like sugar coating on a confection.

He turned to look downstream, eyes alight with the beauty of it, and saw the rolling green of new grass. From up here we could see five miles or so, all of it grass with scarcely a scar made by road or darker green streambed growth, and over it all the intense, clear blue of an unmarred sky.

The kid shook himself as if a cold chill, perhaps of excitement, had come over him, and a slow smile took possession of his lips.

I grinned at him. "Yeah. It is, isn't it?" He gave me a startled look. "Unwrap your hat and put it on, Kid," I said, signaling the horses to ease ahead until the breeching straps put the weight of the big wagon against their broad rumps. "Let's go home."

# CHAPTER 4

The kid was skinny and not very strong, but I could not fault him on willingness. I pulled the wagon around behind the cookhouse, between the kitchen with its big storeroom pantry and the root cellar so the stuff could be sent in both directions, and he got right to work with the unloading. He had a devil of a time with the barrels of flour, but at least they would roll. It was the big, hundredweight sacks that were so funny to watch. He draped them over both shoulders and his bowed neck so that he looked like a mushroom cap atop a toothpick and he walked bandy legged and staggering. But he got it done.

He had shucked out of his hat and shirt and was running sweat before he was done. By around three o'clock, though, the last box had been unloaded and the last items stowed where I found them handiest to be.

"Take a breather, Kid," I told him, and he

was not long in flopping to a seat on the stool I use when doing the busywork that keeps a person in one spot for a while. I took one of the wooden crates we'd just unpacked and plunked it onto the big worktable in the middle of my kitchen. I began piling into it the things Mrs. Senn had asked me to bring from town and some others that I figured she would want for the house kitchen.

"Grab your shirt and hat, Kid. It's time you meet some of the family you're working for."

He pulled his shirt over his head but didn't bother to tuck it into his britches. He set the hat — much improved in appearance now — on his head and hefted the crate onto his shoulder. "I'm ready," he said.

He followed me to the rear of the big house. I gave one sharp rap of my knuckles against the doorjamb while I held the door for him to go through with the box. The kid was sort of a mess. His face was flushed nearly red enough to match his hair and it was running sweat. His shirt, plenty dirty, was hanging out over those mud-streaked new jeans. With the sweat plastering his clothes against his skin in so many places, he looked like a fence post with wet laundry draped on it. I motioned toward the family

52

eating table and the kid set the heavy box on it, careful to set it down gently so he would not scratch the polished oak surface.

"Natalie?" I called through the doorway into the rest of the house.

"Just a minute." Her voice came floating to us, thin and insubstantial, from somewhere in the upstairs part of the house. The kid swept his hat off and held it nervously before him, both hands clamped on the wide brim I had so carefully shaped and that he now threatened to ruin.

A moment later her footsteps clattered down the back stairway that came direct into the kitchen. She was wearing an oversized, bib-top apron over her everyday dress. And a warm smile. Natalie Senn was a plumply pretty woman with gray beginning to streak her brown hair and put swirls of silver in the tight bun at the nape of her neck. "Did you remember . . . ?" She caught sight of the kid and came to a halt, burying her fingers in the folds of her apron. The kid dropped his eyes and looked sheepish.

"This is my new cook's helper, Mrs. Senn. Last fall George told me I could hire one. Well, I did. He's called the Keystone Kid, ma'am, and I think he'll work out."

Her smile came back and she swept toward the kid. She took his arm between her hands and looked up into his boyish, still red face. "I'm so very happy to meet you, Kid, and I know you will do a good job here. You could not have anyone better to work with, and I know you will do well."

He stammered something polite, and although he seemed quite embarrassed about meeting her, perhaps because of the way he was dressed, she pretended not to notice. Instead she focused on the crate atop her large, round table.

"Why, how marvelous. You brought our things already," she chattered. "I'll just bet you carried all this, Kid. That was very thoughtful of you. Indeed it was. And it's heavy. My, you must be stronger than you look." She laughed. "And we will fix that soon enough. Hard work and solid food will have you bursting the seams of that handsome shirt in no time at all. Just you wait and see." She patted him and scurried to the table.

The big box I had packed was soon empty, the contents scattered over the table top amid Mrs. Senn's cooing exclamations. "Katy? Katy! Come down here, child. Here are the snaps you've been wanting." She turned and gave me a bright smile. "You even remembered the thread. Good. And the shade should be ex*act*ly right. She will

54

be *so* pleased. However did you get just the right color?"

I laughed. "With all the time you women-folk spent on describing what you wanted, I'd have been in bad trouble if I hadn't got it right, and you know it."

"I know no such thing," she said lightly. "Besides, if we ever did get angry with you, you would crawl off and sulk for days. And wouldn't we be in trouble *then*? All the work to do and all the hands upset with me. Why, we would lose half the crew. And before roundup is over, too. I thought you had more loyalty than to start such a thing at a time like this. Humpf! You ought to be ashamed." Her eyes were sparkling. She was in a really good humor.

Katy came into the kitchen in time to hear the last of her mother's teasing. The girl leaned against the doorframe with an imp-ish look about her. "Have you been giving Mama problems again?"

I rolled my eyes and did my best to look innocent. "Not me, Miss Katy. I'm as in-nocent as your average lamb, I am. Your mother's off on another tirade. Making ac-cusations. Next she'll be throwing things. Cursing. You know how she is." If Natalie Senn has ever shown her temper or uttered a word more harsh than "darn," I am not

55

aware of it, but this was an old routine among us.

Katy managed to make herself look disgusted. "You should be ashamed of yourselves, both of you. What set you off this time?"

"It is all your fault, Katryn Elizabeth. You are the one who wanted the thread." Natalie beamed then. "And look how absolutely perfect it is, too." She held the spool up, and Katy squealed.

"It *is* perfect, too. Oh, I can't wait to finish this dress. I'm going to be positively *rav*ishing." She danced forward to exclaim over the thread, pirouetting on her toes and laughing. She danced herself right up under the kid's chin and let out an embarrassed little yelp of surprise. I had forgotten about him for the moment, and I guess Natalie had too. Katy turned as red as the kid's hair almost.

"Katy," I said quickly, "this is our new cook's helper, the Keystone Kid."

She eyed him with suspicion and then with quick anger. "You don't have to stare," she said belligerently. Which sort of surprised me, for she is not normally so aggressive or so hot-tempered. But then she hadn't had much practice at finding total strangers unexpectedly in the room when she was clowning with family. The kid dropped his eyes and muttered to himself, or maybe to her, and made another attempt at rending his hat brim into shreds. Katy sniffed loudly and stuck her chin out. She stalked out of the room stiff-necked and dignified. But I guess she forgot about how sound travels down a stairwell. Not two seconds after she swept out of sight onto the back stairs, we could hear one loud sob of purest mortification and a flurry of shoe-stomps on the steps.

I grinned at Natalie and gave the kid a wink. Natalie was having trouble keeping a straight face. The kid was just plain having trouble.

"I think we'd best be getting to work now, Mrs. Senn. If you will excuse us?"

"Of course. And thank you. The thread really is perfect." She was still smiling. By the time I reached the back porch the kid was halfway to the cookhouse. Now I know what a scarecrow would look like if it got run out of a cornfield by a bunch of imper-tinent crows.

I let the kid work off steam by splitting stove lengths of wood — of which there always seemed to be a shortage when I'd been away for a few days — while I set about destroying the fruits of his labor by getting my oven heated ready for baking.

This business of having a helper was something I'd always resisted before, but by golly it wasn't so bad. I pulled my stool over to the broad and much scarred worktable and got comfortable. As I needed something, all I had to do was ask for it and the kid fetched it. And what with telling him where to find things and, no, that wasn't right, it was the next drawer down and, no, that bag is cornmeal, I asked for sugar, why, I don't think it took more than twice as long to get things done with his help.

I put a half-dozen pies in the oven and as a matter of sheer laziness made some biscuit dough to set for use that evening instead of going to the trouble of baking bread. I had time for a smoke before the pies were done and could be set aside to cool. I left the kid with a paring knife and a stack of potatoes while I went into the pantry with my best knife and a sharpening steel to cut meat for supper.

That is another of the many good things I can say about George Senn. He is not shy of feeding his crew plenty of beef, and unlike most I have known he is a bearcat on the subject of making sure every beef slaughtered for home use has to be carrying the FR-Connected Bar. There are standing orders that whenever I want fresh meat to hang I tell Jess, who personally chooses a cull from the herd and has it driven in to headquarters, where I supervise the slaughter and butchering. And woe unto the poor waddie who suggests that he's seen a Rafter Pine Tree or a Box 88 or a Slash WT in a thicket nearby, for when he does that he is just asking for Jess to tear into him before the old man hears of it and orders the boy's string of horses turned out with the loose bands of mares and other unused stuff.

I cut enough meat to go around and a little extra and laid it on the big table and got it salted and peppered and covered with towels ready for use, and then it was just a matter of waiting for time to get things going. I settled into the rocker I keep near enough the stove and the woodbox that I can keep the fire fed without moving and stoked my old pipe again. The kid was still peeling and quartering potatoes.

"That was a mighty pretty girl at the house," the kid said after a while. "Is she the owner's daughter?"

"Katy, you mean? Uh-huh. She's George's oldest, youngest, and only," I told him between puffs.

I hadn't thought of it before much, but I guess the young bucks would soon be thinking of Katy as a girl instead of a child. She was — I couldn't hardly believe it when I counted it up — seventeen now and soon eighteen. Hell, she was most a woman grown already even if I did keep thinking of her as a pert and curious youngun.

And I guess the kid was right. She *was* a pretty little thing. She was as tiny as the kid was tall, just a mite of a thing, slender and quick and as gay as a wood sprite is supposed to be. Delicate little features and soft, yellow hair that she mostly wore loose and flowing even if that was not considered the fashionable thing to do. Sweet. And loving. And feisty. Lordy, but that child had herself a temper. I don't doubt that she'd light into a bear with nothing but a spatula for a weapon if she had her dander up, which she did get up pretty frequent.

Not that I am trying to give the idea she was coltish or — what do they call it — tomboyish. She was a hundred per cent little girl, small and soft and fragile-looking, so that she always reminded me somehow of a new kitten curled up in a sewing basket.

Which is not quite the right impression either, for I have seen her work long, hot hours in the garden in heat that would make most men keel over, and she can help pull a foal with the best of them — though she

60

doesn't care enough about the cows to mess with them. I believe she figures that for men's work. She sure is horse crazy, though, which is one of the reasons why the FR-Connected Bar has such fine saddle stock. The child just naturally loves horses, anything to do with them, and is always vexing her father about upgrading his mare band, and a good many of our mares are gentled for riding so she can spend hours wandering around on a horse. Even then she is all girl, though, riding a sidesaddle the way a lady should. But taking those mares of hers about anyplace a waddie could push one of the using horses.

Anyway, when I thought about it, the kid was right, and pretty soon Jess and I would have to start keeping a closer watch on the crew to make sure none of the hands got to thinking they could spark the boss's daughter. I reminded myself to have a talk with him about that sometime when there wouldn't be any stray ears in the neighborhood.

The old man and Jess came clattering in a while later and stuck their heads in to say hey and see had I picked up the things they'd asked for. Jess had wanted me to bring him some twists of chewing tobacco. George had needed some shaving soap.

61

They stepped inside and took their hats off in my kitchen. They wouldn't have bothered in the chow hall part of the building.

"Glad to see you made it back all right," Jess said with a strong note of concern in his voice. "The boss was getting worried about you. Said he thought you were getting so old you might've forgot the way." George nodded his head in agreement with that tale.

"Now, boys," I told them, "I know you would never repeat a secret that could be embarrassing to someone, so I will tell you the truth. I did forget the way. But I stopped at the Widow Ramsey's place, and she pointed out the right road. She said she's been watching it real careful, Jess, hoping you would be coming down to visit soon." I smacked my lips. "She does make good crullers. You oughta try them. Or maybe you have been." That paid Jess back. The widow has set her cap for him, and at times he gets to feeling a bit trapped by it all. She is a nice enough person, I suppose, except that she is almighty bossy and has nearly as full a mustache as Jess does.

"Boys," I said, "I guess you should meet this fella hiding in the corner. Since you're gonna be paying him. This is my new helper, known as the Keystone Kid. Kid, this little gray-haired fellow with the potbelly is your boss, George Senn. The skinny, ugly one is Jess Barnes. He's the foreman of the working crew. Which means you can ignore him most of the time, same as I do."

The kid came forward to shake and howdy them, and they were polite enough to not make any comment on his shirt, which even when dirty was loud and sassy.

"It's about time you found someone you could get along with," George told me. "Maybe now we won't have to listen to you bellyache about being so overworked."

"Better yet," Jess said, "maybe now my crew won't get so many bellyaches. Teach this old fella how to cook if you can, Kid, but I'll warn you. He's been resisting learning how to do that for years now."

The kid grinned and bobbed his head. At least he had sense enough to keep from blurting out immediately that he wanted to be a "cowboy."

I heard the first of the hands ride in from wherever Jess had assigned them for the day and knew it was time to start frying the potatoes and set the meat to burning. If it wasn't ready when they were, they might storm the building, and if I had to rough a bunch of them up, Jess would never get over complaining about the time lost from work. I shooed the boys out and pretty soon the kid and I were as busy as a centipede in an ant bed.

# CHAPTER 5

"Well, you didn't do too bad, Kid," I said after all the animals had been quieted and were gone.

"Are they always like that?" he asked wearily. His face was flushed and running sweat, and strands of damp hair were curling down toward his eyes. He had his shirt sleeves rolled up and was elbow-deep in dishwater in the big tin washtub.

"Like what, Kid? They seemed normal enough to me. Or did you expect them to take little bitty polite helpings like some kind of town dandies?"

He grinned. "No sir. I've seen farmhands eat at threshing time one summer, so I guess I expected that all right. It's just that I sort of thought . . ."

"Go ahead."

"Aw, you'll just laugh at another of those back-East notions I had about the cowboys."

"Probably," I agreed. "What was this one,

anyway?"

"What I had heard, you see, is that cowboys . . . cowhands . . . are about as close-mouthed as an Indian. Hardly ever laugh or anything like that. You know, real deep, intense, silent characters."

"That's part true anyway, Kid."

"Yeah? What part?"

"The part about them being the same as Indians along that line. Because neither is likely to let go when there's a bunch of citified strangers around, but amongst his own kind either one, waddie or red savage, will turn loose and have just a hell of a time laughing and playing the fool and flapping their lips at one another."

"Really?"

"I said it, didn't I?"

"Indians, too?"

"Just the same, Kid. One of these times you're going to learn you can't trust a rumor to be true." I had another thought and smiled at him. "About the time you get that fixed in your mind, you'll find a rumor that is the truth, and then you'll have to start all over."

He thought on what I'd said for a moment and asked, "How come they weren't quiet around me then? I'm a stranger to them."

"You are a little strange, Kid. I admit that.

But in case you've forgotten — as I take it you have, else you wouldn't be standing around with an empty tub when there's another stack of bowls to do before you're done — you work here now. You aren't exactly part of the crew, but you belong here now." I could see that that really pleased him. He was smiling to himself as he splashed the last of the dirty things into the big tub and began scrubbing at them.

I took the heap of meat scraps and leftover this-and-that and piled them onto a coupla pie tins to set out for the dogs and carried them out. As soon as I opened the outside door, a flash flood of cats and half-grown kittens spilled over my feet and darted inside. They gathered around the kid's ankles and began hollering for their supper. The mutts were more polite. They were jumping and yipping but they stayed outside at least. I told them to sit still and waited until they had hushed before I put their food down.

By the time I got back inside, the kid had already found the plate of crumbled biscuits and meat drippings I had set aside for the cats. He was hunkered down amid a mess of waving tails and arched backs, busy scratching ears and listening to the purrs. I noticed that even the old gray-striped tom was allowing himself to be petted, and that old devil is generally on the standoffish side with humans.

The kid snapped upright when I came in. "I'll get these things finished now. Right away."

"There's no big fuss about it," I told him with a wave. I gimped over to my stool and dragged my pipe out. "There's times we gotta hurry and times we don't. This time of day the hurrying is over and done with." He smiled and played with the cats a moment longer then before he went back to the washtub. And I will say that when it came to the cleaning up he really was a help, for we were done much earlier than I could ever manage on my own.

He finished the washing, got a towel, and began pulling things out of the big tub of rinse water.

"Don't bother drying them, Kid. The air will do that just fine if you pull them out of the water and stack them on edge." He gave me an odd look as if he was wondering where I'd learned about what was proper and what wasn't. "Don't ever get wrapped up with work that isn't necessary, Kid. There's enough that really has to be done without you go around creating more." He shrugged and did as he was told.

"That seems to be it then," he said a few minutes later. Everything was stacked to dry, the wash water thrown into the yard, and the kitchen tidied. The kid was standing in the middle of the room. He looked a mite uncomfortable and for a moment I wondered why.

"Hell, you don't know where to bed down, do you?"

"No, sir, I guess I don't."

"We can fix that. Truth is, I've never had me an assistant before. Never gave any thought to details like that either. Why don't you go over to the bunkhouse — you know which one it is — and ask Jess for a bunk you can drag over here."

He looked just a touch disappointed. I guess he was hoping to stay in the bunkhouse with the hands. I wouldn't have minded as far as that goes, but I do walk kind of heavy on one side and would be sure to disturb the crew when I woke the kid — as I fully expected to have to do for a while. Those boys needed their sleep and had to get up early enough as it was. They didn't need to be rolled out on cook's hours, which are even worse than theirs.

The kid came back dragging a wooden-frame bunk. Billy Knowles was following with a limp mattress draped over his head and shoulders. I had the kid put his bunk in a corner of the kitchen where I'd been keeping a coupla empty packing cases for fatwood splinters that I used to start my fires. Those I had him move closer to the stove. Billy went back, the kid thanking him for the help.

"It isn't much for privacy," I said, "but more than you'll get in a bunkhouse if you ever decide to go in for that line of work."

The kid was stashing his gear, the woolly chaps now out of sight, under the bunk. His head snapped up when he heard what I'd said. "Do you think there's any chance I could do that?" He sounded real anxious. I guess he really had his heart set on his cowboying ambitions.

"Not right away. But, sure. I don't see why you couldn't one of these days if you ever learn enough to be useful to somebody. And I'll tell you this. If that's what you really want, there isn't a better man to work for than George Senn. Nor there aren't many who know more about beef than Jess Barnes. Both of them have been at it since the days before cows came bald-headed, and they know what they're about."

"Bald-headed?"

"Muleys, Kid. Beef without long, sharp horns to gut a horse or gore a rider's leg.

These fancy new strains of blood they've brought in from England and such places." I chuckled. "When I was your age I didn't know there was such a thing as a steer without horns. Now it's got so people are cutting the horns off what few animals they've got left to grow them. Seems unnatural to me."

I went into my room and found a coupla extra blankets and a sack that I stuffed with clean rags to make him a pillow. "I hope you aren't used to ironed sheets and such fancy stuff as that."

"No, sir, I guess I'm not, though I did sleep on sheets at a hotel once." He grinned. "Felt sorta funny."

"You'll feel right at home here then. Good night, Kid." I shut the door of my room. That door was one of the first things I'd done — building and hanging it, that is — when I had been hurt and was feeling good enough to be doing something again. There had used to be a blanket hung there, but I decided I wanted a door. This was the only room I'd ever had that was all for me alone, and I was right proud of it. At least that was something good that had come out of my accident.

Come morning I had the kid up and busy by four-thirty. We fed the crew and were well along with the washing up by dawn. While he finished that, I did a day's baking of bread and more pies. By eight everything was done that needed doing for a while, and this being a busy time of year, there wouldn't be many of the boys coming in for a noon meal. Maybe none at all, depending on where Jess had them working for the day. This not being shipping season, they would be making small gathers in widely scattered locations to do the cutting and earmarking and branding of the spring calves. Thinking about it, I could practically smell the stink of the hot irons on hair.

"You all finished now, Kid?"

"Yes, sir."

"Wait here for me then. I'll be right. . . . No, dammit, it might be getting brittle and rotten with age. The ranch can stake you to some educational tools, I guess." I had been going to get the kid my old rope to play with. But when it came right down to it, I couldn't part with the thing. I knew I'd never have need of it again myself, but still. . . . "Come along then."

We followed the path along the creek and crossed the small footbridge. There were sturdy wagon bridges upstream and down as well. I found an open bale of rope in the tool shed and pulled off about thirty-five feet of it and cut it free. There was some waxed thread handy for working with leather. I used some to wrap the ends of the rope. Lordy, but it had been a long time since I'd had reason to be doing something like this.

I tied a honda in at one end and had the kid pull the knot tight, as his hands would be stronger than mine. I thought about wetting some rawhide and sewing on a burner, but this was just going to be a play-pretty for him to practice with, so I decided not to bother. He could learn how to do that later on if he was interested enough.

"All right, Kid. This is your rope. The kind a waddie uses to catch calves with or whatever else he might need to hang a loop on. What you do with it is give it a twirl or two over the head, throw it true, and drop the loop wherever you want it to be. We'll go over behind the lower hay barn and see how good you are at catching corral posts."

He looked as happy as if I'd just given him a present. Well, maybe I had.

We trudged over there, and I positioned the kid about fifteen feet from a likely looking post. "There's your calf, Kid," I said, pointing. "Catch him."

He admired the rope for a minute and at least did have sense enough to run the free

73

end through the honda and coil the rest of it. But he didn't know how to feel the twist of the hemp, and so he ended up with a coil that was acting like a spring, trying to escape in all directions. The kid took hold of the honda, twirled his overlarge loop round and round his head nearly out at arm's length and let fly. He pounded the ground a half-dozen feet in front of him with what was left of his loop — which was a knot about the size of a man's fist. He looked to see and, yes, I was doing some laughing at him. He colored.

"That's exactly what I expected you to do, Kid, so don't worry about it. I just wanted you to see why you gotta pay attention, because there's a right way and a wrong way, and the wrong way just doesn't do a thing."

I took the rope from him and flipped it out along the ground. "Now watch the way you got to twist this to get a nice, flat coil. You can feel the twist of the fibers, and if you look you can see it when it's stretched out. See? So you don't fight the rope. You coil with it." I showed him how and handed him a neat coil so he could feel the difference.

He gave the coil back, and I built a loop. "Mind now, you got to take the twist out of your rope as you make the loop bigger or it won't lay right. See?" He nodded.

"Now. You don't grab the honda, see? Put a handle on it. About a foot or so of free rope and the same on the loop. That's what keeps your loop open when you throw it. Some like more and some less, but start with a foot or so. Then you just spin it, see? With your wrist, never your arm. And throw." The loop sailed out. "Let it run through your hand and take the slack out as soon as she hits so you don't have a calf running through your loop or a rank steer throwing it off. It's easy."

He grinned. "It doesn't look so hard at that."

"Nope. But I expect you'll have to fling it three or four times more before you get the hang of it. So go right ahead. I'm going back to some shade and a cup of coffee."

I left him there, coiling and spinning and throwing for all he was worth. Maybe a little more than that even, for he wasn't worth much at it. He was willing to try, though, and that is mostly what it takes to learn something. When he came back to the cookhouse a coupla hours later, his rope was gritty with dirt and he was not using his right arm very much. I'll bet it was plenty tired. Even a thing as light as a catch rope will get awfully heavy if you heft it and throw it enough times.

He was looking pretty pleased with himself, too, and I was guessing that he'd caught himself that fence post a time or two.

"Get that chunk of cold roast out of the cold-box, Kid. If anyone comes in for dinner, we'll feed them off that. And after dinner if you like I'll show you how to make a breakaway honda out of wire so you don't have to chase your loop every time you throw it right."

He was whistling when he went to bring the beef.

# Chapter 6

The work went forward, and from the talk around the table at mealtimes the calf crop was a good one this year. I could tell it, too, from the number of filled buckets piling up in the icehouse, each jammed full of Rocky Mountain oysters, every two oysters representing one bull calf. And when you figured the heifer count on top of that, you could call it one live, healthy calf per oyster.

It was the grass that did it, of course. With cows everything depends on the grass. And on water. This year the spring had come early and come on strong. The bright emerald spears of new growth already hid last year's dried, brown stems. With that to graze on, the stock cows were strong and healthy. They put solid bone and muscle in their calves and produced plenty of rich milk for the little devils to suck once they got their legs under them.

Better yet — or anyway as good — if the

grass would hold this good in the high country through the summer months, come fall the two-year-old steers and the excess yearlings would be fat and glossy and command a top price on the eastern market. And with the railroad here now, they would go rolling out in cars loaded right here in the valley. None of that weight would have to be walked off taking them out to the main rail line, which was a dry and rough and nearly waterless eighty-five miles further away. Not much of a drive by old-time standards but a big difference in the amount of weight on the hoof when those beeves reached the markets.

It was shaping up to be a good year for sure, and everyone seemed to be feeling that. The crew came in tired but not so tired that they didn't have energy for the kind of pranks that run through a bunkhouse when things are going well on a place.

Billy Knowles was the last one in one evening. His bunk, his war bag, every stick and stitch he owned was gone and not a soul in the place paying a bit of attention either to Billy or to the empty spot where his bunk had been. He finally found it all, the bunk and all his gear set up neat as a pin. In the loft of the lower hay barn. But when everyone was done with the laughing and the ribbing, Billy included in that, he had plenty of help moving it all back.

Casey Timms, who had taken over my old job as bronc peeler, hobbled in to rest his weary bones, flopped onto his bunk, and went clean through to the floor. Someone had replaced the ropes of his bunk with pieces of light string just strong enough to support his mattress and blankets. Casey never said a word. The boys said he slept the whole night right there on the floor.

Most every day there was somebody being accidentally bumped into taking an unexpected bath in one of the water tanks or in the creek, like when someone would be crossing one of the bridges and another fellow's horse would spook all of a sudden just for no reason at all.

Even the kid began to come in for his share, tripping over boots that accidentally got in his way or having a big bowl of gravy spilled down the front of him when a waddie who couldn't have seen the kid coming up behind him suddenly remembered something and jumped to his feet. I wondered if the kid had seen the little flurry of nods across the table made by the boys who could see when he was in position there. The kid took it all right and even had sense enough to stumble forward so that a good

79

bit of the hot, greasy gravy was smeared into the hair and down the shirt of Charlie Uver, who had started it.

It was all a good sign of the way things were going, and Jess and the old man were smiling and in good humor most of the time.

The kid stayed busy, working hard and steady when I needed him and spending his free time in the mornings working with that rope. I walked down a few times to check on him and give him some pointers, and he was getting so that he could catch his fence post as often as he missed or maybe better. So I had him put a bucket on the ground, straddle the top rail of the corral, and begin all over again learning to throw down at that bucket from a height approximating saddle height. He seemed to regard that as a sort of promotion for him.

In the afternoons when we had free time, I got him to making some odds and ends of gear for himself. A proper rope, stretched and rubbed and with a loop burner sewed in place. Hobbles and a halter and a mecate of cotton rope. He had trouble learning how to make a button knot, but he figured it out eventually. Scraps of harness leather became a headstall and heavy reins. As the things under his bunk began to mount into a pile of useful, usable gear, he got to acting prouder than ever, whistling and grinning no matter what work I gave him to do. And as he came to know where things were and what needed doing, he even became a real help to me.

The crew finished their spring branding work, and even though it wasn't quite the end of the month yet, George paid the boys and gave them a coupla days to go into town for a snort and a haircut and whatever else they might enjoy for a bit of relaxation. It was a pretty good idea, really, because at this time of month, Bessie Blue's social-service center and tension-relieving treatment facility would be mostly empty of competing customers. And the haircuts would still look nice and fresh when everyone went in for the firemen's big feed.

Even though the kid had only been working a little more than a week he was paid too. Five minutes later he and a couple of the younger ones in the crew were hemming and hawing at the back door of the cookhouse.

"Something you boys want? Huh? I don't give handouts in the middle of the day. You know that."

"Yes, sir," the kid said meekly. He glanced at the other boys but was getting no sup-

81

port there. "What I was wondering was if you'd, well, be needing my help now. While the crew's in town, that is. I'd be back when they come. You wouldn't have any full meals to get while I'm gone. If you say it's all right to go, I mean." He had his eyes down and acted like he had just asked me to make some big-deal sacrifice, like giving up my birthright or something, just so he could have some fun. Not that he could have all that much of a big time on the ten dollars or so he would've been paid.

"Humph. I got along fifty-odd years by myself. I guess I can for a coupla days more." I got a cup of coffee and gave him an accusing look. "I suppose you figure to hit me up for your transportation too."

The kid looked at the other boys, but it wasn't the sort of problem either of them would have anticipated. They probably never met nor even heard of a grown human male on a beef outfit who didn't own a saddle. And there were always plenty of horses around for anyone who needed the use of one. The kid looked like he was ready to give up on the whole idea and bolt through the doorway.

"I don't suppose you're much of a rider either." The kid shook his head. "Well hell," I said. "Wait here."

I set my cup down and went into my room. My old saddle was there on a stand in a corner. I wouldn't ever sit in it again, but I wouldn't part with it either and kept it oiled and clean. It was a fine saddle. Deep-seated, the tree double-covered with bullhide. I'd had it made special for me in San Antonio and had used it the better part of twenty-five years before the wreck that changed my shape so I couldn't sit it anymore. I picked it up, about forty-five solid pounds of it, and dragged it out into the kitchen. I dumped it at the kid's feet.

"Here. But if you bust it up or lose it, you're in bad trouble. It couldn't be replaced. And if you come back drunk, you'd best be quiet about it too."

"Yes, *sir*!" The kid picked up that saddle and looked at it like it was inlaid with gold and rubies. Well, it *was* a damn fine saddle. The other boys gave him a look that I chose to interpret as being envy. They went off chattering and laughing, the kid carrying my saddle cradled in his arms so that I wondered if he had ever had to tote one before — because that sure isn't the way to do it. I heard one of the boys say he would rope out Big Nose for the kid to use. It was a good choice. The old gelding was strong and sure-footed and dependable enough for even a child to be safe on him. Whatever there was to see, that old horse had seen it before and was long since past the notion of being spooked by buggers, real or imagined.

You know something? It was kind of lonesome around the stove that night.

The Keystone Kid was back the next afternoon. By himself. The rest of the crew wouldn't be back until the following night sometime, and the kid had ridden Big Nose those thirty-five miles back by himself. It did strike me as being odd.

I was sitting outside when he rode in and could recognize his yellow shirt and the old grulla horse as soon as they came into view. I stopped rocking to watch him come in and adjusted my hat against the sun and pulled at my pipe. The kid was holding himself stiff in the saddle so that I was guessing him to be plenty sore, but at least he wasn't balancing on the old horse's mouth and was riding with a slack rein.

He went straight to the biggest horse corral and pulled his gear — or *our* gear I maybe should say — and turned Big Nose loose to roll. Then he lugged the heavy saddle up toward the cookhouse. When he got close, I could see that he had treated himself to a pair of high-heeled boots. Off-the-counter stuff but better than shoes. He wasn't showing them off when he reached me, though.

The kid carried my saddle inside without a word of greeting, and I heard a muffled thump that sounded like it came from my worktable. He came back outside and stood stiffly — formally, really — in front of me.

"Thank you for the use of your saddle," he said in a dull, dutiful voice. He turned to leave.

"Whoa, Kid. Don't run away." He stopped. "Bring a chair out, why don't you?" I invited, and again he did what he was told but with no bounce or life in his movements. Something was disturbing this kid pretty good.

"I see you got yourself some new boots. Not bad." I tried to be admiring about it in the way I said it. And they weren't too bad either but a little plain. Standard, six-dollar work boots of brown leather with no stitching to set them off. The toe was a bit too round for my taste, but then I like a sharply pointed box toe and had had mine built that way for about as long as I can remember.

Anyway, the kid didn't respond the way I would have expected, at least the way I'd have expected it the day before. Now I wasn't so surprised. He barely glanced down at his new boots. Didn't pull up his pant legs or anything to show them to me. "Yeah," he said.

"Bring anything else from town?"

He shrugged. "A knife."

"You remembered then. Good. If you'll fetch out my big rock, we'll put an edge on it. Never have seen a knife come from the factory sharp enough to use for anything more than spreading butter or spooning up preserves."

"All right," he said listlessly. He went into the kitchen and brought out the wooden box that held my black Arkansas whetstone. That rock has gotten so much use over the years that it has a belly curve scraped out deep enough that I have to take it out of the box to use it now. The kid handed me the box and a shiny new folding knife with utility and pen and castrating blades.

"Not a bad little knife, Kid," I told him. "Keep on like this and you'll have yourself outfitted for a riding job in no time at all. Yes indeedy, Kid. I'll have you fixed up in no time at all now."

No matter what was troubling him, I expected that to cheer him. It didn't. He just shrugged again, his eyes not meeting mine at all. I took the knife and the whetstone and concentrated on making three good edges. There are times when busywork with one's hands can be awfully useful.

# CHAPTER 7

"More coffee here." No "please." No smile. No politeness whatsoever in the tone of voice. Jim Fuller — the others, too, for that matter — was acting like the kid was a total stranger. And one they'd rather not get to know, at that.

The kid didn't say anything at all during the meal. Not that I heard anyhow. He did what he was supposed to do, fetched whatever he was ordered to fetch. But he never spoke to a one of the crew. It was hard to tell in the feeble lamplight, especially so early in the morning when I am not really at my best, but he seemed pale too. More, even, than usual. His thin face was strained.

He never let down in his work, though. And those boys did keep him busy hauling in fresh supplies of hot coffee and fried pork steaks and fried potatoes and mounds of sourdough hotcakes and bowls of stewed tomatoes and, finally, pie and pie after pie, enough to keep me busy baking for most of the morning if I intended to have any sweets on hand for dinner and supper. It seemed a long time, much longer than usual, before the crew was fed and gone down to the horse pens to catch their mounts for the day and we could sit down to our own meal — more of the same but with good beef instead of fat and greasy pork for our meat.

"Tell me about it, Kid," I prodded.

"Nothing to tell," he mumbled. He was keeping his attention on his plate. He hesitated and added, "I'd appreciate it if you'd just let it lay now."

Coming from him that was quite a rebuke. And I had surely earned one. Whatever there was between him and the crew was strictly his own business, and I had no right to butt into it, especially when he made it so plain that my meddling was unwelcome.

Still, there are times when I am both nosy and notional. I guess this was one of them. I finished my meal and left the table. "Think you can handle the cleanup by yourself?"

"Sure." He didn't even look at me when he said it.

"I'll be back directly then. The baking will keep me busy this morning. I wanta move around in the fresh air some before I hook my leg irons to that oven." He nodded.

I got my everyday coat from its peg and slapped my old hat on and headed down toward the pens. It was about to be coming dawn, and the air was fresh and crisply cool. An eddying wind was coming down off the mountains above the place. It was not yet light enough to really see those hills, but I could feel them there like some protecting presence. They were one of the reasons I liked this place so much. They sheltered us from the worst of the winter yet trapped the snow to hold it and trickle it down to us as cold, sweet water in the times when we most needed it. The window of my room looks out onto the tallest of the peaks in this little section of the chain. I like that.

The boys had the horses they'd chosen for the day roped and snubbed to strong posts. Most of them were saddled already.

Jess Barnes was moving among them, slipping along quiet and easy, his voice low so he would not disturb any of the ponies. This early in the season most of the beasts, even the older, proven ones, were still feeling pretty rank and would prefer to be turned back onto winter pasture instead of being asked for an honest day's work. It didn't take much of an excuse for one of them to blow up and see if he could talk his way out of being used.

Jess had a word and a bit of instruction for each of the boys, telling them which way to head and maybe mentioning something they might watch out for in particular.

Right now, with the branding just finished, most of what they had to do would be make-work stuff. Checking to see that the fences were secure. Looking for any extra-stupid bovines that might have gotten bogged and needed to be pulled loose, or gashed-up ones that had torn themselves deep enough to need doctoring, or orphaned calves too little to eat grass that would have to be carried in to the bum pen for close handling. It didn't use to be that anyone would bother much with doctoring or trying to save dogies, but nowadays costs were so close and beef so valuable that it paid a man to work his place more. And it did pay off. Nowadays it wasn't all that unusual for a man to get as high as a sixty-five per cent calf crop off his cows. We used to figure on twenty per cent, and twenty-five was something to brag on.

Jess finished with his gentle ramrodding and came over to lean against the rail beside me. I loaded my pipe and offered the pouch to him. He took a pinch of my cutplug and shoved it into his cheek.

"Gotta have something to take away the

taste of that breakfast," he explained.

"If it will do that, I'll take up chewing myself," I told him.

We stood draped over the rail for a while and watched the boys sort themselves out. Pretty soon the rising sun caught the dust hanging in the air and spread a golden glow over the corral area. And there was surely enough dust for it to catch.

Most of the ponies had a few kinks in their backs that had to be taken out before they were willing to settle down. Charlie Uver's horse went to running backward on him and rammed into the rump of a coarse-boned yellow horse just as Pete Chapman was trying to step onto the yellow horse. The two beasts got into a rib-thumping match over it which Charlie rode out all right, but Pete ended up in the dirt about ten feet away. He did cuss a little about that and kept it up when his horse refused to come un-spooked. Pete finally had to blindfold him before he could get into the saddle.

Billy Knowles came loose from his horse twice before he finally got the thing to go-ing in a straight and reasonably level line. I noticed that Casey had eased over close there in case Billy wanted him to give that seal-brown snorter a lesson in good man-ners, but Billy didn't ask for any help.

Though the third time he got up he wasn't too proud to reach for the apple and keep a good hold on that horn until things were under control.

Inside of five minutes they were calling out their last insults until evening and were drifting out the gate to scatter over the winter range.

"Don't see you down here much," Jess said. He was watching Pete and Jimmy Lee Evans top the rise to the north of headquarters.

"I'm a busy man. But I guess I can be more of a man of leisure now that I've got a helper."

"Uh-huh."

"I expect you'll be going up top pretty soon?"

"Uh-huh." It was what I expected. The way the grass was down here it should be good in the high country already as well. Jess would want to ride up to see that for himself, though, before he started the hands gathering the scattered beeves for a push onto the mountain.

"Come to think of it," he said, "you might as well pack me up some eatables tomorrow, and I'll go up the morning after. Say, enough for two men for three, four days."

"All right. Sure am glad I don't have to

eat your cooking any more."

"Sure wish I *didn't* have to eat yours." There are a coupla ways a body could take that. Damned if I didn't get the impression Jess was leaning toward the serious view on it. Maybe we were both beginning to show our age. But it would have been good to be going up there with him again. "You have something on your mind this morning other than when I'm going up top," he said. He wasn't asking a question. When I didn't answer right away he settled some dust with a stream of brown juice and waited.

"I was wondering what's going on between your crew and my protégé," I admitted.

"You haven't forgot how to be blunt, have you?"

"Nope." Hell, if I was going to be nosy I might as well do it proper.

Jess let another stream fly. "I wasn't with them in town, but the way I heard the chatter last night they invited your boy to have a snort over at the Bull Shooter, and as soon as he showed his face in there with them, our hands started getting the needle from the other outfits. They say he's as yella as that shirt he wears. Do you know anything about it?"

"Uh-huh." I told him what had happened between the kid and Wayne Tynell. And in

94

truth it didn't make the kid sound any too good. "I honestly hadn't thought of how that could come back on your boys, Jess. I should have, but I just plain didn't."

"Well, don't fret about it. This is a good, solid crew this year. They'll handle anything the other outfits want to throw at them." He grinned. "Sometimes a few busted heads and skinned knuckles put a crew in good humor."

"If you say so." That was something that I guess Jess had adjusted to with these young kids, but it was still beyond me. When I was a pup, a waddie might pull a knife or maybe even a gun, but he never would have thought of tearing up his hands by thumping on someone else. You just can't do top work with a rope if your hands are all banged up. Of course, most of these boys any more don't even know how to throw anything but the simple loops for heading and heeling and forefooting. The figure-eights and turnovers they never will learn to throw. Why, Casey and Jess were the only ones in the whole crew that knew enough now to protect their hands with gloves before they stepped onto a horse. The other boys rode barehanded.

My pipe hissed and bubbled to the end of the tobacco and I knocked the char loose.

Jess kept leaning on the rail. It was obvious he wasn't ready to quit talking quite yet. I began to feel some sun-warmth on my back while I waited.

"You're a notional old bastard," he said finally.

I was willing to be agreeable about it. I said, "Uh-huh."

"I've noticed your kid throwing a rope now and then," he went on. "And the other day when I rode in, he was sewing a headstall."

"You've heard the sayings about idle hands and all that stuff."

"You figure to turn that kid into a cowhand, don't you?"

"That's what he was set on when he came out here. It was his idea, not mine." I flashed a smile at him. "And if he's going to learn the business, why, I don't know a better man nor a smarter one to teach him all about it."

Jess snorted. His eyes became serious again, though. "If you think *I'm* going to take him on, take him into my crew . . ."

"You can try him in the haying crew, anyway. When the bovines are settled in up top, Jess. Half the hands won't stay if they're not riding. You know you'll need more men then. And the kid's a worker. I can vouch for that."

"On my haying crew? Hell's bells, man, if you're ever going to need help that's when it will be. You can't feed a hay crew by yourself, dammit."

"I already told Kip Barton I'd hire him to help me during haying. His folks'll be counting on that money. And," I plunged on, "you can take the kid on as half a hand. Same pay as he's drawing now." I took a deep breath. "You won't be sorry, Jess."

Jess looked like he wanted to spit again. Something more than tobacco juice. I hoped he was remembering that he owed me a favor or two. "We'll see," he said. He sure didn't sound enthusiastic about it, though. And I didn't want to push him any further.

"Well," I said, "you supervisory types can live a life of ease if you want, but us working folk gotta keep churning it out if we don't want to end up fired and homeless. I've got pies to bake and bread dough to set or your boys will be trying to scalp me come dinner-time."

He grinned and was his usual self again. "Hell, I might have a happier crew if you *didn't* cook for us a few meals' worth."

I started back for the cookhouse, and Jess went to catch a horse. I stayed another

minute to watch, hoping he'd get a mouthful of corral dust, but he just got on the
beast and rode off. What can you expect,
though? The foreman gets to assign the
string of horses.

# CHAPTER 8

"Come along, Kid. There's something I want you to do."

"Yes, sir." His voice still had no life in it. He'd been three days like that. Ever since he got back from town. And I couldn't see any reason for him to change. The boys in the crew still weren't talking to him. Not that they were being nasty about it. They were really pretty good old boys. They weren't taunting him or baiting him or trying to be mean about it. They just didn't have any use for a coward, and so they ignored him. I wondered if he could see the difference there. I hoped so.

When he saw me get my hat and coat from their pegs the kid got his hat. He trailed along behind me, which is hard for someone to do at the slow pace I travel. I led him down to the furthest of the horse pens — down past the little bum pen where Katy kept her hand-fed orphan calves — to the collection of surplus young stuff that Casey was working on in his spare time.

These horses were the three- and four-year-olds that had never been worked before and had not been chosen when Casey broke out the saddle stock getting ready for the spring work. The FR-Connected Bar keeps a long string of mares so there are always spare animals, good ones, enough that when anyone in the valley is looking for some good saddlers they generally come take a look in this pen and often leave some cash behind when they go home again. And once a year the cavalry remount contractors come by. They usually clean us out of solid bays and browns and chestnuts, which is why so many of our using horses are of the wilder and the lighter shades. The plain Janes are sold off.

Not a one of these beasts had ever been touched with a currycomb. Their coats were ragged and patchy, them not having worked up the hard sweats that loosen winter hair and help it to slip. Their tails were un-trimmed and fouled, hanging down below their hocks. Their manes and forelocks were matted with burrs. Right now they would not look very pretty to an unpracticed eye. But beneath all that they had solid, straight bone and nicely made muscle and short, strong backs and plenty of room for wind in their deep chests. The quality of the breeding stock George had brought in showed in these animals and in the ones the boys would be using.

These were not really rough horses, mind. By now Casey would have saddled them a time or two. They would have felt a man on their backs before and should know enough to respond a little to rein pressure as long as you didn't expect them to be light-mouthed, made horses.

"Do you think you could put a loop on one of those?"

The kid looked down and for the first time I realized his hands were empty. Before that ride into town he'd dragged his rope with him every time we moved around the place during the day when the hands were out working. "I'll get my rope," the kid said. He took off for the cookhouse at an elbow-pumping loose jog. He disappeared around the end of the lower hay barn.

I stood and watched the horses a moment. A liver-colored gelding got into a scrap with a thin, nearly gray, pale buckskin and got his ribs thumped for his trouble. The liver horse squealed and bared his teeth but went sulking off to see if he could find another easier to pick on. I heard a sound behind me.

Katy was there trundling a wheeled cart loaded with cans of evaporated milk and a coupla buckets. "Feeding time for my children," she said with a bright smile.

"You really enjoy those little fellas, don't you?"

"Of course. Don't you?"

I shrugged and grinned. "Yeah, I guess I do." I walked with her to the bum pen — there were seven calves in it at the moment — and began dipping water from the creek into the long trough while Katy punched holes in a half-dozen cans and spilled the thick stuff into the water. The calves crowded around the trough like so many overlarge pigs, bawling and slobbering and rolling their eyes as if they feared the next one might get more of the milk.

"Keep this up and I'll have to restock the canned milk way before normal."

"I am getting low. I meant to tell you sooner. Would you get some when we go into town for the fry?"

"Sure." I'd already planned on driving the big wagon in anyhow. The family would be using the light gig, and they might want to stay in town and visit awhile. I'd be needed back at the place when the crew returned.

And Jess wouldn't have the boys stay in too long, especially since they would already be pretty well broke after that first trip to town with their month's wages.

We finished mixing the calves' milk, and I pulled the cart out of the pen for her. I can't manage a wheelbarrow any more but carts are all right, which may have something to do with why any busted wheelbarrows around the place have been replaced with carts these last few years.

The kid came back. He nodded to Katy and took his hat off. From the way he held it I wasn't sure if he was more interested in being polite or in hiding the rope he held coiled in his hand.

"The Keystone Kid is about to get some education, Katy," I explained. "Would you care to watch?"

Now I guess that was a damned dirty thing for me to do, but I don't know of much that will do more to give a boy — or a grown man either — heart than having a pretty girl watch while he tries to keep from making a fool of himself. That will spur a fellow to his best efforts most every time.

Not that he was likely to impress this particular girl. She'd grown up around cow outfits and cowhands and had seen about all there was to see of horses and of men

103

trying to master them. Hell, she'd even seen me at work and watched while I broke out and gentled mares that she had chosen for future pets. And she had seen a good many fellows — me among them — come loose from their horses too, for the only way you can be sure of never falling off is to never step on.

Anyway, the kid was trapped now fair and square, his Adam's apple bobbing up and down and his eyes coming nowhere near either Katy or me.

"I'm not in a hurry," Katy said.

"Good. Kid, slip in there and put your rope on whatever one suits you."

"Yes, sir," he said. If he had any confidence about what was coming next, he was able to keep it out of his voice real successfully.

I thought Katy was being real sweet to the kid, too. She never cracked a smile, just leaned against a rail and watched the same as I was doing.

The kid crawled through the rails and shook his loop out the way I'd taught him. He began edging toward the horses with a little side-step sort of maneuver. That got their attention right away, and they began to bunch and fidget. Everyone else who'd ever handled them just barged in and went about his business, and I suppose it would have been obvious even to a horse that those fellows had no thought of failure in their minds so there was no point in the horses giving them an argument about what would happen. The way he was trying to approach them now just made them nervous. Still, I didn't think this would be a good time for hollering instructions at the kid. I could tip him to it later.

The horses bunched themselves in one corner of the pen, and the kid inched up nearly close enough to throw. The animals snorted and tossed their heads and streamed by toward another corner. The kid moused along behind them.

They did it a coupla times more, and the kid began to look frustrated. He was getting red around the ears and had sort of a haunted look in his eyes. I wondered if he'd be chasing balky horses in his sleep this night.

"Should I catch one for him?" Katy whispered when the kid was at a far end of the pen.

"You do and I'll give you a first-class paddling, youngun. You aren't so big you wouldn't still fit over my knee," I told her. The little imp laughed and stuck her tongue out at me. It had been quite a while now, true, but by golly she'd been over my knee before. The first time I'd spanked her, she'd gotten so mad she looked like she was ready to chew nails and spit fire, and she'd run to tell her daddy how mean I had been to her. Well, George had paddled her a second time for having earned the first one. That was the last time she had mentioned such a thing to George, and it was near about the last time she'd given me any trouble. A coupla more to convince her she couldn't get away with just anything when it came to me and my horses, and we got along fine.

"Just trying to help," she said.

"Fine. Hush up and quit smiling then. I wouldn't want the kid to think we were laughing at him."

"Shouldn't we be?"

"Later, girl. Later." She shut up and concentrated on trying to be good.

The kid was still having his troubles and now he was beginning to get mad about it. He quit trying to sneak up on those horses and began stomping along after them. The animals quit trying to run then and stood in a corner, quivering but standing there.

The kid carefully checked his loop and assessed the distance between him and the twenty or so horses in this bunch and swung his loop a bit — which you really don't want to do when you're grabbing a horse out of a pen, but he didn't know that — and let fly.

I think he was throwing at the crowd instead of at any one animal. As quick as the loop left his hand there were heads ducking and bodies dodging in every direction, but damned if one fool beast didn't blunder into the loop and get his head snagged there. The kid's luck was running a little better now.

The rest of the bunch went thundering down to the other end of the pen, but the bright sorrel the kid had caught stood waiting for some instructions, not trying to fight the rope or tear loose from the human who'd caught him.

"Bring him up to the breaking pen," I called to the kid. In a much lower voice I told Katy, "I sure could use your company awhile longer."

"Okay."

Katy and I went up to the round, solid-walled breaking pen with the stout snubbing post sunk in the center. It was a good arrangement and well built, as I should know. I'd set that post and built that wall myself.

The round pen is above the garden, close to the bunkhouse, which is not real convenient to the corrals now, but this pen was one that had been in place since before the hay barns and new corrals were ever built. Casey kept threatening to build himself a new one but hadn't yet found the time to do it any better than I ever had.

The kid came along behind us, and even at my pace he wasn't keeping up. The sorrel wasn't giving him any trouble, really, but it had not been led much and wanted to dance some and to explain that it didn't know what to expect next. The kid seemed to be under the impression that this was a wild one at the other end of his rope. He kept walking backward, his eyes locked on that beast. I don't know for sure what he was expecting, but the horse was not trying to rear or strike or anything.

The wall of the round pen was too high to see over, but there were always some empty nail kegs and heavy crates tossed down close by for standing-on purposes. Katy gave me a hand onto a crate and upended a taller keg for herself, she not being much for size. We hooked our arms over the top of the wall and waited for the kid to bring the sorrel in.

"Tie him to the post on a short rope," I called when he was finally in. The kid did as he was told, and I motioned him to us. There was no point in shouting when it wasn't necessary.

"Yes, sir?"

"In the leather-working end of the tool shed," I told him, "you'll find a ratty old breaking saddle. I don't think Casey will mind if we use it, and there's nothing you could do to it that hasn't been done a dozen times before. Bring that and a coupla blankets and the heavy bridle you'll find hanging on the wall there."

He nodded and ran off toward the shed.

"You're going to be just as mean with him as you were with me, aren't you?" Katy asked with a sparkle of delight in her eyes.

"Maybe even worse, child. If you remember, I did start you on gentle horses. But then he should be able to bounce better than a kid the age you were then."

She was right, of course. The Keystone Kid was about to buy himself some learning. You see, that old breaking saddle had had the horn removed. The idea behind that on a saddle used for breaking green horses was so if the horse managed to take you down with it — and it's happened to me a fair number of times before that one last bad time — there was no iron-bolted horn poking up to spear you in the chest if you should get caught between the ground and the animal. With a slick pommel up front you might get yourself some broken ribs if a saddled horse rolled on you, but you had a better chance of getting out of your bunk again and of spending time on the green side of the grass.

In this instance, though, I figured Casey would have already taken that kind of really rough action out of the sorrel. The reason I wanted the kid on that breaking saddle was simply that he would have nothing to hang onto when the horse blew up. And he could damn sure expect an animal this green to start a storm with him. Katy knew that because I'd done something right similar when I'd made her learn to ride. Except that time I had pulled the knee hook off her sidesaddle and made her learn to ride without it. Nasty of me maybe, but it sure had worked. She had developed as good a seat as any woman I'd ever seen, as good as some men had even if they did have the advantage of riding astraddle.

There are two schools of thought on how to learn the balance that will give someone a good seat. One of them has it that you should start out bareback so you don't have any stirrups or horn to depend on. It sounds like a good idea, but I've always felt that barebacking makes a person grab with his legs. The leg pressure tells the horse to jump out with you, and the novice rider hauls back on the mouth to keep the speed down.

You confuse the horse and develop a rider who doesn't know how to keep his damn legs off the horse. So I've always liked to start younguns with a saddle. On a horse just rank enough to make it hard for them to stay on him.

And hell, there I go acting like I am some kind of expert at teaching things. The truth is that I helped Katy to learn and once, a long time back, gave some advice to some children at a place where I was peeling broncs one spring. In Texas, that was. A kid named Bobby and another named Alan. Milliken I think their old man's name was. Something like that.

Other than that, why, I don't even know my own self how I used to get a horse to do all the things they can be made to do.

Once I helped deliver some army mounts direct to a duty post instead of to a remount center. It was real interesting. An old sergeant with gray in his hair — maybe as much as there is in mine now — was teaching some fresh fish how to ride. Now that fellow had the words and the explanations for just everything. The army teaches you to ride with two hands. Hold this hand here and that hand there, pull this way and exert pressure so, and the horse does thus-and-such. It works, too. They have a well-worked-out way to do everything, according to that sergeant.

Me, I never was just real sure what signals I should be giving to make a horse do this or that or whatever. I remember once when we'd been doing some cutting, which mostly involves running sideways and some real hard spinning, an eastern visitor asked me how we taught a horse to do that. Do you know? I couldn't tell him.

What it comes down to, I guess, is that you sort of want the horse to do something and so he does it, green broke or mannered either one.

Anyway, the kid came back lugging the saddle and other stuff. I noticed that this time he had hold of the fork and was carrying the saddle like a saddle. I nodded toward the sorrel, and he approached it uncertainly. The sorrel pinned its ears back and tried to shy away, but it was snubbed too short to do more than swing its rump aside.

The kid seemed to take heart when he saw the horse was well captured. He smoothed both blankets in place and slapped the saddle on. The sorrel got a hump in its back but did not do any serious thrashing.

From the way the kid pulled up those cinch straps, he must have been scared half to death and wanted to make damned sure the saddle would not come adrift. He like to cut the poor sorrel in thirds the way he laid into both straps. And from the way he crawled around finding the dangling ends of the girts it was easy to see that Casey had already sacked this horse out good and proper. A rank horse might have caved the kid's skull in for him, which I had not considered when I told the kid to saddle. I guess I'd given him credit for having more sense than he owned. Still, he got the job done, and that counts for something.

We had a lot of fun watching him bit the horse, too. It took quite a while.

That training bridle is not easy to hang anyway because it is sort of clumsy. It is made for sturdiness, not looks, of thick, inch-wide leather. The reins are thick cotton ropes, big enough to really get a grip on and soft enough that it won't burn your hands if the horse takes the reins away from you — which isn't supposed to happen but does anyway. The bit is hard to handle because it is a broken-mouth snaffle made of copper twists. It's a fine bit for training because you can't hardly do anything with it that would hurt a horse's mouth. But being so floppy and having no check pieces to use as a handle, it can be tricky to guide into place.

And that sorrel was no help at all. Short-tied or not, that animal was reaching for clouds with its muzzle as soon as it saw the bridle. I've seen pictures of those African giraffes, and I swear they have nothing on that sorrel when it comes to getting their noses into the air. It would've taken a ladder to reach his head up there, and the kid didn't know how to rig a war bridle to haul him down with. It took the kid quite a bit of wrestling and tugging before he had everything in place.

He got it done eventually, though, and gave us a triumphant look over his shoulder. Well, that was about the main thing I wanted him to learn. That if he set out to make a horse do something, he could damn sure do it. A human person can't hardly outmuscle a horse, but you can sure out-stubborn one.

"Crawl aboard, Kid, and take him around a few times."

"All right." He had a right to be worn down some after all the wrestling and carrying on, but there was more life and determination in his voice now than there had been before.

He slipped the rope off the animal and threw his reins up. He put his foot in the near stirrup; the horse took it out again by hopping away as far as a seven-foot rein would allow. He tried it a few more times with no better result and then showed he was getting half smart in his old age — and likely that he had watched some of the crew mounting their rough ones. He grabbed hold of the bridle, hauled the sorrel's head to the stirrup and stepped on.

"You've aggravated him long enough, Kid," I muttered under my breath. "His turn next." Katy giggled.

The kid gave us a half-grin and a shrug and let go of the bridle. The sorrel stood spraddle-legged for a moment and gave himself a wet-dog shake, which by itself was almost enough to vibrate the kid off. Then the horse took his turn. The sorrel squealed once, bogged his head and gave a few hippety-hops. Nothing mean, just sort of testing.

I hoped Casey wouldn't mind the bad notions I was putting into this animal's head, for he had just discovered that he could refuse to be ridden. The kid was seated in the dirt with a startled expression locked on his face. I don't think he was real sure how he had gotten from one place to the other.

The kid jumped back onto his feet and tried to catch a trailing rein. The sorrel trot-

115

ted away. The two of them made a few circles of the pen before Katy reached out and snagged a rein as the horse came past us. The horse stopped obediently, and the kid took him. He gave Katy another of those shy, almost embarrassed half-smiles. "Thanks."

Katy nodded.

The kid took the sorrel back near the snubbing post, cheeked him, and stepped on again.

After a half hour or so the kid was no longer jumping to his feet. But he was still getting up. The horse was no longer trotting away either. Now it was waiting for the kid to try again, sweat darkening its shoulders and front end and turning the red almost to a brown shade.

The kid crawled slowly up again. He no longer had to cheek the horse, which was just as well. I'll bet he was feeling some deep-seated aches by that time. He hit the saddle and rammed his boots home in the stirrups and hunched his back in anticipation of the storm. Nothing happened. The sorrel stood quietly. Its head was low but not reaching for a jump. The kid shifted in his seat. Still no explosion. He looked at us and grinned his pleasure and surprise.

Katy gave him a wave of congratulation.

I called to him, "I thought I told you to ride him around the pen a few turns, not to just sit on him like a courthouse statue."

"Yes, sir," he called back. He definitely sounded cheerful this time. He touched the sorrel's ribs with his heels, and the horse moved forward.

I believe that was one very tickled kid. And he had a right to be.

# CHAPTER 9

"It won't be long now. How's the ice holding out?"

The kid reached behind him and felt of the sodden, brown lumps of burlap sacking draped over the ice- and sawdust-packed oyster buckets.

"There's still some left. It'll be all right," he said. The church spire and rooftops of Warcry were already in sight. Coming down with no more load than this, we had been able to make good time even with only two horses in the hitch.

The others, of course, the boys on their horses and the family in the gig, had long since been lost to view. They would be in town by now, the family taking rooms in the hotel and the boys staking claims to the hay piles that would have been spread through the big livery barn and in all the storage buildings with room enough to hold a body or two. With the whole valley gathering for the big yearly feed, there would not be rooms enough to hold everyone.

I was wearing my next-to-best suit — I know better than to wear my best to an event that sometimes turns sloppy — and had some clean shirts and smallclothes in my grip. The kid had washed his clothes fresh the day before, hiding in the kitchen until they were dry. He didn't own any others, though he did have clean underthings in his valise. The woolly chaps had been left tucked under the foot end of his bunk back home.

By golly, if the kid didn't watch out, he was going to start *looking* like a hand, anyway. The yellow shirt was faded enough now that it no longer tried to bite anyone walking past, and his jeans were commencing to soften. With his new boots and reshaped hat — which was now carrying a decent amount of corral dust from a coupla days of him playing with the spare horses — he could be mistaken for a regular hand.

He was still pale, spending most of the day in the kitchen and being naturally fair complected, but even that wasn't quite so standout glaring as it had been just a few weeks before.

Come to think of it, it seemed a lot longer than it really was. And in that short time the kid had become a real help to me and had learned quite a bit.

On the road ahead of us were some other south-valley wagons, and every little while a bunch of fellows would come loping past us with a wave or a cheery word of greeting. Everyone was anxious to get into town today.

The big oyster fry wouldn't be until tomorrow, but sometime over the past dozen years or so it had become accepted that everyone came in to start the festivities a day early. Tonight the Masonic Lodge would take over the Bull Shooter for the party they had instituted four years back. It had been such a success, they'd held one every year since, and it looked like that would become a regular thing too. They brought in kegs of beer and set them up on blocks atop the bar and served peanuts and pickled eggs with it. The party was open to everyone, men that is, including the Knights of Columbus boys. I wondered what the Knights would be coming up with to show their open-mindedness. I figured there was sure to be something in another year or two. All of which was to the good for those of us who'd be partaking of whatever it turned out to be.

We clattered into Warcry awhile later and

pulled the team around to Clete Purty's icehouse, where they would be collecting the oysters. Clete runs a dry goods business and is chief of the volunteer fire department. As I expected, Clete was there himself. He probably wouldn't have time to set foot inside his store again until the fry was over. He was there and Handy Cauthorn and Ron Collins and a couple of the other fellows. They were all wearing their dress blue caps with the gold braid and shields and shiny black beaks. They grinned and howdied us when we drove up. I introduced the kid to them, and they gave him polite greetings. I could feel him loosening up a little after they did. I guess he must have been expecting an ordeal or something, and it did seem like he had troubles whenever he entered Warcry.

"What do you have for us, boys? Is the FR-Connected Bar contributing an oyster or two this year?" Clete asked.

"I think the boys remembered to save a half dozen or so," I told him. "I guess you're welcome to them if they haven't rotted already." I hooked a thumb toward the wagon bed and said, "Help yourself. Or do you want me to unload them for you, too?"

"We ought to call you on that an' make you do it, by damn," Ron said with a smile.

The kid crawled over the back of the seat and stripped the coverings away from our buckets. There was enough ice left that I knew the oysters were all right. Clete grinned when he saw how many we'd brought. Seventeen buckets. There could have been a lot more except that some of the boys just plain did not like to be bothered with bringing them in, and sometimes distance and the press of time made it impossible to keep them fresh. And in truth I guess I should admit that the temptations had been too great. I had sneaked a coupla batches to fry up for me and Jess and the old man, though the rest of the boys were not supposed to know this even if we did do it every year.

"Hand them out, Kid. It's about time these lazy town fellas did some honest work," I said and got some wisecracks fired back at me.

They made short work of the unloading. Through the door of the icehouse I could see a good many other containers already brought in from the closer places.

"Will we have enough, Clete?"

"Looks like a good year for it," he said. "I think we'll be able to satisfy even your appetite."

I turned to the kid and said, "Old Clete

there almost lost his job as fire chief a few years ago. Three was it, Clete?" He nodded. "We had a poor calf crop and a terrible hot spell early in the year that spoiled most of what we did get. We didn't hardly have enough oysters to make a dent in what we needed. Poor ol' Clete had to fill out the meal with pork, which I guess is what these town weaklings eat all the time."

"It's true," Clete said. "I never saw a worse year for the oysters, and wouldn't you know there'd be no fresh beef available on such short notice." He shook his head. "Right through the morning of the fry we kept looking for the oysters to come in, but they never did. But we don't have to worry about that this year. We can lay on a real feast this time."

I heard another wagon coming and turned to look. It was Tom Abbot and his family, more south-valley folks, though Tom had the smallest of the cow outfits down our way. There were a lot more shoestring outfits to the north, where the land had been claimed later when there were more people around looking to take it up. Not that I'm trying to knock Tom. He runs a solid little operation and takes an honestly earned profit from it. He's beholden to no man and fair with all, and there is not a bad thing anyone could say about him.

"We'd best get out of your way, boys. We'll see you tonight probably."

I parked the wagon at Wiggins's loading dock again since we would be doing some restocking there while we happened to be in with the wagon. I reminded myself again to buy extra heavy on the canned milk. Katy was really using it up for her orphans.

"I'll take care of the team if you want," the kid said. He leaped lightly to the ground and began unhooking the horses.

"There should be a picket line set up east of the loading pens," I told him. "You'd best find a place for them while you still might find room. You can water them later."

The kid led the horses off. I got my war bag and headed for the hotel. They always held a room for me there. Damned nice of them and plenty thoughtful. It wasn't the sort of thing they had to do, but they always did it. And this time of year I'll just bet they got an awful lot of clamoring for hotel space.

For we enjoyed our yearly get-together so much that I guess we spoke about it to strangers and each year some came back to see. Drummers arranging their visits to coincide with the fry and snake-oil men and gamblers and such looking for bigger crowds to milk the money from and promoters of one thing or another. Not that we minded. We figured they added to the fun of the whole thing, and if any of these strangers was smart enough to fleece us, why, in that case they were entitled to their profit.

Benjie Harris had my room key waiting, the same one I always took when I was in town. I got myself settled and fingered my chin and decided to go ahead and shave and have myself some fun. Benjie gave me a short wave as I went out, but he didn't look real happy at that moment. There were a coupla loudly drunk drummers giving him a hard time about there not being rooms available.

I drifted down toward the TC&W tracks, where most of the excitement would be. I didn't especially want it right then, but a thin, pale figure in a yellow shirt caught my eye. He was sitting cross-legged near the railroad tracks, his back against one of the six-by-sixes of the big loading chute. He was staring westward, seeming to take no notice when someone would walk in front of him. There was something about the way he held himself that made him look lost and painfully alone. And hell, I couldn't just go on about my own business, or pleasure, after seeing him like that.

"Hi, Kid. Are the beasts settled and

happy?"

His head snapped around and for a moment the emptiness was still in his eyes, but quickly that was replaced with what looked like a kind of pleasure. "Yes, sir. And I put some hay down for them. I'll take them to water later."

"Good. Have you seen the sights yet?" He shook his head. "It might not be much by Pennsylvania standards, Kid, but for us this is big doin's. C'mon and humor me while I do some gawking at all the wonders."

The kid grinned and came to his feet. "Whatever you say, boss."

We crossed the shining railroad tracks to some commercial displays set up there. Bright colored sulky mowers and trip rakes and a gang plow that would have taken a four-horse hitch to pull it and a grain drill for seeding oats or whatever. Further down there were some new wagons and a really handsome landau painted red with gold trim. The railroad must have had to add a flatcar to the regular train to bring all this stuff in. We looked them over, and I had to admire the quality of the green and yellow Deere mowers. One of them could cut a six-foot swath at each pass. Talk about making hay. . . .

The kid didn't know what much of any of

it was for, which surprised me for I'd always heard that Pennsylvania was good farming country where they should be more familiar than us with these mechanical implements, but I explained as best I could and he seemed to catch on once he was told.

Closer to town a snake-oil man had set up a platform and tent where he was hawking some marvelous elixir that would cure anything that ailed man or beast. A brown-skinned woman with mighty little in the way of clothing assured him an attentive audience. He was not selling much of his snake oil, but that was just his come-on anyway. After a while the woman danced off into the tent, and with a broad wink the whiskery old fraud explained that this ritual dance from the mystic Orient couldn't be concluded in public. Anyone who wanted to see the rest of it could step inside — for a fifty-cent admission charge. I expected the dry lips and shallow breathing the kid showed, and no doubt he'd have gone inside if he'd had the money. But I was kinda surprised by some of the older fellows who did go in. I wasn't surprised that they would be interested but that they didn't know any better. I never have understood why a grown man would pay half a dollar to look at something in public when for a coupla dollars he could rent the use of that same thing in private.

I half expected the kid to tap me for a loan but he did not, and we walked on down into the town.

It was getting on into the late afternoon now, so I guided us toward Elsie's place. She had gotten into the spirit of things by setting up a long table across the front of her place — the inside was just too small to hold all who would be looking for a meal — loaded with thick sandwiches and chunks of pie and cake and other things that could be carried off in your hand to be eaten wherever you could find room to sit. We got in line, but Elsie spotted us and came hurrying over.

"What do you think you're doing standing out here?" she demanded. "Get yourself inside before I get angry with you." She took me by the arm and tugged me out of the line. "You too, I reckon," she told the kid.

She led us to one of the few empty tables. Most of them were occupied by town fellows wearing fire department caps. "Nellie!" she hollered, pointing at us before she hustled back out the front door. Poor Elsie seemed to be in a regular frenzy today.

Nellie Adams, who helped out on those

few occasions when Elsie couldn't handle the place by herself, came to us practically at a run. The strands of hair that had escaped from her bun were stringy with moisture, and her face was flushed.

"Don't you *dare* tell me what you want," Nellie said breathlessly. "You'll take what we've got." Without waiting for an answer, she spun in a flurry of billowing skirts and apron and was gone again.

"Whee-oo!" I said. "Do you think we should sit, or would that take too much time?"

The kid grinned and shook his head. We sat and in about fifteen seconds here came Nellie again, carrying a tray with four big bowls on it. She put two bowls in front of each of us and was gone with a muttered "back in a minute" floating over her shoulder. One bowl held a thick stew with chunks of beef and potato and onion and carrot in brown gravy. The other was full of beans, soaked and then oven-baked in a sauce that seemed to have molasses and tiny bits of diced onion and brown sugar in it. Mighty good, too. It looked like Elsie had been prepared ahead of time for the inside customers too.

Nellie came back once with mugs of coffee and returned to her work. She was slicing bread and cutting slabs of cold meat, both roast beef and boiled ham, as fast as she could to supply the needs outside. She'd slap on butter and a spill of salt and if you didn't like it that way you could just go rustle your supper elsewhere. They didn't have time today for fussy eaters.

We finished our meal in more of a hurry than I usually like to take, but I guess I was sort of infected by the hurry-up feeling in the place, and I think the kid was too. I drained off the last of my coffee.

"Do you have anything against working on your day off, Kid?"

"Nope. Let's." He led the way to the work counter where Nellie was so busy. "You know where everything is," he said, "so keep it coming, and we'll do the rest." He took one of the long knives and began slicing loaves of Elsie's bread. I found a knife that came near to suiting me — though I have never known a woman who can keep her knives really sharp — and started slicing meat. That left Nellie free to carry stuff out front and handle the tables and bring more bread and meat and butter and other such odds and ends — practically nothing compared to what she'd been doing but enough to keep a coupla people beaver-busy.

And by damn, the kid seemed to be enjoying it as much as I was.

# CHAPTER 10

All the rockers on the hotel porch were taken, so we went on past there toward the wagon. It felt good to sit down again. I loaded my pipe and got that extra-good flavor and contentment that comes when you're tired but feeling good from it. The kid sat silently, watching the people stream past, while I finished my smoke.

"Would it be all right for me to sleep in the wagon tonight?" he asked when I had knocked the dottle from my pipe.

I looked around at the bed of the wagon. It was a mess, burlap and wet sawdust and puddles left from the melted ice. "Nope."

"Oh." He didn't argue about the answer, though it was pretty obvious he was disappointed by it.

Well, hell, I thought. There were men bunking down on piled hay all over this town. If it was all right for them, it was all right for the kid.

Yeah, and there wasn't a single one of those fellows who would have a kind word for him. They would be polite, sure. But there wouldn't be a one of them wanting to buddy up to a tenderfoot kid who was known to be a complete coward too. So what could I do? Turn the kid out to be miserable by himself while I went off with my friends?

"Go water the horses, Kid. I'll take your stuff up to the hotel room. Number one thirty two, same as the last time."

"Yes, sir." He didn't sound overjoyed, though. I guess he figured he was imposing. And of course he was. But what the hell? It was better than the alternative.

The kid took off at a fast walk toward the line of horses out by the tracks. I fished his valise from under the wagon seat and headed back toward the hotel. After that time spent in Elsie's kitchen I felt too greasy to be out on the town, but a wash-up would fix that. And some of the free beer laid on by the Masons would make me feel a whole lot better.

I washed and waited for the kid to come back so he could clean up as well. He threw out the dirty water when he was done and brought in a pitcher of fresh. He was trying to be useful while he was here, the same as he tried back home.

"All done, Kid?"

"I think so."

"Good. Let's go over to the Bull Shooter then. They should've started by now."

He looked uncertain. "The Bull Shooter. That's the saloon where . . . I had that trouble before. Maybe I better stay here."

"Aw, you don't wanta sit here in an empty room while there's a free bash going on, Kid. C'mon. You'll be all right."

He shrugged his shoulders and stood.

"That's the boy." I pulled my coat on and got my hat, and we were off.

The kid didn't really want to go. It was my meddling that put him there.

The Bull Shooter was surrounded by men and by boys trying to convince each other they were old enough to be there with the men. Most everyone already had a beer in his hand and most carried paper sacks of peanuts or squares of paper folded wetly around the pickled, hard-boiled eggs. Everyone was trying to talk to everyone else, all at the same time.

I elbowed my way through the crowd, having to pause every step or two to pass a word with someone. Some of these fellows I hadn't seen since the last big get-together, which would have been the Fourth of July past. The valley only got together for big holiday celebrations twice each year. Once for this fry after the close of spring branding and again for the fireworks and speechmaking to celebrate the Fourth. There were other special occasions, of course. And socials and dances and such from time to time. But only those two when the whole valley was sure to turn out for it.

The kid followed behind and eventually we made it to the doors and inside. It was close packed and hot inside, smelling of tobacco smoke and toilet water and beer foam. Already some of the Masons were carrying out an empty keg while others rolled in a full one. They muscled it onto the bar, and Hiram drove a spigot into the bung. Hiram wouldn't be making any money this night, but he was in there helping. And he wasn't even a Masonic brother.

Monte Tillits handed us each a canning jar when we reached the bar. "Bring 'em back," he said. "We're already out of mugs."

Hiram was manning the tap. He filled the quart jars with a flourish and pointed us toward the barrels holding the peanuts and the eggs. I didn't feel like fighting through this mob trying to carry anything in my left hand so I popped an egg into my mouth and filled a coat pocket with peanuts. That sort of thing was why I never wore my best suit to town for the fry. The kid loaded up behind me.

Bill Dean had a chair that he offered to vacate for me, but I thanked him and refused. The air was too close inside with so many people packed in, taking every seat and about all the standing room too.

We squeezed through to the side door and carried our jars of beer to a nearby wagon tailgate, where a coupla youngsters hopped down so I could sit.

"Cheers, Kid." The beer was downright good. We sipped at it and watched people pass. Everyone was in a good humor, smiling and talking and clutching at each other's elbows.

Jess and Tom Abbot and Warren Tynell's foreman, Fletcher Lewis, came by and stopped for a chat. They were carrying mugs with them.

"I don't suppose you've seen Daisy May wandering around?" Jess asked.

"Not yet, but if you stay put a little while he's almost sure to be by," I told him. He was referring to D. Z. May, the other south-valley man who had high summer pasture in the same general area that we used and Abbot and Tynell. I've often wondered what the D and the Z stand for, but as far as I know the only man in the whole valley who has the answer to that one is Daisy May himself. I'm not even sure his wife knows what it is. All I've ever heard her call him is Mr. May. And he always refers to her as Mrs. May.

"You boys trying to decide who goes up top first?" I asked.

"Uh-huh," Jess said. "Tom figures to start his next week, and I'm going to move ours about as quick if there's no conflict with Daisy. Fletch hasn't been up yet and wants to hold the Slash WT down low awhile anyhow. So if Daisy's agreeable, we'll go as soon as Tom is through."

There is a power of good grazing up on that mountain, and through long use we have all worked out who will put his herd where and about when he will need to do it. But because of some steep slopes at the break between the foothills and the mountain proper, everyone uses the same lower route getting up there. It saves a lot of confusion and extra work to make sure there aren't two separate herds trying to occupy the same funnel at one time. The four outfits co-ordinated their moves this way going up each spring and again coming down each fall.

Tom and the two ramrods had finished their beers. "Could I bring you gentlemen a refill?" the kid offered. He collected their mugs and took them inside, leaving his own nearly full jar on the tailgate beside me.

"Pretty nice kid," Tom said. "One of yours?"

"Old ugly's new helper," Jess said, hooking a thumb in my direction.

"He's a good kid, Tom. Good worker."

Fletch raised an eyebrow. "Would he be the one I heard Wayne talking about a few weeks back?"

"That'd depend on what Wayne was saying, but more than likely it would've been the same kid, I guess," I told him.

There was a lot more I might have volunteered on that subject, but there are some things you just don't say to a man about his employer's baby boy, especially if you respect the man you are talking to and the loyalty he should give to his outfit. And there wasn't a thing wrong with Fletcher on those points.

Fletch's other eyebrow went up. "Maybe not such a good kid after all then," he said. Which got Tom Abbot's curiosity up. It was obvious he hadn't heard about the fuss between Wayne and the kid.

"My opinion is that he's a good kid,

138

Fletch," I said before Tom could step in with a bunch of questions. The kid would be back soon — with a beer for Fletcher among his burdens — and if we got into an argument on that particular subject, he was almost certain to feel some strain.

Fletcher looked me in the eye for a moment before he said, "All right. You know him better than the rest of us."

I glanced at Jess in time to see his jaw muscles relax. His jaw is a dead giveaway when Jess is tensing up about something. Jess might have had his little crew troubles connected with the kid, and he might not have a hell of a lot of use for the kid himself. But by damn, if anyone was fixing to put some bad talk on one of our boys, old Jess would be in there ready to argue or even fight on his behalf.

I don't think Fletcher had caught any of the warning signals, but it looked like Tom had. He must have been curious about all this, but he dropped it cold and began talking about the prospects of the hay crop this year and when we should start laying on our haying crews. Everyone was of the opinion this would be a year for early cuttings, possibly early enough to give us a third cutting at the end of the season though we do not often get to take more than two.

If so, we would be in good shape for winter feed and could carry some two-year-olds over for the high spring market prices next year.

The kid came back and distributed the now full mugs to their owners. He perched on the tailgate and leaned back as if he didn't want to push himself into the conversation but wanted to be close.

I finished my first brew and was thinking about asking the kid to bring another. I sure wish I'd been drinking a little faster and had sent him off already. Or maybe that would only have delayed things by a short while.

Wayne Tynell caught sight of Fletcher standing with us. He was carrying a glass jar too, but his was not holding beer. It held maybe a pint of colorless liquid that was certain to be corn whiskey. If the last few times I'd seen him meant anything, Wayne was pulling a cork pretty hard and pretty often.

"Hey, Fletch, ol' boy," he said. He draped an arm familiarly over Fletcher's shoulders. To my mind that should have earned him an elbow in the ribs. Boss's son or no boss's son, a ranch foreman of Fletcher's age and experience was entitled to more respect than having a whelp like that paw at him.

But I guess they did things differently at the Slash WT. I couldn't help thinking what a good thing it was that Warren hadn't bought out old Fred's estate, for I would've been homeless a long time ago if he had.

"You're makin' sure no one's gonna interfere with the movement of our herd, aren't ya, Fletch?" Wayne wanted to know.

"I'm making sure none of us will ruffle anyone else's feathers, Wayne," the ramrod said. But there was no hint of correction in his tone.

"Fine, Fletch. Fine. I . . ." Wayne finally got a look at who was beside me on that tailgate. "Well I'll be go to hell," he said. "It's the dude with the yellow belly, right? Sure, I'd remember that shirt anyplace. What are you doing here with the menfolk, kid? Say, isn't that the name I tagged you with? Kid? Some kind of kid. The Yella Kid?"

"The Keystone Kid," the kid said mildly. "I liked it so much I decided to keep it. Thanks."

Wayne shifted closer to the kid and took a swallow from his whiskey jar. He was a long way from being drunk, but he'd had enough. I hoped he was not going to start anything, but the indications surely were otherwise.

To top it off, Billy Knowles and Jim Fuller

141

and Bean Simon were wandering past at the moment. Billy spotted Wayne and the kid and the rest of us. He stopped and poked Jim, who poked Bean. They came over to join the party.

Normally I'd have thought that was just great, because normally that would guarantee that no member of our bunch would have to take a beating. The boys would stop it way short of that. If it came to a scramble now, the boys would still help. If only the kid would throw just one punch into Wayne Tynell's face, the boys from our crew would be tickled to break it up before anyone got hurt. What I was afraid, though, was that our crew was about to get themselves a demonstration that would match the secondhand stories they'd already heard.

Wayne looked at our boys and grinned. It was a nasty grin. "Are *all* your hands cowards? Or just some of you?"

Bean and Jim began to bristle and in another minute there'd have been some fists flying, but Billy, of all people, stopped them. He was usually the feistiest of the lot. He stepped close to Wayne and shoved his own pug nose practically into Tynell's chin. "Not a one of us is, Wayne-boy, an' any of us'll be glad to prove it to you."

Billy turned to the kid, and I just knew

what was coming next. I looked to Jess, hoping he might stop it, but all he could do was shrug and hold his palms out. Wayne Tynell wasn't going to start the fight. Billy was going to force it for him.

"Prove it, Kid," Billy said, a hint of pleading in his voice. "Bust this big son of a bitch in the mouth one to show him the FR-Connected Bar don't back off." Billy stood swiveling his eyes from Wayne to the kid and back.

The kid stayed where he was.

"Well?" Billy demanded.

"Aw, Billy," the kid said. "Anyone could see he can whip me. It won't prove anything to either of us if I start a fight. That doesn't make sense."

Billy looked like he was going to explode. And Wayne, with his usual tact, chose just that moment to laugh in Billy's face. Billy balled his fists and would have started swinging if Jim and Bean hadn't taken him by the arms and pulled him away.

"Cut it out, Billy," Bean said loud enough for us all to hear. He gave the kid a dark look. "That yella dough-puncher ain't worth it."

Billy shook himself and glared at the kid. "Watch what you say about the *rest* of us, Tynell," he warned. He and his buddies stomped back into the Bull Shooter. They had the sound of Tynell's laughter to spur them along.

Jess and Tom, even Fletcher Lewis, looked embarrassed by the whole thing. As I guess I was myself.

The kid was about the only one — except for that Wayne — who *didn't* seem to be embarrassed by the performance he'd just put on. He merely looked confused.

"C'mon, dammit," I told him. I left my empty jar on the tailgate and headed for the hotel after one free beer. A second one would have gagged me just then. Or having to sit in public with the entire valley population there to question my judgment. Not that they didn't have a right to be questioning it. I sure was.

# Chapter 11

Four o'clock came earlier than I wanted it to that next morning in spite of my getting to bed hours before normal the evening before. I guess what it came down to was that I just was not anxious to face the day. I thought I'd gotten over feeling like that years before. There wasn't any going back to sleep, though, so I found the lamp and struck a match.

In the glare of the sudden light the kid's eyes stood out like a pair of tiny mirrors. He was wide awake, lying there staring into the darkness. He hadn't been awake all night. I knew that for a fact because I'd had to put up with his snoring quite a spell before I could sleep.

The match burned down to my fingertips and I cussed some before I lit another. This time I remembered to use it on the lamp-wick instead of myself.

I got dressed and still the kid hadn't

moved. So far as I'd noticed, he hadn't even blinked his eyes. I thought about shaking him to get his attention. But for what? I left the lamp burning and went out.

It was still way too early to wake poor Elsie after the day she'd just had, and I didn't have anywhere else to go. I just wanted out of that room if the kid insisted on lying there staring off into space. I went down to the lobby and onto the porch. At least the rockers were empty at this time of morning. I eased down into one and enjoyed the smell of the clean, night air. Though I could have used a heavier coat than the one I was wearing.

I rocked for a while, just sitting and listening to the late-night sounds. Roosters beginning to warm up their lungs. An occasional dog answering them. The faint slap of some distant outhouse door.

Someone passed along the other side of the dark street, heading from the direction of Bessie Blue's place toward the horse line. The hollow thud of his boot heels hitting the board sidewalk was loud. It was a lonely sound. He was lost in the shadows within half a block.

I was feeling a little restless, though usually I am pretty well content whether there are other folks about or not. I thought about firing up my pipe but didn't really want the taste of it on top of yesterday's leftover flavors. That was bad enough without adding more. So I just sat, waiting for nothing except the passage of time, thinking about nothing in particular.

After a half hour or so the hotel door opened. It was the kid.

"Mind if I sit down?"

"Suit yourself."

He slumped into the chair next to mine and sat for a while and looked at his hands. "I guess I had another wrong idea about this country," he said at last. His voice was very low, thoughtful.

"How's that?" I grunted.

He sounded bitter now. "I heard that out here a man was free to be anything he wanted to be. I guess that isn't so either."

I wondered just what in hell this kid had expected. It was really none of my business, but I could not help saying, "Kid, it looks to me like you had all the opportunity in the world to show what you are made of. Well, you made your own choice; you were free to do however you wanted. Now it's up to you to live with that choice. And, Kid, no one else laid that on you. It was strictly your own doing."

"What about that fellow that keeps picking at me? I never asked him to do that. That wasn't my doing." There was no whine in his voice, but there was some anger.

"No, but if you ever find a place where there's no idiots to creep out of the woodwork, you let me know. I'll throw over everything I've got here and move to that place with you."

"No one looks down on him for being the way he is, though," he persisted.

"Maybe," I said, "but he has damn few friends, probably no really good friends. And you have to remember that Wayne grew up here. Good or bad, he's still part of this valley. Folks don't like him a hell of a lot, but they accept him as part of the place. You came in cold. Like it or not, you've got to live with that."

The kid shook his head. "I don't know," he said. "I just can't see any sense in letting someone like that pull me into a fight that I'm going to lose anyway."

I was getting kind of impatient with such talking. As far as I can see, a man does what he figures he should do and takes whatever comes of it, and that is that. Talking about it doesn't change the facts, not when you get right down to it. So maybe I was a little quick to snort at that.

"Hell's bells, Kid! What happened the first

time you ran into ol' Wayne? He slapped you around good, that's what. Do you think he'd have hurt you any worse if you'd stood up to him? Or yesterday. Which do you want more? To avoid Wayne Tynell or to have the boys take to you?" I stood and gave him a hard look. "Think on that awhile."

I decided Elsie'd had enough sleep and went to get myself some coffee.

They started the fires under the big iron grids about ten o'clock and had coals enough to start cooking before the declared serving time of twelve o'clock noon. The volunteer fire company sure turned out for this. They were all busy, rushing around like crazy with their slicing and cooking and serving and carrying things back and forth.

They didn't offer much of a selection. Fried Rocky Mountain oysters and baked potatoes, some butter and salt and your choice of coffee or lemonade to drink. No beer today, and about half the people in line were kids and more women than you would have thought lived in the valley. The serving line was open all afternoon, and on the flat north of town and west of the tracks were foot races and three-legged races and egg-tossing contests and apple bobbing and such for the kids. Further out some of the men were matching horse races and staging bronc-riding and team-roping contests. I got my first plateload of oysters and a mug of coffee and went up to see how our boys would make out in the riding and roping events.

We never brought any horses in to race, mostly because the normal distance of a run at these things was two miles, one mile north to the red, white, and blue pole that had been set there years before and then back again. Our ranch stock was heavy on quarter-mile running blood, sprinters with a lot of cow sense but no competition for some of the fellows from the north part of the valley who had bred a lot of English blood into their animals.

Now the riding and roping. That was something else again. Our boys would be right in there for those.

Sam Jasson and Farley Hunter, both north-valley men, were matching a race when I got there. Sam was running his good stud horse against a lean, hard-muscled red gelding of Farley's. Both were wearing light saddles and had fifteen- or sixteen-year-old kids on them. It would've been considered poor form to use a flat racing saddle or to import a regular jockey, but shaving all the weight possible was just part of trying to win.

The stud horse was flaring his nostrils and dancing on his toes. He had been here before and knew what was coming. It coming onto breeding season probably did not help to calm him. The stud would not have to understand Sam's talk with the owners of favored mares to realize that much. The coming of spring would be enough to have him hotted up and ready.

Farley's gelding was a horse I'd never seen before. He was full grown and fully muscled, but there was no way to tell if he was freshly broken out and showed a flair for running, or if Farley might have brought in a seasoned runner from the outside. Whichever, the horse didn't show that he had a nerve in his body. If he weren't in such hard flesh, you might think he was too sluggish and lazy to move out of a trot, but a horse doesn't get that hard in the chest and shoulders from standing in a corral. Anyway there was something about the horse that hit me right. I was taking his calmness for confidence and thought I'd follow my hunch.

Fletcher Lewis was standing nearby and was looking a bit disgruntled. When I asked him why, he said it was because he couldn't find anyone who wanted to back the gelding against Sam's stud horse. Well, I knew how to fix that. We haggled a bit until Fletcher sweet-talked me into laying fifty of mine against his sixty-five-dollar wager. He sure was anxious. Mostly we just picked a horse and bet them even-up.

Sam and Farley got done with their bragging and strutting and got down to business. They waved everyone aside from the scratch-line start toward the pole and told their boys to bring the horses on. The buzz of conversation came to a halt, and everyone turned their attention on the horses.

It was an ask-and-answer start. The kid on Sam's stud asked, "Ready?" and the youngster on the gelding answered, "Go!" and they rammed their spurs in with a whoop and a holler.

The big stud just seemed to explode. All that muscle bunching and pushing, and bits of turf flying in the air behind him. Putting spurs to him was like putting a match to gunpowder.

The gelding was nothing like that. His start was like his muscle, sleek and refined. He just began picking them up and laying them down, each stride reaching further than the last one. He was so smooth he didn't seem to have any speed, and it was some little time before Sam's supporters noticed that the gelding was running right alongside their favorite. And by that time he wasn't running beside the stud horse any longer; by then he was out front and moving away. He was a good five lengths ahead at the pole according to the reports of some boys with field glasses, and he coasted in virtually alone at the finish line, still running smooth and easy. The stud horse by then was fifteen lengths behind, lathered and so tired he was starting to paddle his forefeet. The boy on him had marked him hard with whip and spurs, but the horse just didn't have enough.

"I will be go to hell," Fletcher said as he handed over my sixty-five dollars.

"You're welcome to take it back on the team roping," I told him.

"Your team against the Slash WT?"

"Uh-huh."

"Who's working for you?"

I shrugged my shoulders. "Don't even know, Fletch, but you can know we'll have a team in it. And I didn't ask who's doing your throwing, did I?"

He grinned and checked what he had left in his pocket. "You're on. Sixty-five, against the clock."

I watched a few of the young fellows ride

down some rough stock. Billy Knowles came unglued on this third jump and would have some laundry to do when he got home. Casey rode his down to a quivering, polite mount inside of two minutes and — probably out of habit — began teaching the beast to give to rein pressure before he got off.

My plate was too long empty and I was thinking of making the trek back for another when someone shoved a heaped refill of still-steaming oysters under my nose and took the empty plate out of my left hand. It was the kid. He looked apologetic and stubborn at the same time.

"I don't intend to quit," he said.

"I didn't ask you to."

"People can think what they damn well please, but I'm not going to quit. I want to stay in this valley and learn about the cow business."

"All right," I said. "In that case you'd better get yourself some oysters. Build up your strength."

He smiled and took off running.

Oh yes. That bet. I had a short chat with Jess and convinced him to get in there and show these younguns how to do it. With Jess heeling and Charlie Uver heading, the FR-Connected Bar had the low time of the day

154

by two full seconds. They were nearly four seconds better than the Slash WT's time. I did not at all mind going home with a hundred thirty dollars of Fletcher's hard-earned money.

# CHAPTER 12

It was not like Jess to hang around the cookhouse after the others had eaten and gone. He liked to get out where he could keep an eye on things, see how the boys were handling their string, see if anyone was getting too rough. If they were, they would be among the ones cut from the crew when they came back from up top.

Him dawdling over coffee now, that had me kind of worried. I wondered if the kid had gotten into some sort of trouble. I couldn't think of anything out of line. He'd been on his best and busiest behavior for the past week. Stayed out of the way of the crew and did his work and spent his free time off by himself with the string of spare horses. I couldn't think of a thing that Jess might bounce him for.

"Go ahead with the cleanup, would you, Kid? I need to do some walking."

"Sure thing." He already had most everything cleared away from the table and had a good start on the washing.

"You might as well fix yourself some breakfast, too. I might be a few minutes." I got my hat and joined Jess.

We walked down toward the pens. I didn't want to keep Jess away from his work any longer than necessary. He stopped by the lower hay barn, though, and leaned back against it.

I braced myself for whatever was coming. And then I wondered why. For crying out loud, I told myself, that kid shouldn't mean anything to me. He was just another wet-eared kid and one that would crawfish away from a fight at that. The country was practically overrun with starry-eyed younguns, and most of the rest of them had some backbone. So why had I picked this particular one to worry about? Still, it looked like I had. I was really worried about what Jess might be fixing to say.

"I want to talk to you about your pup," Jess said for openers. Something must have shown in my face. Jess gave me a close, curious look. Then he smiled and slapped me on the shoulder. "You're getting as fretful as a damned old woman," he accused.

"It's 'cause of the people I got to put up with around here," I told him.

"So quit worrying," Jess said. "I just want to ask a few things about him."

I lifted my right shoulder and let it drop. "Ask then. I might even answer."

"I've noticed the kid working himself sweaty in the horse pen when the crew is out. Can he ride?"

Again I had to shrug. I was not going to be telling Jess any lies, and he knew it. "He can manage the older, better broke stuff if it's just a question of getting from here to there. I wouldn't say he could work off a horse yet. As for the green ones, well, he's on top now more than he's on the ground, which is an improvement, but I wouldn't turn him loose on one without a nurse-maid."

"He could handle Big Nose, though?"

"Big Nose or Old Glory or the Yellow Runt or any like them, sure."

"How is he with handling them on the ground?"

"You mean is he scared of them?" Jess nodded. "No. Not a sign of that now. He has a lousy seat, and I'd guess he hasn't ever ridden hardly at all. But he isn't afraid of them."

I guess we'd both seen enough visitors and city people and such who weren't used to saddle stock and who just plain ran from any horse that wasn't hitched to a wagon or tied up. They seemed to think any loose horse might strike at them or bite, and of course they were right. They'd never learned to be willing to take a fist or maybe a fence post and knock a horse down before something like that could happen. Once you are willing to do that, the beast will know it, and you probably won't have to carry out any threats. Not often, anyway.

"Can he rig a pack?" Jess asked.

"I don't know, but if you mean the old-style rigging then I would doubt it. Except for you, me, and Casey I doubt there's anyone on the place who can. If you mean the saddles and pockets, though, I wouldn't know why not. Anybody who can hang a hat on a peg can do that." Which is oversimplifying it maybe but isn't far from true. It took some talent to build a secure pack out of ropes and blankets and sacks, but nowadays we were using army-style packsaddles with canvas bags that you just loaded and hung in place and tied to the saddle. And I began to see what Jess was driving at.

"Can he cook?"

"Enough for what you want," I told him. "Hell, you can put up with almost anything for a week or two."

Jess seemed to want to gnaw on his

thoughts before he went any further, so I pulled out my pipe and tobacco and fussed with that awhile. Jess took a healthy pinch of my tobacco and shoved it into his cheek.

"Going to take them on around to the Squawman, are you?"

"Uh-huh." He shifted his chew to the other cheek and let out the first, weak burst of juice. It didn't look hardly ripe yet. More yellow than brown.

The Squawman Valley was a hanging pocket of grass south toward the pass. With the graze on the mountain coming good so early, Jess would take the beeves there first. The natural movement of the herd then should carry them higher and back north toward the route they would have to use in the fall when we brought them down again. If we were lucky the early start in Squawman — named for the remains of an old cabin that could still be seen the last year I was in there — would save the trouble of midsummer movement of the cattle. The thing was, you can't reach the Squawman with a wagon, which is the only way I can travel anymore.

Jess nodded, more to himself than to me. "I'll carry your Keystone Kid along as cook then. Teach him what you need to. We start the gather tomorrow."

"Is Tom clear of the gap?"

"He will be by the time we move them that far. I've had the boys keeping an eye on their progress."

"Have you told Fletcher?"

"I'll send Chapman over today."

That was courtesy and custom more than necessity, really, because all four outfits going up this part of the mountain cross the west end of the FR-Connected Bar to get there. If George ever really wanted to throw his weight around, I suppose he could make everyone else go when he told them to. Hell, he might even stop them from crossing our range to get up there if he ever wanted to be that way about it.

I've heard all sorts of wild tales about feuds between neighbors caused by the breaking of fence lines, and for all I know maybe that sort of thing does happen in other places. When I worked outside the valley, though, there weren't any fences to be breached, and around here we've just never had any problems like that.

We all sort of took to fences as a convenience rather than a form of legal barrier. They are useful for keeping your stock where you want them. And if someone has a reason for crossing your fence, he just lays it down, drives his animals over, and then puts the fence back up behind him.

"Daisy May will go up behind us," Jess said, "and the Slash WT last unless they've changed their minds for some reason. Which reminds me, I'd better send someone over to tell Daisy when we're going, too. I think he wants to come up right on our heels."

"You'll sure be too busy next week to spare anyone."

"Ain't that the truth. Well, I better get to work. The boys'll be twiddling their thumbs soon if I don't get down there. Thanks for the chew."

"Sure."

The kid was as tickled as a kitten getting its belly scratched when I told him. Nothing would do but that I hunt out the pack-saddles that very morning and show him how to load them.

It was kind of lonesome around the place once they'd gone. I guess it did not help that I still felt some pangs when I saw a re-muda gathered and driven toward the high country. The everyday comings and goings didn't bother me, hadn't for a long time now. But trailing them up to the moun-tain . . . that was different somehow. Maybe because it meant I wouldn't be able to keep up with how things were now. Were the cows with calves holding their flesh, or were the calves sucking them hollow? How were we doing for losses? Did the twos look like they were filling out to shipping weight, or should some be carried over as threes?

Not that I could do anything about it anyway. But I liked knowing just the same.

For lack of anything better to do, I baked some goodies for the family and carried them over to the big house, and I damn near plucked the spare horses rat-tailed gathering hair to be braided into belts or hatbands or mecates or whatever. I wanted to teach the kid how to do that when he got back. I figured he could probably use a fancy belt, and I'd found that Earl Crane had had to leave his yellow horse behind with a stone bruise on one foot. Its mane and tail provided me with a nice supply of cream white hair. Though Earl would likely spit when he got home and saw how much was missing. In truth, I did get a little carried away there.

After a few days that sort of amusement was starting to pale, and while I might be slow I am no damned invalid. And it'd been some time since I'd paid a visit to Bessie Blue's place. I went over that evening and told George I was going to take the wagon into town for a few days.

"You're not going to tell me you are low

on supplies so soon, are you?" George asked.

"Nope. Don't need hardly a thing. I just wanta go to town."

"Natalie!" George roared.

Mrs. Senn stuck her head into the room. "What is it, old man?"

"Need anything from town, Nat? The gadabout is going in tomorrow, so if you women want anything you should speak up."

"A piano would be nice," she said without hesitation. There was a cheerful sparkle in her eyes.

"Put that on your list," George told me casually.

"A player?" I asked, just as casual.

"That would be all right," Natalie said. She thought for a moment and looked a bit more serious. "Oh, I'm sure there must be a dozen things we need. Katy and I will make up a list tonight if that's all right."

"Fine."

I waited until a respectable hour before I hitched the team the next morning, and Katy brought the list out to me. It wasn't a long one. A few odds and ends, a new potato ricer. And more canned milk. I shook my head.

"I know what you're thinking," she said as I folded the paper and jammed it into my

164

coat pocket.

"I'll just bet you do, too."

"Would you mind some company part way?"

"Of course not."

"Okay. Be right back." She ran lightly toward the long shed. She was back in ten minutes or so leading one of her mares. She handed me the reins to tend while she went in to tell her mother where she'd be. When she came back, she climbed onto the wagon box and stepped across onto her saddle. "All set," she said.

I put the team into a trot, and she jogged along beside.

"I don't think I remembered to thank you for those cinnamon twists," she said.

"You're welcome, child. I'm glad you still like them."

She grinned. "When I get married, that's one of the things I will look for. A husband who can make cinnamon twists as good as yours."

"It's a good thing you have plenty of time, then. That might take a while."

"Plenty of time? I'm practically an old maid already." She tried to look indignant but couldn't quite manage it.

"Bah! You've got years and years yet

before you start thinking things like that, child."

This time her nose did come into the air a bit. "It might not be as long as you think. Or anyone else either." She almost sounded serious.

"Bluebottle flies are the first ones drawn to honey, child, but they aren't much account. You can afford to take your time and be choosy, pretty as you are." She liked the compliment but not necessarily the advice that went with it.

"Maybe so, but when I find the right boy, I'm not going to wait. And it just might not be so long coming, either. You'll see."

"Yup. And when it does, you know I'll be wanting only the best for you, Katy. So mind you pick him carefully, or I might not approve."

She showed her dimples in a smile and changed the subject to a pair of larks that got up in front of us. And I put the conversation out of mind. I figured as long as she was still talking about finding the right boy and not the right man, she was all right.

She turned off when we were down on the public road and put her mare into a brisk lope across the shallow, green swales that were empty of cattle. She made a pretty sight in her riding skirt and bonnet.

Me, I drove on in to Warcry and checked into the hotel. I managed to get rid of twenty-three dollars of Fletcher Lewis's money in Bessie Blue's place the next coupla nights and spent some time talking with the boys in the Bull Shooter and found an even better use for some more of Fletcher's money before I went home.

Damned if Edwin Dart and his wife — whose two daughters were grown and gone now — didn't have a secondhand player piano they were wanting to sell. I gave them fifty dollars for the piano and a trunk nearly full of music rolls, and I laughed most of the way home thinking about the way the family's eyes would pop when I drove up with that thing in the wagon. I was right, too, and it was worth every bit of it just for that sight alone.

# CHAPTER 13

"My gosh, have you ever . . . ? Oh, of course you have. I forgot. You've been on dozens of drives like that, haven't you? Well anyway, let me tell you about . . ." The kid was really wound up, beaming like a bull's-eye lantern and full of chatter. He had the canvas packsaddle panniers piled all over the work space of the kitchen, and I don't think he ever once shut up while he was unloading them and stowing the stuff away.

I got practically a step-by-step description of the drive and a bite-by-bite account of his meals. He couldn't have been any more excited if he'd been named trail boss. From his point of view it had been a roaring success.

The kid sure was dirty, though. He looked like he hadn't washed his face since he left. It was positively black. And in the midst of that it even looked like he was getting some whiskers. I hadn't noticed that before.

"Finish putting that stuff away, Kid, while I get down to some serious cooking. If that damn Jess had thought to send a rider ahead, I'd have been ready with something special. As it is, they'll just have to make do."

I fell to and pretty soon the kid was working along with me. We sliced huge steaks and got a mountain of biscuits in the oven, enough to dang near compete with the mountain they'd just come down off of, and fried enough potatoes to strain the backs of two men to carry it, and set some dried corn to boiling in salted milk and water. And for the trail-end meal I always mixed up some cakes instead of their usual pies. There wasn't much time, but we got her done.

The whole crew was in a good humor this night. They were picking at each other like so many strange roosters thrown into the same coop, but all of it in fun. A couple of them were even mildly twitting the kid again, although these were older hands like Uver and Chapman and inclined to be more tolerant than the younger boys. I was awfully pleased to see it.

They gobbled up everything in sight and leaned back to smoke and talk over coffee refills, which was also tolerated on special occasions like this. I would've taken my plate in to join them, but the kid didn't want to sit at the big table, so I stayed in the kitchen with him. When we were done, I told him, "You're through for the day now, Kid. Take off. Get yourself a wash-up and hit the slats. I'll be quiet as I can."

"No, sir. No need for that. I'll help, and we can both get to bed early." He was on his feet and working again before I had a chance to argue with him.

I'll guaran-damn-tee, though, he wasn't awake very long after we got done with the dishwashing. He didn't even wait to fill the wood-box but mumbled something about "in the morning" and stretched out. I think he was sound asleep halfway down to his bunk.

I turned the big lamps out and cut the flame on the last one to a flicker so I would have enough light not to stumble over anything and maybe disturb him. I slipped outside with a package under my arm and headed for the bunkhouse.

Jess's room takes up one end of the long building, with its own doorway so he can come and go without bothering the hands. It also helps that that way anyone who might want to talk to him can do it without everyone else having to know he's in with the ramrod.

170

"I was about to decide you weren't coming," Jess said.

"You sure get set in your ways."

"Don't give me that, old man. I know you've been goofing off in town while we were up there working. This is the least you could do to make amends."

"If you want to be like that, I can go back to the cookhouse and turn in." I took the bottle out of the sack — absolutely, strictly and utterly forbidden here at the headquarters — and pulled the cork. I took a swallow and handed Jess the jug before I sat down.

He squinted at the label and licked his lips before he drank. "Did you just inherit some money, or have you always had more class than I've given you credit for?" It was twenty-four-year-old sour mash whiskey and about as good as anyone could ever hope to find. Fletcher's money had bought that too. Jess took a sip, swished it around in his mouth and let it slide down. "Ah-h-h. That's sweet as any nectar."

"Not very accurate, but the sentiment is all right. You can hand it back any time now."

"How did you hang on to it until we got back?"

"Nothing to it," I said with a wave of my

hand. "That's the last one left out of a case." Which was a lie, of course. Even if I could afford it, I wouldn't buy anything like that by the case. It's too fine to be made commonplace.

I got out my old pipe and let Jess hang on to the jug awhile. I'm not that much of a drinker. Neither is he, for that matter. "So how was it up there?"

He spreads his hands. "What can I say? You know there's no place else like it. The grass is even better than usual. Hock high already, even in the Squawman, and the water running cold and deep." He shook his head. "Real special, old man."

"Sure would like to go up to the Squawman again sometime."

"For another jug like this one I might carry you up there on my back." He took another swallow and smiled. To look at his face you'd have thought he'd just gotten a peek at the Holy Grail.

I puffed on my pipe and watched him nibble lightly at the mouth of the bottle and after a while he asked, "Aren't you going to ask me?"

"Ask you what? Hell, you don't know anything. I learned that a long time ago."

"Huh! You don't even care enough about the outfit to ask how our trail cook worked out. You laid around here drunk and forgot all about us working men."

"None of you looks too gaunted up, so I calculate you had enough to eat. An' if you give a waddie enough, it doesn't hardly matter how poor it might be."

"If you're going to take that attitude, I should just keep my mouth shut then. Or has the kid already told you?"

"He told me what he cooked, and he told me what he could about where you went. If there's any more, I don't know it."

"Oh, there's more all right. He didn't say anything about Billy Knowles?"

"Not a word."

Jess chuckled to himself and had another nip. "You know how feisty Billy can be."

"Uh-huh."

"He was pretty upset with our cook after that display of his at the oyster fry."

"Sure. Billy was robbed of a good scrap." Which was an unkind thing to say. "He was all set to defend the outfit," I added quickly. "Did he throw that up to the kid?"

"Yep. Every meal for the first three days till even the younger hands were getting tired of hearing him." Jess grinned and sat back and gave his attention to the jug.

"So what happened, dammit?"

His grin got broader. "The cook got hell

beat out of him, that's what."

"He got . . . !"

"Oh, calm down, old man. He asked for it." Jess chuckled again. "Know what he did?"

I glared at him.

"Your timid little shadow got fed up, I guess. After supper the third day he finished his cleanup and packed his sacks so everything was just so. Then he marched himself over to Billy an' looked him square in the eye. He said, 'Billy, I don't rightly know how to go about this, but I'll try it.' An' then he wound up an' bopped old Billy one right on the button. It wasn't enough of a punch to swat a fly hardly, but he meant it and he threw it." Jess sat back again, his eyes glittering.

"Well?"

"Well nothing, really. Billy naturally beat hell out of him. Pete Chapman had to do the cooking next morning. But it's a start. Maybe the kid isn't completely worthless after all."

"I never thought he was," I snapped.

Jess got serious again. "I did," he said softly.

"Oh." I honestly hadn't realized that. Good Lord, the things a man will do for a friend. For Jess Barnes to keep someone at the FR-Connected Bar and him thinking the fellow worthless — that was more than I ever thought he would do. And much more than I ever would have asked of him.

I got to my feet and looked at the skinny, big-nosed bastard who was our foreman. He was getting about as much gray on his head as me. "Go to sleep, ramrod. The morning's rushing after us."

"Don't forget your bottle."

"Save it for me. We'll finish it another time." I turned my back and got out of there. Damnation but a man is blessed when he has a friend.

I got a closer look at the kid the next morning and found that a lot of that dirt on his face was not the kind that will wash off. It was the remains of some pretty fair bruises. I guess Jess was right about the way Billy'd got to him, for that fight would have been more than a week before, and the kid was still nicely colored.

The kid didn't volunteer anything about it, though, and after a while, while he was busy turning griddlecakes and making little tiny ones on the sly for the kittens, I pretended to notice his face for the first time. "Did you have some trouble with the horses up there? You look like you got kicked in the face."

"Something like that." He poured more batter onto the griddle and let more drips fall on it to cook into animal treats. That was all he ever said on the subject of his bruises.

The crew went clattering off toward town after breakfast, and I took the kid over to the working-stock pens so he could show me some of the pack animals. I wanted a look at their backs. I really expected to teach him a lesson by doing some pointing and cussing, but the only one of the pack string that didn't have a clean back was one short-eared, mouse-colored little devil with withers so low he was always letting his pack slip. Even he didn't have more than a coupla small galls the size of quarters. The kid must have been real conscientious about his loading.

"Do you want to keep on learning how to ride?"

"Yes, sir. If it's all right with you."

"It's not my bones you're risking, so go ahead. Rope out that scruffy-looking bay with the wire cut on his near shoulder and bring him up here." He gave me a close look. "Uh-huh," I said. "The one you've been avoiding up to now."

He grinned. "I didn't know it showed."

"I've seen it, and so has the horse." The

bay was one of those animals with a naturally foul disposition. He was quick to kick or strike or bite, and I'd seen the kid pass him up once when he would have been the easiest to catch.

The kid got his rope, though, and headed down there. I watched from a distance so he would pay attention to the animal instead of thinking about being watched. I felt someone at my side and turned. Katy was standing there.

"You're up and about awful early, child."

"It's too nice a day to stay inside. Even for practicing on the piano." She grabbed my arm. "And guess what? Mama said I can ride in once a week and take lessons from Mrs. Carmady. Isn't that wonderful?"

"I guess it is, Katy. It seems that joke turned out all right."

She laughed. "I've never seen *any*one look as surprised as Mama did that afternoon. Daddy is still teasing her about it." She looked down toward the lowest pen. "He's learning, isn't he?"

"Everybody has to start someplace, and he sure started at rock bottom. But he is doing better."

The kid was in the corral now. He walked into the middle of the small herd and split them. He turned with the group that the

177

bay was with. The horses in that bunch broke past him to rejoin the others. As they went by he flipped his loop out, with much less fuss and windup now that he was learning how. The first throw was wobbly, the loop larger than was needed, but it slipped down onto the neck of the bay. The horse twisted and pawed at the ground.

"I don't like that one," Katy said.

"Oh?"

"It's a kicker. I saw it when Casey was breaking them. I hope the army takes that one."

"Recommend it to them," I told her. "If you smile pretty, there's no officer could refuse to buy your horse."

"Pooh!"

"It's true, I swear. They're all gentlemen. By act of Congress, no less. They could be demoted to private if they refused a lady."

"*Sure* they could." Her eyes were bright and gay.

The kid drew the bay in close to him, and the animal struck at his shoulder with a slashing, snake-quick forefoot. The kid dodged aside and used his coil of rope as a flail, whipping the hard manila across the head and chest of the bay. The animal began backing, its hind legs spraddled and low as they tried to keep up with the backward churning of the front legs.

The kid followed, his left hand firm on the neck rope and his right steadily pumping with the coil. The bay threw its head, the ears pinned and eyes walled.

"Try it again, you son of a bitch," I could hear across the distance. I suppose I should have worried about Katy being there, but, hell, she was an accomplished cusser herself at age ten and caused all of us a good bit of concern until she learned what was proper and what wasn't.

The bay flew backward until its rump, tail tucked low and tight, was jammed against the fence. The head reached higher, and it started to raise a forefoot again but got another slash of the rope across the legs. The horse stood quivering and running sweat.

The kid was sweet-talking it now. I could see his lips move. The bay's head came down and the ears perked upright. The kid turned his back on it and led it up toward the breaking pen.

"He's doing better than I thought," I told Katy. "Another day or two and I'll turn him outside. See if that bay can wear some holes in his jeans or if he can run some of the snort out of that animal."

"Mind if I watch?"

179

I patted her on the shoulder. "Why, little girl, I want you to make yourself right at home around this place. If anyone asks what you're doing here, just tell them I said it's all right."

"Thank you, kind sir," she said with a nicely done curtsy.

# CHAPTER 14

Jess trimmed the size of the crew when the boys got back from town. He always held over anyone who was willing to stay for haying, but from now until fall we would have little need for riding hands. He always kept Casey Timms and four others. Casey'd been with us long enough now to deserve year-round work and would help with the horses when any buyers came around.

The other four boys would take turns going up top, two at a time, to stay with the herd as line riders and general, all-around nursemaids. They would pull bogged animals or doctor any that needed it, brand and cut any late-born calves they spotted, push the beeves a little if they started overgrazing an area, and do whatever else they might see needing done. It was an easy, comfortable work compared with branding or driving and was a point of some pride for those chosen to do it.

Billy Knowles was tapped to stay this year, the first time he'd been chosen although this was four years now that he had ridden for us. It was a good choice, for Billy is a worker, quick and smart and determined. With a few more years of experience under his belt I figured he would make someone — maybe even us — a permanent top hand.

Pete Chapman would stay, as he had for the past several years. Chapman is a real Mr. Dependable. Not so much fire and dash as Billy and not as good with a horse or a rope, but he knows the bovine mind and just seems to feel it if one is coming sick or has wandered off and gotten into trouble. And he can take a plug of tobacco, a tin of kerosene, and a pocketknife and cure damn near any ill that can come to a cow.

Charlie Uver was offered a job but said he hadn't seen Montana and North Dakota for a few years and thought he might like to visit around in that country again. He packed his war bag and chose a horse and sloped out of the valley.

Jim Fuller, another young one but savvy, stayed, and so did Earl Crane. Earl probably has been chousing cows for twenty or more of his thirty-five years and is solid and steady. Jess would match one youngster with one older hand when he divided them for the nursemaiding, I knew. That would steady the young ones and give Chapman and Earl someone to keep up with, because those youngsters sure had the energy.

No one wanted to stay over and work on the ground this year, although I believe Jim Fuller might have if he hadn't been kept as a rider. He has a lot of loyalty to the brand although he is more quiet about it than Billy. I suspect in the long run Jim might turn out to be the better hand, maybe even ramrod quality, while Billy is and will stay a top hand but not a boss. He has more temper than a foreman can afford. In a way Billy reminds me an awful lot of a fellow I used to know real well, the way this fellow was before something made him sit back and do some serious thinking about things.

Anyway, the other boys packed up and drifted, and we settled to a slower pace. Chapman and Billy took the first two weeks up top, and all the others had to do was mind the horses and work on the fence.

I guess I will never understand why or how a bob-wire fence can take so much fixing. You would think that any inanimate object like that could be put up and then forgotten. Not so. Somehow there are always broken strands, whole sections washed out or fallen down, loose wires to be tightened, missing staples to be replaced, and rotten or broken posts to be dug out and new ones put in their place. This time of year the boys working down in the valley could have left their ropes at home, but they'd have been lost without a fence tool and a sack of wire staples. Still, it was part of the business now and no one thought of it as ground work any longer.

The kid kept on messing with the horses, and when he saw that the kid was determined about it, Casey began showing him a few of the finer points. Things that I could tell him about that needed a demonstration to really be understood. After a few weeks of that, Casey admitted that he was developing a tolerable seat for such a raw youngun.

As May drew toward the end, the valley began filling with beardless kids from towns and farms as far away as the Sand Hills, all of them trying to be the first to hook on with a haying crew so they would have some cash to take home at the end of the summer. Jules Sidlow's boy even brought a bunch of his college chums home with him for haying, although I suspect they regarded it more as a lark than as a job. Jules took them all on anyway — his hay crew ready made for him — and later he said they surprised him by being the hardest-working, smoothest-functioning crew he'd ever had. And I think he felt a lot better after that about his boy having chosen an eastern school.

As for us, for two weeks before we signed our crew we had the long table filled every meal and the bunkhouse filled every night, even down at the end of the valley like we were. And a lot of those youngsters had walked down from the railhead looking for jobs. With the TC&W just in, this was the first season we had got them coming to us afoot like that. I noticed when Jess did his hiring it was mostly from the ones with gumption enough to show up without a horse. The quitters and the sluggards would not have made it so far on their own.

I sent for Kip Barton the last week in May and turned the kid over to Jess.

Kip was fifteen or so and a good-enough boy, but he sure taught me how much I had come to depend on the kid knowing what needed to be done and where to find things. Kip had to be told everything and directed with care. Whenever I assumed he could do something on his own, he was able to prove me wrong.

Most of our haying is done close enough to the headquarters that the grounds can be reached from there every day, so it was not too bad. We fed a big breakfast, fixed a traveling lunch and drove it out to wherever they were, drove home and started preparing supper. Busy, but not all that bad.

I never used to like haying when it might take me away from what I considered to be important work, although each year I'd had to make sure we had enough horses broke to work in harness. I hardly ever went by to see how they were doing, though. Now I kind of enjoy it. The activity and the heat and the smell of cut and drying grasses.

We keep four mowers and two rakes working and all the wagons we own or can borrow. This time of year, though, everyone was in a tight for wagons, so we had to use the family's gig to carry food out.

Jess had put the kid on a loading team. After the hay was cured enough for storage, it was forked onto the wagons — rigged now with stake sides — and brought in to fill the big barns. When they were full, the rest of the hay would be stacked, the stacks scattered around the winter feeding grounds where the beeves could reach it. Hay from the barns, all from the rich first cuttings, was for the horses. They need more care and better-quality feed to bring them through a winter with fat left over, even if they are smarter than cattle when it comes

186

to taking care of themselves.

I got a kick out of the way the kid looked during lunch breaks. Red and running with sweat and just absolutely covered with dust and bits of broken stems and a hundred kinds of irritating seeds and stickers and little bits of this and that, things that collect like malevolent live creatures under trouser waistbands or anywhere else where they can be the most nuisance and cause the most discomfort. People who call a flatland farmer a hayseed know what they are talking about, all right. I know, for one year to settle a bet I spent a day stacking with a big fork, and I have never forgotten the scratchy, sticky feel of it by the end of that one day. I knew what the kid and those other boys were feeling.

When there was a run of water close enough, they would sluice themselves off before they came dripping to collect their lunch. Other times they would still be dripping, but with sweat, the trickling runnels of warm sweat making mud tracks down bare, sun-reddened backs.

But the hay began to come in. The big wagons trundled back and forth from field to barn like a procession of huge caterpillars, each rig creaking and groaning under the weight of the new hay, the horses lathered and flaring their nostrils in search of more air by the time they made it in.

Our stock is too light for this kind of work and more than one has been ruined for saddle use by straining its spirit out against the harness tugs of a heavy wagon, but there is no help for it. We couldn't feed that many heavy drafters the year round just to have them used for haying. The rest of the year they would be useless. So we keep only the single four-up of heavy horses to use on the freight wagon and for any winter sledding of wood or feed or salt or whatever might be needed. For the haying we just have to make do, the same as everyone else in the valley.

At this time of year Casey was mainly busy shoeing the horses and doctoring them. For the thin hides of saddle stock do not take well to the chafing and rubbing of harness, and he was steady busy with grease and swab trying to keep the horses in useful condition. His word became the law on which animals could be hitched or which must be held out of harness for a rest, which of them might be given light duty with rags jammed under straps or collars for extra padding.

One thing was sure. The kid was finished playing with and learning from any rough stock this year. The ginger would be gone from this crowd now, and there would be no rough ones in the pens until the next crop was brought in for breaking.

Crane and Fuller went up to take their second turn on top, and four days later Chapman and Billy were down again. By then the upper barn was full and a respectable green pile was building at the creekside end of the lower barn. As riding hands they were entitled to tease the sweating, miserable hay crew by idling along the fences in sight of whatever stands were being mowed and raked just then. When they got tired of that, they went into town for a few days.

A boy from outside the valley named Jeremy Powers, no relation to George Powers of Warcry, had a wreck with one of the mowers. One of his horses got spooked by a lark forced off her nest and scared the other horse and they tried to bolt in opposite directions. The Powers boy fell off his sulky smack onto the mowing bar, but it turned out not near as bad as it might have been. He lost a piece of his right ear and had his scalp laid open like a pants pocket, but Casey sewed and greased and tied the cut and in a few days the boy was back on his mower, where he insisted on being. He said he was too weak yet to work a fork and if he had to sit around he might as well be useful while he was doing it, and he would be damned if he was going to come down in the world by driving anything less than the mower. So Jess let him go ahead, and he did all right.

Casey felt responsible, of course, for it was up to him to choose the mower hitches. If he had been careful before, he was an old maid about his pairings after that accident, and he fretted something awful until the Powers boy was well mended again.

Kip finally settled down to knowing what he should be doing by the time the barns were full and they dragged out the big stacking pushers.

For that the heavy horses are needed. To build the big range stacks, a ramp is placed in front of the anchor posts. The hay is piled at the foot of the ramp, and the horses push a big sweep up the ramp to drop the hay from the top. You can stack quicker and higher that way than with any number of men trying to pitch with forks, and we had gone to the method several years before.

The kid began showing up for lunch with a little less dirt on him, and it turned out he had been given a rake to drive. One of the other boys just hadn't been doing too well handling his teams so that Casey was having to doctor too many of the animals he used. Jess let the kid have the rake and found that Casey wasn't muttering and fussing so much after he did. The horses were coming back in better shape and with fewer galls. It pleased the kid and it pleased Casey, and it pleased me too.

We went at a dead run like that for weeks, right smack up until the Fourth of July, only once getting hit with enough rain to spoil the drying and pack the hay, so we were pretty lucky. And then it was over. For this cutting anyway.

Jess paid the boys and told them when to be back if they wanted on for the next cutting — and most or all of them would — and the kid moved his stuff from the bunkhouse back into the kitchen.

"I'll be going back over there one of these days," he told me. "More than for the next hay cutting, I mean."

"I wish you well with it, Kid. I really do."

We had our blowout for the Fourth with the comfortable feeling of knowing our haying was going well and the stock was in good shape this year.

# CHAPTER 15

We didn't get the third cutting we had been hoping for. The summer rainstorms just didn't come, and while there was still enough runoff from the high country to keep the creek and most of the feeder streams flowing, there was too little water in the ground down here. The grass browned up and turned brittle and lay waiting for water that now would not come until next spring's melt.

The haying crew was gone and the waddies began to drift back in, knowing they were free to stay and eat and use the bunkhouse until Jess decided it was time to assign a string of horses or else had a word with the fellow off to one side to tell him there wouldn't be room for him this time. Most of the jobs he held open for boys coming back from wherever they'd been. He held one last spot open right down to the wire, but Charlie Uver never did show and in the end Jess hired a hard-looking yahoo who called himself Slick. I didn't like the man and I don't believe Jess did either, but Slick could make a rope stand up and talk to you, and we would need a good catch man.

Slick had been there about a week when the kid happened to see him working a rope the first time. Over the supper wash-up that night the kid asked me in an awed tone, "Did you see that fella with the rope this afternoon?"

"Who?" I asked, though I knew damn good and well who he was talking about.

"I didn't catch his name, but he's one of the new hands. Heavy fella, in his thirties maybe. Wears a low-crowned brown hat."

"With a telescope crease? Sure I saw him. His name is Slick. He was showing off for some of the youngsters this afternoon as I recall."

"Yeah. Boy, I never saw anyone who could do all that with a rope, all that spinning and jumping and stuff. Why, he's better than any of the rope-trick artists I ever saw in the Wild West shows back home."

"Could be," I said. "I've never seen one of those shows." I grinned. "Seems they don't come out here much, though circuses and stage shows and the little opera companies do all right out here."

"I wonder why that would be?"

"Simple, Kid. You can't make yourself out as someone special if the thing you're doing for big money is the same stuff a waddie does every day for his living. And anyone dressed up like you were when you came here would just get a horselaugh."

He looked sort of puzzled. "No one was laughing when I got off that train."

"You just couldn't hear it."

"Anyway," he said, "we were talking about Slick and the way he can handle a rope. You can't deny he's good with it."

"Nope. There's no denying that."

"I was wondering if maybe he'd teach me some tricks."

"Can you make all the throws I showed you yet? The cow-working kind of throws?"

He fished around in the dishwater tub and came up empty. He reached for a fresh stack of dirty things before he answered. "Most of them."

"Most?" I'd seen him practice recently.

"Well . . . I can head 'n heel 'n forefoot, anyway."

"Figure-eight?"

He grinned. "Not yet."

"Work on that awhile then."

"It wouldn't hurt to ask, would it?"

194

"It wouldn't hurt." I knocked my pipe cleanings into the stovebox and went to see if Jess had a jug he wanted to share.

I guess the kid did ask because pretty soon every time he had a few minutes to spare he was grabbing his rope and looking for Slick, learning how to spin with it, his hand away back from the honda, doing fancy stuff that he could never use for anything but trying to impress boys even less experienced than him — if he could find any such creatures, that is.

Things were in good shape down below, and pretty soon Jess had the crew molded together the way he wanted them. We packed the heavy wagon with food and a lighter wagon with bedrolls and the pile of stamp irons and all headed up the gap toward the top.

This time of year was something special, thickets forming great walls of gold and red, the light brown slopes dotted with dark green shading into blue where the needle-bearers grew. The air so crisp that just breathing it was like taking a drink of icy water from a mountain stream. The big horses in my hitch seemed to feel it, too, for they threw their heads and nipped playfully at each other while they hauled the heavy rig up the steep slopes.

The May and Abbot outfits were already down by the time we moved. We hadn't heard anything from the Slash WT about when they wanted to come down, though Jess had sent word of our plans a good week ahead of time in case they wanted to squawk.

The summer crew had done a decent job of keeping an eye on the beeves, not trying to keep them bunched but knowing where they were and making sure they were all in the same general territory as they moved. And they had already been started in a slow drift downward.

I set up a camp and saw to my three squares a day and had time to catch a few fish while the boys cleaned out the highest pockets and began pushing the bovines into a loose herd. As soon as the last hidey-holes had been cleared, they eased them together into a herd and began driving them down, the wagons leading the march so we would have time to stop and cook while the herd passed and the boys dropped back then to eat.

It was a good little drive. No excitement among the beeves and so no weight run off the way they will do when they get in a panic about something. It's amazing the way cattle will shrink when they get excited about something. That wasn't of much consequence — or at least we never much thought it was — when they sold by the head, but now that buyers pay by the hundredweight it can make a big difference to the outfit.

We took them through the gap, put the fence up behind us to prevent any fool critters from drifting back up and moved them a decent ways down onto our own range so Tynell would have room to pass behind us when he decided to come down. Then the boys got down to some serious work.

There were not enough unbranded calves in the herd to require more than a day's work, and I knew Jess would be pulling the summer boys aside to tell them what a hell of a fine job they'd done.

In a way it was a shame there wasn't more branding needed, for even I enjoyed watching the way Slick could peel a calf loose and drop it just where and how he wanted it. He might play with the fancy stuff, but he could do the work too. I think the kid spent more time that day watching Slick than he did helping me, and I could not really blame him. Hell, the guy was better with a rope than I'd been on my best day, and I was not exactly a slouch with one. Once upon a time, as the saying goes. And a man should be willing to give the devil his due.

The kid had been spending a good bit of time with Slick since before we'd left headquarters, even more since we were up top. He spent his evenings listening to Slick tell how there wasn't any country that could compare with Arizona when it came to real cow country and real cow people. Which kinda made me wonder, if he thought all that much of it, why wasn't he down there? I mean, I'm real fond of Texas too. It birthed me and it taught me, and I've liked well over half the people I've known from there. But if I thought it was as close to Eden as old Slick seemed to think Arizona was, I'd damn sure be there right now.

Which is neither here nor there, I suppose. Anyway, they got the last of the branding done and began cutting.

They pulled out the wet cows with calves and the yearlings and scattered them first. Nearly all of the dry cows were bunched separately and held close, as George does not believe it pays to carry over the ones that aren't producing. Only a few of these, the very best ones, were turned loose and given another chance at calving.

All of our few three-year-old steers — we prefer to sell them as twos — were put in with the dry cows and the heifer threes that could not meet Jess's approval. Finally Jess went over his tally books and thought about the state of the grass and the amount of hay piled in the big stacks and consulted with the aches in my old bones and decided how many twos to carry through the winter. The remaining twos — most of them — were put in with the other steers and dry cows. And we had our market herd.

Jess gave Chapman a good horse and some instructions and sent him off toward headquarters to report in to George on what we had. Chapman was back in another five days with the old man's blessing and a confirmed railroad-car order that would be met in Warcry in eight days.

They moved the herd down past head-quarters to the public road, let them eat their way north to the edge of our land rights and held them there until time to move off toward town.

We stopped one night in Barton's largest pasture, the use of which gives the man some cash money each year, and by the next night the beeves were in the TC&W pens, which were freshly vacated by someone else's outfit judging by the condition of the ground.

The boys let out a holler when the last gate was shut, and I guess I did too.

I parked the big wagon at Wiggins's dock and had the kid leave the light wagon there too, for it was time to start laying in winter supplies. We could take both of them home loaded and get a jump on it.

"You coming over to the hotel, Kid?"

He kept his eyes on the harnesses he was stowing under the wagon seat. "Well, if you don't mind, I sort of promised Slick I'd . . . well . . . show him around Warcry tonight. So I guess I won't be going over with you." He quickly added, "Unless you need anything. If you do, why, let me know."

I straightened the tarp over the cooking gear and the mostly empty food boxes in the wagon and told him, "No, I've been getting along under my own power so far. I guess I can manage tonight again. You go and have yourself some fun. I'll see you in the morning."

"Yes, sir." He gave me a grin and a wave and was gone.

I got my bag from under the seat and headed straight for the barber shop, as I felt as shaggy and as filthy as an old buffalo bull. Or as shaggy and as filthy as one of them used to be, anyway. I don't know if there are any of them left now that aren't stuffed and kept behind glass.

I was feeling sort of like that myself when

I reached the barber shop, but Tom fixed me up to human condition again, and I even treated myself to one of his shaves to go with the haircut and bath. They have bathing rooms on each floor of the hotel nowadays, with slipper tubs and boiling-stoves in each one, but I still think of the barber shop as the place for that. Tom keeps his tubs and stoves for those of us that are set in our ways. I changed into clean, presentable clothes there, too, and was feeling much better by the time I checked into the hotel and dropped my gear off in my usual room.

Elsie was in a mood for talk and so were the boys over at the Bull Shooter, and I had a pleasant evening of it. I turned in about eleven or so without ever running into the kid or Slick.

# CHAPTER 16

"*Good* morning." All I got back was a scant bob of the head. The kid never once looked at me. He kept his eyes away the whole time he was hitching both teams.

It isn't like it was so early in the morning that he shouldn't be feeling friendly. What with finding the crew after their night on the town and loading the wagons, half the morning was gone already. We would be home late and having a cold supper for sure.

Then the rest of them gathered around, and I could see that this was going to be one fun day. Every man of the whole crew was just as solemn and subdued as they could be, and Jess had his face set as firm as a cigar-store Indian's. Whoo-boy, this was sorta interesting.

I guess there is some of the Old Ned in me yet, for I could not help grinning and whistling and just making like I was having a grand old time.

Now those boys should not have been boisterous, exactly. They hadn't been paid yet. But they should have been feeling loose and cheery. And old Jess should have been feeling plenty good, too, with the market herd delivered and off our hands. So, yes sir, it was interesting.

When everyone was ready, the crew moved out, and I waved the kid ahead with the light wagon. I gave Jess a come-here look. He did.

"Well?"

"Well what?"

"Are you going to tell me what caused all the smiling faces? I thought we'd had a pretty good fall work, myself."

Jess shook his head, but more in disgust than anything else. "I'll tell you one thing. When that kid of yours isn't in trouble himself, he's somewhere close by."

"Aw, *hell*. Did he . . . ?"

"No, he wasn't flying his yellow flag this time. His part of it was bankrolling that damn Slick. It's a good thing we don't need a catch man any more this year. And a poor thing we won't be able to use him next spring. But that yahoo is leaving just as soon as he gets back to where he can grab his own horse and his gear, and that is a fact."

"The kid wasn't directly involved,

though?"

He shrugged. "Not really. Apparently ol' Slick talked the kid into standing treat for an evening at Bessie Blue's."

"It sounds like he earned his name honestly then. Sort of."

"Ain't that a fact," Jess said. He rummaged in his coat pocket for a chew and popped the nasty stuff into his mouth. "Anyway, it seems that Slick can't hold his liquor any better than he can hold his tongue. Do you know Lucy over there?"

"Sure. Nice gal." She was, too. A black girl, the only one in the valley, though from time to time a black-skinned waddie would drift through and stay as long as the work lasted. Around here that wasn't considered to be anything either for or against a man so long as he could do the job. Which had taken me a while to get used to, to tell the truth.

Anyway, Lucy was a soft-speaking, quick-smiling little gal who did her best to make a man comfortable and happy when he was with her and so was as popular as any of the girls at Bessie's and more popular than some of the greedy, sullen types. Those girls never lasted long, though, soon being chased off toward Cheyenne or Denver or some other, bigger place where people would put up with such unpleasantness.

Jess spat and said, "Slick decided he was better people than Lucy and proved his point by knocking her around."

"Were any of our boys there? Besides the kid, I mean?"

"A couple were. Enough. They took care of it. Not that your kid was much help. They said he was doing some shouting and pulling but wasn't throwing any punches."

"Somebody should've been throwing some kicks to where they'd be felt the most," I said with a bit of cursing. It wouldn't do to have our crew barred from Bessie Blue's, and she was damn well capable of closing her doors to every rider we had if they couldn't act like gentlemen. She had done it once to the Rainbow outfit, kept them out for a whole season. It was several years before they could hire any experienced hands again.

"I went by this morning to apologize," Jess said, "and assure them Slick wouldn't be riding for us anymore."

"Is Lucy all right?"

"Bruised and battered some, but she'll be okay. She'll lose a coupla nights' work." He hesitated. "I promised them the outfit would make up for it."

I nodded. "If George balks, let me know.

I'll talk to him too."

"I don't expect he will, but thanks. If it comes to that, though, I'll pay it myself. I'm the one made the promise."

"You won't pay more than half," I told him.

He nodded. Jess knew what I meant, and if it came down to that he wouldn't be shy about asking for my half then. But I didn't think we'd have to pay. We can put some pressure on George when we have to, and he knows we'd never crawl him about anything that wasn't in the best interests of the outfit. And generally him knowing that is enough to make any real fussing unnecessary.

Jess rode along beside me for a while, spitting and glaring. It should not have been about having to fire Slick. That was just something that had to be done, and while our ramrod does not like having to give anyone his time, it is something that must be done several times each year anyway when the crew size is cut if nothing else.

"Something is still gnawing on you," I told him a few miles out.

"Maybe," he admitted.

"You aren't mad at the kid again, are you?"

"Maybe. Some."

"Aw, come on now, Jess. Nobody can tell how someone else will hold his liquor until he's seen the fellow with a skinful a time or two."

"Dammit, though, he was right there. If he'd done something right away, that girl wouldn't have been hurt. And it wouldn't be costing the outfit cash money to keep us in good standing."

There was nothing I could say to that, and well he knew it. After another minute or so he bumped his mount into a lope and swung wide around the light wagon ahead of me. The crew was already out of sight.

We reached home early in the evening and found everyone else already at the table. Mrs. Senn and Katy had started cooking when the crew came in.

The women were encased in a couple of my big aprons, their faces flushed and dampness pulling spiky tendrils of hair from their buns. The kid and I had no sooner set foot into the kitchen than they were shooshing us toward the dining-hall table.

"Get out of here now," Natalie fussed. "You'll just be in our way if you hang around in here. Go on."

"I sure wish you wouldn't spoil these boys so," I told her. "Once they get a taste of good food, I'll have trouble with them forever more."

"Quit grumping and thank us," she ordered.

"Yes, ma'am. Thank you." I nudged the kid and he mumbled a thank-you too, though I think he was directing his more to Katy than to her mama, who was sure to have done all the real cooking. Much though I hate to say it, Katy is a god-awful cook despite everything Natalie and I have tried to teach her.

It was sort of nice to be sitting at the big, noisy table again, and damned if old Casey, who was sort of an unofficial segundo, didn't shift his plate so I could have my old spot at the foot of the table. Jess, of course, sat at the head. Not that anyone but Jess and Casey would know what Casey was doing, but by golly I appreciated it aplenty. It was mighty thoughtful of him.

The kid carried his plate around to the side of the table away from Slick. At least the crew did not seem to be down on the kid about any of this, for they did not give him the freeze-out that Slick was getting.

Talk about good meals and welcome ones. That one qualified on both counts. I sure had not been looking forward to laying on a big meal when we got home, even a cold one, which was what I'd planned. Somehow that drive from town was wearing at me more than it used to.

When we finished gorging, the kid and I ran the women back to the big house and went to washing.

"That Katy sure is some cook," the kid said while we worked.

"Yes, indeed," I told him. "I've never tasted food quite like hers." And I will guarantee that that was the truth.

"She's pretty, too," he persisted.

"Uh-huh." Well, that *was* the truth. "But don't you go getting ideas there, Kid. You're nothing but a cook's helper. Don't forget that."

He got a stubborn look on him. "I won't be a cook's helper forever. One of these days I'm going to be a cowhand, a regular hand and a good one, too."

I couldn't help laughing. "Hell, Kid, don't you know *any*thing? As far as being good enough for the likes of Katy Senn, that would take you about as far as a ten-cent ticket on the TC&W. Why, to you being a waddie may be the biggest ambition of your lifetime. But she's been surrounded by punchers since the day she was born. Another one of them would be about the last thing she would look at."

The kid scrubbed at a pot, newly built

muscles working in his arms. And along his jaw. "I guess I make a lot of mistakes," he said.

"You make your full share at the very least, Kid."

He looked at me. "Like with Slick, huh?"

"I would have to agree." I guess I was a bit more tired than I'd realized. My game leg buckled and I lurched to the side. I caught myself on the counter and the kid jumped to help me to my rocker. "Sorry, Kid."

"I'll finish this," he said. "Do you have your pipe and stuff?"

I patted my pockets. "Yeah."

"Fine. Take it easy. I'll finish here and unload, but you don't have to stay up. I know where everything goes all right."

"Tomorrow, Kid. The stuff won't rot sitting in the wagons just overnight. We'll put it away tomorrow. In the meantime, I guess I will go on to bed." I got to my feet and gave him a mock glare. "And mind that you don't make any noise while you finish doing my job." That got a smile out of him. The first I'd seen from him all day.

I felt considerable better in the morning, woke up feeling pert and lively again at four as usual. I dressed and ran a hand over the stubble on my chin — I hadn't shaved the night before — and decided I could let it go awhile longer. One of the few advantages of being a graybeard is that a little negligence in that area is no longer so noticeable. As early as I was up and about, though, the kid was up before me. It was the first time that had happened, and I hadn't even heard him.

The kitchen lamps were flaring already, and there was a pile of goods nearly covering the worktable. He'd been busy.

The door swung open, and the kid clumped in with another armload of canned goods and a cheerful "Good morning." His cheeks were bright red, and I could see his breath hanging in the air at the doorway. He heeled the door quickly shut but even so a cold draft washed in behind him. I hadn't noticed before, but the fire was already going in the big stove.

"Chillier than usual?"

"Chilly! It's plain cold out there. Last night's dishwater is solid ice. I like to busted my tailbone when I stepped on it. I just hope none of this canned stuff split open and got ruined."

I cracked the door open for a look outside and found that he was right. It was plain damn cold. The sky had that peculiar emptiness and special clarity of a really hard-freeze night. Pale, pale moonlight was shining on a thick frost.

"Does it always get cold this early?" the kid asked.

"Not hardly," I told him. "Wait a minute." I went back to my room and found an extra pair of gloves. I tossed them to the kid and got back a sigh of relief.

"They sure will feel good," he said, "and I guess I'd better get a heavy coat the next time I'm in town."

"If you have any money left," I said without thinking. It was a foolish and an unkind thing to do. The boy's face fell, and he lost the cheery brightness of the brisk morning. "Hey, Kid, I'm sorry. I didn't mean it like that. Hell, I was just teasing you."

He gave me a weak smile and said, "Okay," but it wasn't. He tugged the gloves on and got back to work at the unloading. I gave myself a few mental kicks and figured I had earned the shocking discomfort of being the first one on the backhouse seat on so cold a morning.

I fixed an extra-big, belly-heating breakfast and put on more coffee than usual before I clanged the iron to call the hands across from the bunkhouse. They came in shivering and stamping their feet, patches of color high on their cheeks and a lot of laughter

212

spilling out of them. The horses would be in a mood to hump their backs and act playful this morning, and the boys were already getting wound up ready for it.

However far down they might have felt the day before, this cold had snapped them out of it. The only one who still had a long face was Slick, and he should have known what was coming.

That wasn't enough to button him up, though. Maybe Slick thought he could bluff his way through if he talked so much there wasn't time for anything but listening to him rattle. Anyway he launched into a long windy about Arizona, something to do with the ranger companies they have down there and the time good ol' Slick had saved the mortal lives of two or three or maybe it was a dozen of those boys with his quick thinking.

The rest of the crew ignored him, joking with each other and letting Slick's voice boom past their ears without touching them.

It is something of a wonder that anyone had time to speak the first word, much less to fill the chow hall with good-humored noise, judging by how fast they put the food down. Seeing those platters empty was like watching a tent-show magician make little balls disappear. Awesome, it was.

Slick ran down finally and looked around, blinking owlishly. His plate was half full, the others so empty they were practically clean. The other boys looked over at Jess, and the ramrod cleared his throat.

"Slick," he said, "I want to put that white-footed sorrel you've been riding into Billy's string."

The rope artist sucked air through his teeth and bobbed his head curtly. The sorrel with the white forefeet was Slick's top horse. Taking that — or any other — horse from his string was the customary way of saying he should draw his time before the foreman had to bluntly tell him to clear out. And normally it would have been said in private, not where all the others could hear too.

This was a scene that I would think Slick had played before. He poured himself more coffee and eyed Jess. He faked a laugh and said, "Fine. Works out just right then. Too damn cold here to suit me. I figure to head for Arizona quick as you'll pay me out. I was gonna tell you after chow anyway, see."

Jess nodded and continued the fiction. "Sorry to see you going, Slick."

"Huh, well, *my* bones'll be warm this winter. I'll give a thought to you boys freezing up here." He put his attention on his plate and ignored the other boys.

With the show over the hands shrugged into their coats and pulled their hats low over their ears. They headed out to catch their horses in the early half-light and commence the frosty fun of that first cold-weather saddling. Jess left, too, but he would be going to the big house to get Slick's wages, unless he had calculated what was owed the night before and put it aside in his room. Only Slick remained at the table, and for once he was not talking.

We cleared the table except for one coffeepot and some cups, and I set the kid to washing. Neither of us was liable to keel over in a faint if we delayed eating a little longer. I poured myself a cup of the no-longer-hot coffee and sat beside Slick.

"What do you want, old man?" he demanded.

"Just a few words, Slick. Just wanta give you some advice."

"That's just what I need. Advice." He scowled into his coffee cup. The cold air outside carried to us the rising yips and yells as the first of the boys topped off their mounts.

"I sure am glad you agree, Slick, old fella, because there's something you need to do when you get your pay."

The scowl shifted my way. "Let me guess, old man. You want me to pay back that pup you wet-nurse in the kitchen. Kid's too stupid to take care of himself, so you figure you gotta do it for him, is that it?"

"Nope," I said. "You, now. You don't learn from your mistakes, Slick. If it was you that'd been taken by a slick-talking yahoo, I just might figure that would be the way to handle it. As for the kid, well, I figure he bought himself some education the other night. If he learns from it — and I figure he will — it will be well worth the price."

I looked at him square and said, "No, what I had in mind was that the outfit is going to have to pay for that girl's lost work. I figure you caused it, so it's rightly your place to pay for it. For the outfit, Slick. Not for the kid."

"I don't owe this outfit a damn thing, old man. Not with the way they've treated me, I don't. Keep your advice to yourself an' keep your yap shut, or I just might take a notion to stomp on you some before I leave. An' don't think that yella little pup of yours would do a thing to protect you, neither. He couldn't, even if he would."

"Slick, old son — an' I use the word as a short form of what you are — I have got along just fine so far without asking anybody

216

else to do my fighting. I reckon I can manage for another day or two."

Slick shoved his jaw out and swelled the heavy muscles in his arms. "Listen to the old crip brag." He wagged a fist under my jaw.

"It's a good thing you are such a thorough son of a bitch," I said with a grin, spelling it out this time since he seemed to have missed it before, "because otherwise I might start to feel sorry for anyone as ignorant as you."

He looked more puzzled than angry. And maybe he had caught something of the anticipation in my eyes.

"You see, Slick, I'm an old-fashioned kind of bastard. Not near as civilized as you younger fellas. So does some slimy lump of muscle like you come after me, I won't bother to make a fist. I'll just drag out the old hoglaig I used to wear an' blow a hole or two through your gut. So come ahead if you want. If not, pay the foreman for the trouble you've caused and get the hell out of here." I got to my feet and stood over him. "Make up your mind."

He thought about swinging. I could see it in his eyes. Then he seemed to think again. And I will guaran-damn-tee I was not bluffing him. Maybe he could see that. He

217

folded, turned back to his coffee cup muttering something that I couldn't make out.

"You have fifty-five dollars coming," Jess said from behind us. I hadn't known he was there, and I'm sure Slick hadn't either. I don't know just when he had come back in. He crossed to the table to stand beside Slick. "It will cost fifty to cover your damages," he said. He peeled a five-dollar bill from the sheaf in his hand, wadded it, and dropped the bill into the dregs left in Slick's coffee cup. "Any argument about it?"

Slick looked from one of us to the other. "No wonder," he blustered. "There was two of you all along." He didn't believe that, I wouldn't think, but it would be easier to tell himself that than admit he'd backed down from a gimpy old fella like me. He pulled the bill from the cup and shoved it, still wet, into his pocket. "The hell with all of you. I'm going back to Arizona." He grabbed his hat and coat and got out of there.

Jess gave me a wink and a slap on the arm before he shoved Bessie Blue's fifty dollars into his jeans. He turned for the door, too. There was work to be done.

And me, I was plenty hungry now. I was overdue for breakfast. When I entered the kitchen, the kid was starting to fry a coupla huge steaks. I noticed there was a heavy roll-

ing pin lying on the counter. I hadn't had
that particular article out to use it since
before we left for the fall working.

# CHAPTER 17

Another week and things were pretty well settled for the winter. The beeves were scattered along the north end of our range, scattered enough that they would not be so likely to overgraze themselves into trouble while there was still grass to be eaten. And any storm drift would be toward the south end of the place, toward fresh grass and fresh stacks of hay. As soon as we had some snow they would be all right for water. In the meantime a few men with axes could keep the water open for them. And really it was too early to be worrying about hard winter anyway.

Jess paid off most of the crew and kept just a short bunch for the winter. He offered winter work to the same boys who'd been with us over the summer. Only Billy Knowles refused, saying he'd promised his folks he would be back for Christmas but that he planned on showing up in time for the spring work. A likely boy by the name of Phil Cline was given the job in his place.

Jess also kept a pair of brothers from Montana, Abner and Ross Eason. During the winter we kept two line cabins manned, one northwest and the other southeast of headquarters. That left Jess, Casey, two hands and us peons at home. Unless something unusual came up, the line-shack pairs stayed out two months and in only one in three.

The other boys drifted, and Jess had the remuda turned out and driven upcreek to some cottonwood breaks where they would winter untended along with our big mare band — save, of course, for Katy's pets. At headquarters we kept a short bunch of using horses and the heavy drafters. When the winter got really hard, though, the loose horses would start yarding up near the pens, and we would hay-feed them over the fences.

It was too early to be manning the line shacks, but there was sure enough to do. We had to make more trips into town for supplies, get the snacks heavily stocked well in advance of the need. After all, it was not impossible that the first boys up could get caught in a freak snow and not show up at headquarters again until the spring thaw.

And the rest of the boys needed to be snaking wood to the buildings and starting the sawing. So there was plenty to do.

It was all delayed, though.

Two days after the crew was paid off, the hard cold was still with us. Not quite so deep as it had been but still below freezing. The dishwater the kid had thrown out was still there as a film of ice, scratched and scuffed now so that it was no longer so treacherously slick. The clarity of the sky was going, though. A low, dense haze was building, which accounted for the slight warm-up.

By ten o'clock that morning we could no longer see any part of the mountain.

By dinnertime we had trouble. Just as we were ready to eat, Pip Foster came fogging in on a Slash WT horse that was dripping lather.

I happened to be near the door and looked out to see him coming.

"Forget about the chow for now, Kid. I think the boys are fixing to get busy. I want you to take that wet horse down to the shed. Turn one of Katy's mares out, rub this one down with some sacking, and put it in a stall. Then get yourself back up here on the run."

He grabbed his coat and hat and went out

to take the reins from Pip.

The door from the dining-hall end of my building opened, and a shirt-sleeved arm waved Pip inside, so I went to join them there and see what was going on. I snagged a pot of coffee as I passed the stove.

Pip looked to be half frozen. He didn't even unbutton his coat at first, just stripped his gloves off and wrapped his hands around a hot mug of coffee.

"It started snowin' last night," Pip said between pauses to sip the coffee and to let his teeth rattle. "We're caught in it, boys. The whole damn herd. Still up top. If the cut drifts full, we'll be losing beef, boys. We need help."

Jess nodded immediately. "You've got it. The big crew's been paid off, but we'll be coming." He turned toward our hands. "You heard him. Get your gear and pick two horses each. The heaviest and toughest you can find, and don't be proud about taking them out of your own strings, either. Take whatever looks best."

The boys grunted their understanding and streamed through the door.

"Are you able to guide us back up, Pip?"

The Slash WT rider tried to grit his chattering teeth and grin at the same time and mostly just looked sickly instead, but he said, "I'll be with you, Jess."

"All right. We'll switch your gear to a fresh horse and rope you a spare. You stay here. Get yourself warm and have a bite to eat." He grinned. "Lord knows, there's enough sitting on that table getting cold. We'll be back for you directly." Jess turned to me and raised an eyebrow.

"It will take us awhile longer," I told him. "Don't try to wait. We'll catch up later. You don't wanta waste what time you have before the gap fills."

"I could leave someone with you," Jess said, giving me a dubious sort of look. Pip was already at the table wolfing at the meat. I wondered how long he'd been in the saddle. All night more than likely.

I shook my head. "We'll make it or we won't, and you'll need every man. If I see we can't get through, I'll get down on the flat and wait for you. Either way, I won't get stuck in your path."

"All right, then." He started to point toward the table.

I interrupted with, "Run them past. I'll have sandwiches or something ready. And if you get finicky about it, you're in trouble."

Jess left, and I got busy slicing thick slabs of bread to wrap around the steaks I'd cooked. That would have to do since there

224

wasn't any way for them to carry anything else to eat on the move. The kid came back and pitched in to help. Between us we had enough ready in the few minutes until the boys were lined up, already mounted, between the cookhouse and the bunkhouse.

"They're ready, Pip."

"Okay, thanks." He crammed a last bite into his mouth, buttoned his coat and took a sandwich off the stack as he went out the door.

The kid distributed the sandwiches, and the boys headed up the creek at a long-traveling trot.

The kid paused on the doorstep and tilted his head back, his eyes squinting nearly shut and his nose wrinkled. "Starting to snow," he said.

"Good."

He gave me a look like I was crazy.

"They'll need more food, shovels, saws. There's no way we could get a wagon through up there now on wheels, and snow down here will let the runners travel freer. We won't tire the team so bad getting there."

"We're going too, then?"

"You just bet we are, Kid. Now I've got some work for you to be doing while I take care of the inside part."

He looked pleased about the prospect of going.

I sent him back to the wagon shed with a double armload of instructions. He had to pull the wheels off the light rig and fit the runners on. The long-unused tandem harness had to be located and run out to fit a pair of the big draft horses, and the tools had to be loaded. Meantime I was packing food and stuff. As it was, it was a coupla hours before we were able to get under way, both of us encased in old buffalo coats that I'd had kicking around practically forever. They smelled awful, but I figured we would be glad to put up with that soon enough. And I was right.

Down here the snow was still light, powdery stuff that barely covered the earth, although it was enough to let the steel sled runners travel better than they might have. Up top, though, it could be bad and must be or Fletcher would not have sent for help. The big question now was the wind. It was calm so far, the snow falling at only the very slightest angle off the vertical. If that kept up they would be all right. Cold, but all right. Wind was the thing to worry about. Anything driving down from the north or swirling up through the pass to the south would pick up accumulated snow and drop it into any protected depressions the wind was crossing. That would include the lone gap that was our path to and from the summer grounds. If that was plugged, the Slash WT beef would have to stay up top until there was a melt, whenever that might be.

The big draft horses were hard-muscled and sleek after their summer's work, and I was glad we had them. The rig looked strange with those two huge beasts — each of them would weigh twenty-one hundred pounds at the least — hitched one behind the other in the tandem harness, the wheeler squeezed between poles and the leader in loose harness. But I was glad now that George had bought the odd trappings when he had.

That would have been ten years ago or maybe longer, when Natalie Senn and Katy, just a bit of a thing at the time, had seen pictures of such an outfit drawing a hack in England or some such exotic place. They had thought the outfit so handsome they asked for one and hit George at a time when he was feeling particularly indulgent. I don't think they'd used it more than two or three times since. It worked all right but drew an awful lot of comment from spectators as everyone here was used to side-by-side pairs with regular old tongues and doubletrees.

Shafts, they figured, were meant for single-horse courting rigs. This strange contraption was all right by the big horses, though.

I used to be plenty down on the drafters. They are big and slow, heavy on their feet, and kind of awkward. I guess I just thought them dull and beneath my notice, but over the past few years I have come to respect them. They aren't dull so much as they are honest, and they have as much heart as a good cow pony, and no one could ask more than that.

The devils are slow, though, and it was dark a good many hours before we reached the gap although I had pushed the animals for all I dared take out of them so early.

"We'll spend the night here," I told the kid when we finally did reach the foot of the gap.

He peered into the darkness and shook his head. "Don't you think we should go on? The wind is already blowing pretty hard. By morning this could be blocked."

"It won't take that long, Kid. That's why we wait. If we try to make it now, we won't get halfway through, and any drift bucking we get done will be closed off behind us. We can do those boys a lot more good now by waiting. They've got enough to worry about right now without adding us to their burdens."

The snow was coming down at a sharp angle now, slanting in under our hat brims to drive tiny spikes into exposed flesh. I turned my collar up higher and tore off a piece of coat lining to tie it up. The kid watched me and after a minute or two did the same.

"Unhitch, Kid, and tie those animals on the lee side of the wagon. That's about all the protection we have to give them right here."

"Yes, sir." He climbed down and started to work. I got out and leaned into the back of the wagon, pushing against the vehicle and then drawing it back a few inches to rock it in the hope the runners wouldn't freeze down too solidly.

The kid settled the horses and gave them each an armload of the loose hay he had crammed into the bed of the wagon before we left. He had put in a coupla sacks of oats, too, I noticed. He went to search for something burnable while I began piling packed snow, more moist now than that first powder, for a windbreak.

He found a coupla long, dried-out limbs that had been tumbled down by the spring flows and then were left high and dry when the water disappeared. He dragged those close. And we sure had enough saws to cut them with. I had put in a coupla long crosscuts and four bucksaws.

"What'd you bring these things for anyway?" the kid asked while he pumped with one of the bucksaws. "Nobody could use that much firewood unless he wanted to heat the whole damn mountain."

"Not wood for burning, Kid. For eating. If that herd is for sure stuck up there, they might save them, some of them anyhow, by cutting trees so the beeves can chew the bark. It makes lousy feed but better than snow, I'll tell you."

I wondered how they were making it up there. From where Tynell summered they would be moving south across the slope and then down. Most of the way they would have the protection of firs or spruce, so they should not be in any real trouble until they reached the unprotected gap. Down here the growth was mostly leafed stuff that now would offer no shelter.

The knobs lying above the gap — worse luck — were bare. It occurred to me that we might have been able to avoid something like this if we'd thought ahead, planted something up there. Maybe cedars, as those pesky things will thrive anywhere, especially if you don't want them to. Too late to do anything about it for this year, but it was something to think about for the future.

I looked up into the darkness, seeing in my mind's eye the places they would be now, where there was some cover. Even an "easy" run in this kind of weather would be no pic-nic for them. The beeves would want to turn tail to the wind no matter what direction it might swing, and they would be nervous and balky. The horses would have poor footing. The less experienced ones would be paying more attention to the footing than to the beeves. And the cow-wise ones would pay so much attention to their work that they were apt to take tumbles. And cold? You can't huddle up to a fire when you're in the saddle.

Lordy, I could remember it well enough. Come in in the evening with no feelings in your hands and less in your feet. Step off your horse knowing you were going to fall flat because you hadn't known where your feet were for hours and couldn't begin to control them now that you needed them. Hack and punch at cinch straps that seemed to have turned to iron since you pulled them tight that last time. Pack your nose and ears in snow before you got close to the fire lest you thaw them too quick and end up losing some chunks of yourself. Oh, I remembered, all right. And damn but I wished I could've been riding with them now. Instead, I hitched my collar higher and shifted closer to our fire while the kid cooked us some meat and coffee. We'd forgotten to eat earlier.

Morning came with scarcely enough difference in the light to tell it was daytime. The snow kept falling, and the wind kept blowing. The kid protested, but we stayed put. I had him use one of the big horses to drag more wood close, but that was all the movement I allowed him. He kept staring up toward the gap.

"There's nothing to see up there, Kid. Won't be until the wind quits. Those boys might be ignorant, but they aren't stupid. They'll stay up in the trees until it's calm. Then they'll make their try."

"How can you be sure?"

"It's what I'd do, Kid. And I damn sure don't think I'm any smarter than Jess Barnes or Fletcher Lewis. They'll do what's best for that herd."

"The men could get down, couldn't they?"

"The boys? Sure. The horses probably couldn't, but the hands could I guess. Why?"

"Nothing, I guess. I was just curious." He kept on staring up through that snow-curtained gap. It looked white and innocent and empty as far up as we could see.

# CHAPTER 18

The wind finally died late the second afternoon we were in camp there. The snow had quit falling that morning.

I don't know about the kid — he wasn't complaining about it anyway — but I had almost forgotten what it felt like to be warm. It is odd how when you are living out in the open in weather like that you can remember the fact of warmth but not the feel of it. The cold seems to sink deeper and deeper into you until the desire for warmth is itself only a vague and generalized notion.

The kid must have been as cold as me, though, for he sure was conscientious about keeping the wood coming for a roaring fire. Under other circumstances I might have fussed at him for building a tenderfoot blaze. As it was, I appreciated his efforts, futile though they had been.

Now that the wind was no longer robbing

us of heat, I began to get some good from all his work. I unbuttoned my smelly coat for the first time since I'd put it on back at headquarters and spread it to trap more of the warmth. I sighed and gave the coffeepot a contemplative look.

"Shouldn't we be doing something now?" the kid asked. I guess the inactivity was making him impatient to do something, anything.

"Why?"

"The wind stopped," he said, as if that answered everything.

"Yes, I guess it did at that," I agreed.

"Well? You said we couldn't go until it quit. It quit. Shouldn't we be going now?"

"Nope."

He grimaced and began packing snow into the coffeepot to melt. It sure takes a lot of fillings with snow to make one pot of water. Worth it, though.

Since he had quit asking, I told him. "They'll need time to bring the herd down out of the trees, and we don't have any guarantee that the wind and snow won't kick up again tonight. There'd be no point in wearing ourselves out getting up there only to have it close in again behind us. If it's still clear in the morning, it will be time to try breaking through."

He looked up through the gap and shuddered. I don't think it was from the cold alone, either.

"Is that what we have to do?" I will admit it looked pretty bad up there. In some places the gap was nearly level with drifted snow.

"That's it, Kid. Break it down, trample it, shovel it. Whatever we have to do. But they'll need our help. Their light horses will already be dead tired from working cattle now." I grinned. "At the very least, I think you'll find it interesting."

"I'll bet."

That night by the fire was a lot more comfortable than the last two had been. Almost bearable.

At least it was still calm the next morning. And cold. Hard, bitter cold again, enough to make the snow squeak under our boots and to coat the hairs inside a man's nose with prickly little sheathings of ice.

A slick, glazed crust had formed on the softer deep snow, and I gave some thanks for the heavy feathers of hair that made the lower legs of the draft horses so damned ugly. Ugly, but useful. Those skeins of tough hair had been bred into them for just such conditions as this. The broken ice surface would not cut their legs so easily when they crunched through it. I hated to think what would be happening to the legs of the cow ponies up above. They didn't have such protection.

"Do we start?" were the first words out of the kid's mouth when he wakened.

"We do. How much grain do we have left?"

"Sixty pounds or so."

"Okay. Give each of them twenty pounds and get the harness on them. I'll fix us a heavy feed, too. You'll be needing it before the day is done."

We ate and hooked up, and I handed the kid a wide-bladed grain scoop shovel. "Your weapon, sir."

"Do you mean I've got to shovel the whole way up?" he asked nervously.

"Lord, no. Just sit tight. I'll tell you when I need you."

I took up the reins and got a light contact on the big horses' mouths. They pulled, were checked by the drag of the frozen runners and leaned forward into their collars. Their big hooves plopped, and a spray of snow and ice flew. The wagon broke free with a lurch, and we slid forward.

The first quarter mile was not too bad. The snow was about knee deep here. The big horses simply waded through it in their slow, powerful way, trampling the crust and packing a narrow path under their feet, each hoof damn near the size of a dinner plate and plenty of weight about it.

We began hitting deeper stuff then. The first bad pocket was chest-high on the lead horse. He snorted and flared his nostrils but waded ahead several yards before even his great strength was not enough. I let him rest a moment before I gave a series of tugs on the driving lines. Both horses tucked their heads and began shoving the wagon backward.

"Do I shovel now?"

"I'll tell you when."

I slapped the lines against their rumps and hollered. The big horses surged forward, driving hard into the path they had already made. The leader hit the wall of snow. He hit it like a railroad snowplow. The crust was shattered for five feet around, and loose snow sprayed over his withers. He drove himself up and over, crushing down onto the snow and packing it beneath churning legs and feet. He made four or five yards before he could go no further.

We backed, and the big horse charged the drift again. He had the idea of what we wanted now. In all he had made about seventy-five yards before the snow was so deep he could no longer go over it. I backed him away again, further this time.

"Now, Kid."

"Yes, sir." He grabbed the scoop shovel and floundered forward into the path broken by the horses.

"Just take off the top coupla feet," I told him, "and don't try to throw a full scoop each time. You'll last longer and move more snow in the long run if you throw just a little each time. Full scoops of that dense stuff would have you passing out on me in no time."

He got to work, and I got down to change the horses in the tandem hitch. Here was where that rig would have its value. It was the lead horse that had to do the hard work of breaking through. The wheeler just lent his weight to packing down what the leader had already broken, that and pulling the wagon, which for these horses was nothing. By switching their places in the hitch, they could take turns resting, yet we could move steadily forward. With a conventional hitch both would have to work all the time. Rest stops — necessary if you didn't want to kill your horses — would make the work that much slower.

The kid shoveled past the hump of the drift and into a more shallow area. I laid the horses into their collars, and the fresh leader smashed ahead. Two more charges and we broke through into wading-depth snow again. The kid climbed back up, and we slogged on.

It got no easier and seemed to go endlessly on, with the drifts getting deeper and wider. By late morning both horses were sodden with sweat and melted snow. Steam rose from their wet, matted coats. It hung above them in the cold air like a pair of tiny clouds.

The kid looked to be nearly as tired. He held his arms like they were so much lead, shaped and painted to resemble human limbs. When he shoveled he took smaller and smaller loads onto the big scoop shovel and threw them barely aside from our path. He had long since learned to shed the bulky and, under these conditions, overwarm buffalo coat while he was shoveling, putting it back on as soon as he could turn the job over to the horses. Even so, his hair was plastered flat with sweat. The wet hair over the nape of his neck had frozen into clusters of oddly shaped icicles, each with its own little core of red hair. Still, he didn't quit. He plugged at it as steadily as the horses did.

I wanted to call a halt for a while. Both

the kid and the team had earned a rest, had long since earned one. But I could not. The kid needed food. All right. He could eat it while the horses were doing the work. It was as much of a rest as I could give him. If I let the horses cool off too long in this cold, they would sicken, maybe die. Worse, they would stiffen up and do it before we had done all we could. And there were some two dozen men and I didn't know how many hundred cattle up there in need of our help. We had to give it now or not at all.

I backed the horses and shuffled them forward every so often while we waited, to keep their muscles active while they waited for the kid to finish this latest patch, this one over his head so that he was having a hell of a time getting it low enough for the horses to tackle. There was nothing I could do to help him, though. It was times like this when I felt like a bunged-up cripple, having to sit and watch while someone else did the work.

He broke through and waved the wagon forward, slumping into the snow while he waited for the rig to reach him. That was bad. The snow would melt and saturate his trousers. He could be taken bad sick if he wasn't careful.

The drift here was so high that the wagon

wedging into the narrowly shoveled and horse-broken path toppled snow across the driving box and into the wagon bed. We had to shovel it out to get rid of the excess weight.

Another, shallower stretch was ahead where less snow had clung to the rising slope of the long gap. The kid sat wearily with the buffalo coat draped over his shoulders. Steam from fresh sweat lifted out of his collar. He chewed without interest on a piece of jerky, one of the few foods that can still be chewed without having to thaw it in such weather.

"We'll make it, won't we?" he asked.

"That's a damn fool question," I snapped at him. "Don't ask it again, nor anything like it."

He shut his mouth and went to looking everywhere but at me for the next little while. And maybe I had been too snippy with him. After all, this was a lot harder on him than it was on me. All I had to do was sit here and keep from freezing.

The lead horse came to a head-hanging halt again, and the kid crawled out. I backed the team and changed the leaders again. They were needing it awfully frequent now. The kid hefted his shovel and went to scooping. After a while he stood the shovel in the snow and knuckled the small of his back. He shook his arms to relieve what I could just bet were shooting pains across his shoulders. He leaned backward. He was looking up the gap when he did.

He wheeled to face me, a broad grin on his face, the exhaustion hidden now. "Hot damn!" he yelled. "Look up there." He was practically jumping up and down in his excitement.

I looked where he was pointing, and surer than hell there were some dark figures moving against the stark white of the endless humps of snow. Some of our boys or the Slash WT. The beeves would be coming along behind the trail-breaking crew.

"Look at 'em come, Kid. That's the ticket. Them working down, and us busting our way up. By damn, we'll get those critters off this molehill yet."

And so we did.

Oh, don't get me wrong. It still was no snap. When we came in sight of them, there was yet a half mile of deep drifts and constant step-by-step work separating us. But somehow it was easier now that we could see how close we were to breaking a route through.

We made it before dark, even. Our hard-working drafters bucked the last few yards of clinging, freezing snow. The leader made it into the break pushed down by Earl Crane's pony. Earl backed gratefully away to give the big horse room, and the exhausted lead horse stood, dripping wet and steaming, and shook itself like a huge dog.

Earl slipped down off his horse and came forward to shake our hands and make some glad words before he took the shovels and carried them back toward the rest of the boys.

There was still a deal of shovel work to be done. We had to clear a turn-around for the wagon and heavy horses. But then it was clear sailing to single-file the Slash WT down through the path we had forced.

I sure was glad to see those boys, and I guess they were ready to see us too. Even with spare ponies they could swap onto, they were in rough shape for horseflesh. If our horses were tired, theirs were ready to lie down and give it all up. With so much less weight to use in bucking those drifts, and no grain feed to give them strength and body heat, they were in poor shape. In just a coupla days the flesh had sloughed off their ribs at an unbelievable rate — and FR-Connected Bar horses just are not kept like that.

Worse yet, their chests and lower legs were

seeping blood and were caked with more from older wounds where the ice had sliced into them like so many dull knives. The cuts were not all that deep, but there were sure enough of them.

The boys got the turn-around dug, and I swung the patient drafters to point them downslope. Far up the gap I could hear the yips and yells as Slash WT riders began lining the cattle into the narrow track. Much of the way coming down the beeves would be in a narrow, soft-walled chute, part of the time so deep a man on horseback could not see over the sides. But by damn they could get down now.

The drafters led the way down. It sure was easier than going up.

We reached the coals where our fire had been for the past coupla days and the wood the kid had stockpiled for us there. We didn't waste any time in setting up there again but got right to it.

The kid dragged some sacking — snow-covered and stiff but better than nothing — out of the back of the wagon and gave both draft horses a good rubdown before he grained them. I got at the fire to restart it and soon had several big pots of coffee boiling. As soon as that was cooking, I went to chunking bacon from the slabs I'd brought.

I had to use a hand ax to get it off. The pieces were not exactly neat slices, but I didn't think anybody would mind that greatly.

Our boys were sniffing around the coffeepot even before it was done cooking. They were so cold they poured it weak and half-boiled and began gulping it like that.

The Slash WT crew began drifting in one at a time a half hour or so later as the first of their animals began to clear the gap and scatter onto the flatter land of our range. Their boys kept dribbling in and heading for those coffeepots like bees for their hive through most of the night. It was close to dawn before the last of Warren Tynell's white-faced steers was out in the open. Their cook wagon was the last thing down, Fletcher Lewis and Wayne Tynell riding just ahead of it to see that everything and everyone had made it down before them.

I was a little surprised when Norman Hanes, the Slash WT cook, turned his rig, still running awkwardly on deep-biting wheels, down toward the Tynell range without stopping. I surely had figured Norman would want to add his skillets to the fire so we could put a proper breakfast out for the two bunches of tired boys. But he didn't. It was too dark in the dim moonlight to make out what, if anything, he was doing on his driving box, but he sure never turned his team toward our fire.

Fletcher and the Tynell whelp did come over, though. The Slash WT men at our fire scattered like a covey of quail and headed for their horses. Jess stood up to meet the incoming riders, and it occurred to me that he was holding himself awfully stiff. His jaw was stuck out, and he had that cold, expressionless look on him that he gets when things are in a tight. I commenced to wonder just what the hell was up here. We should be celebrating, not getting set like a pair of feist dogs meeting in an alley.

Fletcher stepped down by our fire, but Wayne kept his seat. Fletch's hands kept toying with the buckle on his chaps, and he looked downright embarrassed. He started to say something, choked the words off short, and shot a look up at Wayne. He drew himself upright — I hadn't realized until then how hunch-shouldered he'd been standing — and gave Jess a warm and friendly grin.

"By God, Jess, I appreciate what you boys did for us. We'd have lost beef for sure if it hadn't been for your bunch. I don't guess I'll forget it."

Jess nodded. "You'd have done the same

for us," he said. "De nada." He looked up at Wayne and after knowing him so long I could tell Jess was bound and determined he was *not* going to say whatever it was he was thinking.

It would have ended there, I am sure, if that Tynell lout had had the first scrap of brain in his head.

Instead he sat there looking haughty and sneering, the play of the firelight making the expression all the uglier in the bitter cold night. He looked straight at Jess Barnes, as fine a cowman and as good a man as has ever set foot into this or any other valley, and said, "Don't expect any thanks from me, you son of a bitch. We wouldn't have had any trouble if it hadn't been for you. And mark my words, Barnes, you might as well pack your gear and pick your traveling horse. You're through in this valley." He wheeled his mount and headed down toward his herd and the speck of firelight I could see beginning to flare down that way.

Jess had given no reaction at all. He turned his unblinking stare toward Fletcher. Fletcher was the one who looked like he'd just been slapped in the face.

"This is not my land," Jess said in a low, controlled voice. "If it was, Fletcher, no

Slash WT hoof and no Slash WT rider would ever again touch it. You tell Warren that for me, will you?"

"Sure, Jess, I . . . I'm sorry. My God, but I'm sorry." He gathered up the reins of his horse and swung into the saddle. He turned back once, his head almost obscured by the frozen breath hanging there, making him look distant and unreal in the shifting light. He mouthed the words softly again, so softly we could see them better than hear them, and turned his horse away.

# CHAPTER 19

"By damn, Jess ol' hoss, I am proud to know a fella like you."

He gave me a blank, hard look.

"Yes indeed, Jess. Any man who can bring freak storms down from the heavens is a good man to know," I said.

He didn't say anything at first, but I was in no hurry. When he had chewed on this enough, he would be ready to talk about it I'd still be there when he was ready.

The rest of the boys were sleeping. They would sleep well into the daylight, but they had earned the privilege. And I figured it would be just as well if no one else was awake when Jess wanted to talk.

I sat and drank coffee while I waited, pouring frequently from the big pot, a few swallows spilled into the cup each time so the predawn cold would not have time to do too much damage before I drank it.

After a little while Jess began to get restless. He had been sitting on his saddle. Now he got up and paced to the wagon and back several times. He came back and sat again, looking dog tired. It was about to come daylight.

"Do you have any idea what that silly bastard decided?" he asked.

I shrugged. "I'd believe most anything of that boy."

"Can you believe it? I hogged the use of the gap. Wouldn't let them use it in time. So it's all my fault."

"I agree," I said real seriously. "Obviously you knew we'd have this storm a coupla months early. And of course you got on your high horse and wouldn't let them into the gap no matter how much Wayne begged and pleaded. It makes sense to me, all right."

Jess snorted. "You *know* I sent word over there. Twice. Never heard the first thing back from them either time. Hell, I couldn't know what they wanted to do if they didn't tell me. I've got all I can pray over running this outfit. I can't try to second-guess what's best for the Slash WT too." He shook his head.

"Anyway," he said, "that bum kid of Warren's blames our outfit for the whole thing. And dammit you know what Warren thinks of that boy. Anything the kid says has to be the way it is. This could really cause trouble between George and Warren, and Lord knows I wouldn't want that. But I swear I've had all of that kid I can stomach. I mean it. I am flat fed up with him."

"Aw, I wouldn't worry about it, Jess. You didn't do anything wrong, and neither did Fletcher. Nobody could have known we'd get a crazy snow like this, and that's what it comes down to. The breaks of the weather, is all, and that's the whole story of the cow business. You take what comes and do whatever you gotta do to meet it."

"I guess, but I sure wish it hadn't happened," he said.

"Sure. So does everybody else, but that won't change it. Anyway, there's no point in worrying about it. Fletcher knows the boy is taking potshots at the moon with this thing. You saw how he felt about it. He was embarrassed half to death. He'll tell Warren — if he has to; after all, Warren has been in the business awhile too — and it'll blow over. If I were you I wouldn't ever expect to hear an apology out of that whelp, but I think you can count it a closed deal, Jess."

"I hope you're right. I sure do." He sighed and got up to put more wood on the fire.

The pull of habit began waking the boys not long after daylight. Maybe the cold, dropping again now that it was clear, had something to do with that too. Whichever, we had a quick breakfast and headed for home with the big horses setting the pace for everyone.

We made it that afternoon. We had no sooner pulled into the yard than George and his womenfolk were running out to greet us.

"Is everything all right?" George asked anxiously. "No one's been hurt? Our herd's all right?"

"*Our* herd?" Jess asked. "Sure. Why wouldn't they be?"

"Why wouldn't they . . . ? Okay, then let me ask this," George said. "Where the hell have you people been all this time?"

Jess looked at me and I looked at him, and I'll bet I looked about as sheepish as he did.

"I guess it's my fault . . . ," he began.

"No, you had to scat," I put in. "I'm the one who had time and just plain didn't think about it."

"Quit that," George told the both of us. "Where have you *been*?"

So Jess explained what had been going on, being awfully flattering about the little part the kid and those big horses had played, and George calmed down. Jess didn't mention anything right then about the fuss with Wayne, which I figured was appropriate. That sort of thing would best be discussed in private. And in warmth.

The boys headed for the horse pens. We unloaded the wagon, and the kid took it and the drafters back down to the shed.

It was good to be home, and I lost no time getting a fire going in my oven. That is one good thing about cooking. You generally get to keep warm regardless of the weather. It didn't feel too bad to get some clean clothes on either. I was beginning to feel a bit rank, and it was some kind of relief to get cleaned up and shaved again.

The cold continued for another two weeks, and we had one more snow before it broke. When it did warm up, though, the temperature climbed all the way back to normal. The snow melted completely off the flats, and the drifts began to shrink. In another week there were only some crusted patches of dirty snow left under a few trees and on the northern slopes of the steeper cuts and gullies. To just glance around without having been there, you wouldn't hardly have known we'd had such a turn of weather.

As soon as the road was clear again, the kid put the wheels back on the light wagon, and we began hauling back and forth to Warcry. He drove the light rig while I stayed with my heavy wagon. I know those seats are built the same, but the big one seems more comfortable somehow.

We stocked both line camps with enough to feed two men for half a year and practically bulged the walls of our storage spaces at home. I considered that first storm to be fair warning and was not going to be taking any chances of running out. Of any damn thing.

I didn't really need much help in the kitchen with so few hands to feed, but the kid managed to stay busy with odd jobs, things the regular hands didn't like to do like sawing and splitting and piling the mountains of wood we would need to heat the big house, our place and — less since the boys were mostly gone — the bunkhouse. He spent a good deal of time, too, helping Katy pull the last of her garden. She liked to leave some things like parsnips and salsify until after we'd had a freeze but then never wanted to do the work of digging them. This fall her garden was right thoroughly dug up by a very helpful Keystone Kid.

The cold weather came back, at a more normal time this second time around, and

Jess sent his line-camp crews out making my job even that much easier. To me that was always the official start of the winter season. As soon as the line riders left for the cabins, the cold weather slowdown was on.

# CHAPTER 20

Jim Fuller was bubbling over with the news he carried. He and Earl had been so anxious to tell us the news from town that they'd come home in time for the evening meal instead of dragging in in the middle of the night after squeezing the last howl from their two days off.

"They have it all set up, I tell you. They're hiring big tents and stoves and everything, a whole special freight car full of stuff, and they're going to bring a band in all the way from Kansas City. Real fancy, this is going to be," Jim said. "Barrels of duck packed in brine from Maryland and some sort of fruit punch and . . . just everything you could think of."

"It is going to be *some,*" Earl told us.

And I will say, when the Knights of Columbus decided what they were going to do for Warcry, they surely had done it up brown. The boys said the lumberyard was already hard at work fixing up a portable dance floor to put in one of the big tents and a regular raised platform for the musicians. The whole works. Peter Schweisgude would do a top job on it, too. He was one of the founders of the Knights here as well as running the lumberyard.

Christmas Eve the dance would be, and a big dinner beforehand, though the boys said they were going to charge an admission fee for the dinner part of it. But hell, it sounded like it would be worth it.

"Jim, you go down to the south camp tomorrow," Jess said, "and make sure they have their calendar straight. They can come in the twenty-second. The Eason boys are due in the twenty-first anyway, but Earl, you'd best ride over and let them know ahead of time. Those cows can get along without us for a coupla days or they aren't worth keeping."

"Don't forget to tell the family right away. The women will want to be making new dresses for this, I'd bet," I warned.

"I'll tell them tonight. The old man wanted to talk to me about something anyway," he said.

I was looking forward to it, too, and I am not one to drive all that distance for your average social. But this was going to be something purely special. I wasn't about to miss out on it even if I would not be dancing. You can just bet I wouldn't miss it. I even decided to wear my best suit for this one.

The kid got his brand-new best put together for it too. He dragged out a never-been-worn striped shirt and a fresh, new collar and packed them into his battered valise, and for riding in on the twenty-third he brought out his old yellow shirt — not so bright any longer but still kinda spiffy with its red trim — that I hadn't seen on him for several months now. He didn't own a proper suit, but he did brush his coat and black his boots and had me trim his hair. So we were pretty well set.

The only one who wasn't wound up about it was Jess. I tried to josh him out of whatever seemed to be bothering him by teasing him about saving all his dances for the Widow Ramsey, but he never even rose to my bait. Whatever it was, he was keeping it to himself.

We went in on the morning of the twenty-third. The family took the gig, and the kid and I followed in the light wagon, both rigs fitted with runners and on this occasion both teams hung with clusters of bells that jingled with a high-pitched tinkle at each hoof-fall and added to the festive mood of the day.

It could not have been a nicer day for the trip. Enough snow on the ground to be pretty but not so much as to be a nuisance traveling, and there was a sharp, clean nip in the air that made even me with my heat-loving bones feel good. The horses seemed to feel as good, for they moved at a fast jog with their feet lifting high, their heads up, and their ears perked.

Usually going into town we go pretty much on our own with the crew loping ahead and then the family with their fancy harness team and lastly us drag-alongs in the wagon, but today we all stayed together as we went, and I was kind of proud of our little group as we met others heading in to Warcry.

We trooped through the main street in a group and split up at the hotel. The family took rooms there and I did, but the rest of our crowd — this time including even the kid, by damn — headed for one of the big tents that the Knights had set up for sleeping purposes, with coal-fired stoves and mounds of straw scattered around so the men would be comfortable. They were providing three tents for the event. Two for sleeping and one monstrous thing big enough to hold a circus for the dining and dancing.

The ladies, of course, would stay under roof, with the unmarried belles nesting up in big sleeping parties like so many pullets on a roost and even their mothers doubling up when they had to.

From the number of people and rigs and saddle horses roaming about in utter chaos, it looked like this Knights of Columbus bash was going to rival the firemen's oyster fry for bringing the valley together. Something that had never happened in the wintertime before.

For a change I could park the wagon behind the hotel stable instead of at Wiggins's place. This trip we didn't hardly need a thing except to have fun. The kid had already disappeared with the other boys, in his excitement forgetting the team, which was usually one of his chores. Not that I minded. I'd been getting along by myself a good many years, and if I was too lazy to do it yet, why I would deserve some comeuppance.

I put my things in my room and headed straightaway for the Bull Shooter. After all, a nice day for late December or not, this was no weather for rocking on the hotel porch.

Hiram had the lamps lighted and a cheery fire going in a potbellied stove near the center of the room. The fellows in town judged the seasons by Hiram putting in his sandbox and stove. Most folks will just buy a stove, set it in place, and leave it there, greasing it in the springtime and then ignoring it until it was fired again in the fall. Not Hiram. He had a thing about his stove and made practically a ritual out of bolting it together or unbolting it with the change in season and giving free drinks to whoever helped him move it in pieces to or from his storeroom. Now, of course, it was purring softly with a coal fire inside.

I took a seat close to it, and Handy brought me a hot buttered rum from the huge sack bowl at the end of the bar. Hiram also insisted on heating his rum punches with genuine irons that he kept by his stove. The only break he made from the old way there was that he didn't use a poker. In honor of his customers he kept a supply of branding irons hung on his wall and chose a different one each day to use for his rum heating. There was one of ours somewhere over there in his collection.

The rum went down smooth and sweet,

and I saluted Hiram with my mug after the first couple swallows. He was half the length of the room away but didn't need to speak. He grinned and gave me a little bow and went on about his business, knowing I was pleased by his efforts.

Pete Chapman and Earl Crane were already at the bar making up for what they couldn't get at home. The other boys hadn't come in yet or maybe had decided to go straight over to Bessie Blue's so they wouldn't be having thoughts about that to mess up their Christmas Eve partying tomorrow.

Pip Foster and a couple other boys I recognized as being in the Slash WT crew were at the other end of the bar. When Pip came idling over to see whose iron was being used in the punches today — it turned out to be a J Bar C — I motioned him over.

"Where's Fletcher?" I asked, thinking to razz Fletch about his racing losses last spring and see could I take some more off him.

Pip gave me a queer sort of look and glanced around to see who else was in the place before he dropped into a seat next to me. He leaned close and said, "I thought you'd've knowed. The ramrod left us."

I was absolutely floored by that, and it

took me a moment to register just what he'd said. "But . . . Fletcher had been around here near as long as me. Why'd he ever cut loose, man?"

Again Pip gave me a strange look. "You were there when the blowup started."

At first I could not think of what he meant. "I was?" I asked stupidly. "Aw, no. You surely don't mean that snowstorm business. You can't."

"I guess I can," Pip said. There was a touch of sadness in his voice. "Him and the old man had a helluva fight about it. Them two and Wayne, that is." He shook his head. "Fletcher pulled stakes and took off soon after."

Pip's voice dropped lower. "He had Kyle Horne ride with him to town so Kyle could take the horse back. He took a train out. I guess he didn't even want to ride a Slash WT horse again."

My God, I never would have thought such a thing. And if he wouldn't even leave with a horse — every paid-off hand is entitled to a saddle horse when he leaves a place, if he hasn't worked more than one lousy payday — it must have been really bad on Fletcher.

But to just leave like that, after so many years, and him being number one on the place . . .

I guess I could understand him not coming around to say good-bye to people, though. I was willing to bet he hadn't even made the rounds of the fellows in town when he left. For it would have been a painful thing for him. He would not have wanted any sympathy, and no matter what might have happened between him and Warren, there would've been too much loyalty to the brand left in him to allow him to complain about the outfit.

But to be gone now. I couldn't hardly believe it.

"I sure am sorry to hear that, Pip. His friends will miss him. An' I'll bet you boys who rode for him will be missing him even more."

Pip snorted. "Ain't *that* the natural truth. Not that I'll be missing him for long," he said. "I cain't afford to throw over a winter job unless I really have to, but come the spring work I'll be hooking on somewhere else. You can bank on that."

He shut up and got a faintly embarrassed look on him when he realized how that would sound, him talking about his outfit out of school like that. Then he stuck his jaw out and gave me a tight grin. "It's the damn truth, though. See you." He got to his feet abruptly and left the Bull Shooter.

Fletcher Lewis. Gone down the trail now. He wouldn't be back to this valley again. Likely I would never see him again, and that was a shame. He was a pretty good old boy, and there are never so many of those around that you can afford to waste one. Somehow I felt that Fletcher had been wasted.

Handy pulled his chair close again. He had been polite enough to turn away while I was talking with Foster, but I guess he'd heard the conversation.

"I thought you'd have heard about that," he said, "you bein' neighbors and all."

"Strained neighbors lately, I guess. More than I realized we were. Anyway, I hadn't heard a word about it, and I'm sure if any of the others had, I would've been told about it. He was a friend, you know."

"Yeah, I know. An' as nosy as you are, you don't miss much, you old devil."

I pretended to grump at him, but my heart wasn't much in it. I kept thinking about Fletcher. It sounded like Handy knew something of it, though. "Who's running the show for them now? Old Warren take it over himself?"

Handy's eyes gleamed with amusement. "Whoo-boy! Even better'n that. The son and heir is now foreman of the Slash WT." He laughed. "Sure am glad I don't hold any shares in the bank. Yes sir, they just may be holdin' some thin notes all of a sudden."

"Jee-zus! Even Warren can't be that blind, Handy. That boy doesn't know enough about the cow business to make a pimple on Fletcher Lewis's butt, and the old man tries to put him in Fletcher's shoes. No wonder Pip said what he did."

"Uh-huh. He won't be the only one neither. Just let the weather break next spring and there won't be a top hand left on the place. The word is all over town already. The old hands feeling bad about it an' all the half-grown younguns with notions of drawing riding wages already planning on this as their chance to catch on with a cow crowd."

"It sounds like they'll get their chance, all right. I sure hate to see it, though. Warren and his boy deserve all they get, but that's a hell of a way to treat a good spread. Oh well. It's none of my nevermind. Tell you what, Handy. I'll spring for the price of two more of these if you'll bring them."

"About time you offered," he said. "Free booze is the only reason I'm willing to sit with you."

He brought the hot buttered rum drinks and we changed the subject, but I could not keep it completely out of my mind. As soon

267

as that second drink was gone I slipped out and went looking for Jess.

I found him in Tom's barber chair and waited until he was done getting pretty. "C'mon over to Elsie's and buy me a dinner," I told him. "It's about time you provided a meal." I tried to make it light but either I hadn't or Jess wasn't in a mood for it. He didn't argue or badger at me, just said all right and led the way quietly.

He hadn't heard about it either and was as shocked as I'd been. There was a bleakness in his eyes, and for a long while he did not say a thing. From the way he went through his food, with all the enthusiasm of a steam engine at low throttle, I'd bet he never tasted a thing that went into his mouth.

I was hoping he would open up and talk to me about whatever was bothering him, but if I had thought that talk about Fletcher's troubles would make him loosen up about his own, I was surely wrong. If anything it seemed to make things worse.

It was an awfully quiet meal.

# CHAPTER 21

I didn't see the kid at the roast-duck feed the next day, but he was one of the few people of the valley who didn't go to that part of the festivities. It could have been that we all, like I did, wanted the Knights to make a go of this so they would do it again the next year.

The dance, though. Now that everyone, just everyone turned out for.

They had set it up to be a most refined and elegant event, too. The ladies were there in their finest and their fanciest. The gentlemen were dressed to match, and no one had better act on any but his very best manners this Christmas Eve.

Someone had gone to a lot of trouble preparing for it, too. Not just the obvious things like the tents and the dance floor but little things like the evergreen garlands draped along the tent walls and wrapped in long spirals around the support poles. There

must have been three wagonloads of green-
ery that someone had cut and wired together to do all that with. Every lamp globe
was spotless clean and every wick trimmed.
Judging from the numbers of lamps hung
all through the dance tent, the Knights'
homes must have been awfully dark this
evening. You wouldn't have thought they
could've found so many in the whole town.

It was surely a success, too. Everyone you
looked at had a big smile. I had a cup of
fruit punch and was pleased to find that
none of the young bucks had tried to im-
prove on it. That was a sure sign of best
behavior. Of course the boys had been
smart when they put the tents near the
depot. Easy for unloading things from the
rail cars but, maybe more important, the
dance was close enough to the Bull Shooter
that anyone who wanted a snort could step
over there for one without making a big
thing of it.

There were chairs spotted around the
edges of the dance floor, and while most of
the fellows chose to stand and leave the
chairs to the ladies, I was for sitting down
myself. I figured to be here a spell and
intended to be comfortable while I watched.

The band they had brought in from so far
away was . . . decent enough, I guess I

should say. At least it was interesting to know they had come so far. There was a piano, a violin, bass fiddle, saxophone, and a fifth fellow who switched off between an accordion and a guitar. They were dressed in matching suits. And really they were pretty good. I guess I was just expecting something way beyond the few touring groups that came through once in a while, and that they were not.

The family arrived, George looking awfully proud with Natalie on one arm and Katy on the other. They nodded and smiled their way through the earlier arrivals and took chairs straight across the floor from where I was sitting.

Natalie was wearing a maroon dress that I hadn't seen before. And Katy. Her dress was new too. I had seen the material once before when I carried it out from town, but I sure wouldn't have recognized it if I didn't know where it came from. Katy looked tonight like she'd been doing her shopping in New York or San Francisco.

The material was a dark blue velvet that looked like a moonlit winter sky. The dress was long and full, of course, but fitted close from the waist up. She had made it with long sleeves, but the neck was cut kind of low. She had made a little choker or collar sort of thing of the same material that made her neck look slender and white and lovely. Some sort of bauble was hung from the choker. Something I hadn't noticed before. I wasn't close enough to see what it was for sure, but it was certainly not the pale cameo her folks had given her for her sixteenth birthday. She sure looked grown up.

And I sure got one hell of a shock about a half hour later. The band had been playing pretty steadily ever since folks began to show up, and now people were beginning to form into squares and get onto the floor. Sam Hinglemann took the hint and got up to call the dancing for those that were interested.

Wayne Tynell oozed up alongside of the family, smiling and radiating charm and looking handsome in a fine suit and shiny hundred-dollar boots. He bowed over Natalie's hand and then over Katy's, and then that fool girl got up to dance with him. I guessed maybe no one had told her about the trouble he'd caused, but she still should've had better sense than that.

They danced three sets in a row, and I didn't like it. Not the way she kept peeking over her shoulder at him when they changed partners nor the way she kept giving him big-eyed looks that would make even a nice fellow have improper thoughts. And she did look cute as a calf's ear out there in her new party dress and neck bauble and her cheeks rosy red — though whether from the cold outside or the dancing inside or from Wayne Tynell I could not have said.

After the third set Wayne left her chattering with Mrs. Daisy May and headed for the fruit-punch table.

The kid came in about that time, and I could see why he probably had missed that good duck dinner. He likely had his last two months' pay on his back. He'd gone and bought himself a suit and vest and looked as well turned out as any gentleman in the crowd. His red hair was slicked down and his boots gleaming. I'd have worn shoes this night if I'd owned any, but I guess he had figured that would make him look less the cow-country man. Anyway his shoes were back home. And in truth he did look just fine, dandy and dapper as a whiskey drummer.

The kid spotted Katy first thing and headed straight for her. The band was tuning up for another go, so I could guess what he was going to do. Sure enough he planted himself in front of her and gave her a stiff little bow and was about half smiling when he said something to her.

I still don't know how she would have replied. Wayne came back just then with two cups of punch. And he did not exactly like the kid to start with.

Wayne came up behind the kid, carefully transferred one cup so he was holding both in one hand, and gave the kid a vicious elbow in the back. I don't think anyone else noticed the short, quick movement, but I sure did. Then the two-faced son of a bitch patted the kid on the shoulder and seemed to be apologizing for the "accident."

The kid's face was dead white but he gritted his teeth and nodded and tried to smile. He was sure to know it was an out-and-out lie, but Katy never tumbled to it. She just smiled and shrugged and shook her head about something they were saying over there. She took one of the cups from Wayne with a pert little smile and turned away to lead off toward some empty chairs over by the tent wall. It would be colder over there but more private — which I did not especially like.

Wayne paused to say something into the kid's ear before he followed Katy. There was a cold-eyed, tight little smile on Wayne's face when he turned away.

The kid stood still for a few minutes more, watching their backs as they walked away.

He didn't look scared, though. Just thought-ful. Finally he turned from them and drifted, smiling at a few people here and there and stopping to have a word with someone every twenty paces or so. It seemed he was beginning to get acquainted now.

He joined me eventually but never said a word about Katy or about Tynell, so I didn't bring it up either, and after a time he went on about his business elsewhere, without ever getting into the dancing like the other boys from the outfit.

All in all, the Christmas Eve dance was a success and Christmas morning about as much so, with the children of the valley drawn together in town for the first time so they could receive their presents in full view — or close to it — of all the other kids and then run around making comparisons.

I gave George a watch fob and the ladies each some gay colored cloth and Jess a hat and Casey a pair of spurs and got some lovely, useful things from them in return. I gave the kid a horsehair belt and matching hatband that seemed to genuinely please him. And damned if he didn't have some-thing for me, too. A handsome little penknife with my initials inlaid in the handle in gold letters. He'd had to plan ahead for that, you can be sure, and I considered it almighty thoughtful of him.

I would have to say that when we went home we were all feeling pretty good. Even Jess's mood seemed a little lighter than it had been for a while.

# CHAPTER 22

On the morning of February 23 the whole blessed world fell apart, or our piece of it did anyway.

We were just fixing to have breakfast, all of us in the long chow hall at the table that would hold many times our number. Jess at the head and Casey next to him and Pete Chapman and Phil Cline. I was sitting with them, as I liked to do during these slow winter months. The kid was carrying in a bowl of gravy.

The outside door swung open and Natalie Senn stepped inside. She was wearing a lightweight housecoat and carpet slippers. Snow crystals coated the slippers, obscuring the pattern of the material, and her ankles were bright red from the shock of the cold. She left wet, melting splotches behind on the floor where she walked. Her hair was falling loose around her shoulders; one side had been brushed out but the other was still night-tangled. She seemed calm and very composed.

"George just died," she said. Her voice was flat, without a hint of emotion. We all stared blankly at her. "He was shaving," she said, "and he just . . . fell down. He's dead."

Jess was the first to reach her side. He put an arm around her shoulders and guided her to a chair. He had to push her down into it. I put a cup of coffee into her hands, I don't know whose, a cup already full and sitting nearby. Pete got his coat from a peg and wrapped it around her shoulders.

Natalie looked at each of us and drew in a short, shuddering breath and smiled. "Thank you, boys."

"Are you sure, Nat?" Jess asked.

"I am," she said. "He's gone."

Jess nodded. But he slipped outside and I could hear his boots crunching on the snow with muffled thuds as he ran toward the big house. He was back a few minutes later, leading Katy. The child was crying and was near to being hysterical. She was dressed but her hair, too, was loose. Her face was red, her eyes puffed and draining. The effort of her crying sent waves of anguish racking through her body. Her shoulders leapt and fell irregularly. Jess sat her next to her mother and she clung fiercely to Natalie, hiding her face in Natalie's bosom.

"We'll go over to the house, Nat," Jess said softly. "Well . . ."

"No!" she barked sternly. She drew herself erect on the chair and raised her chin. "It is my place to lay out my man. Katryn Elizabeth will help me." She leaned back and took Katy by the shoulders. She shoved the girl an arm's length away and told her sharply, "Get yourself together now. We must do for your father."

She was unbending now, even harsh. Having no one of my own, I suppose I will never fully appreciate the awesome strength of the control she placed upon herself, but I could not doubt that that was what it was, for Natalie Senn had always been a warm and loving woman, given to laughter and affectionate play when she was with her George.

She nodded to us without focusing her eyes on any of us. She rose and lifted Katy with her.

"You will notify the neighbors and the town?"

"Yes, ma'am," Jess said softly.

"We will need food when they come to call," she said, still under that terrible control that blocked emotion from reaching her voice.

"It will be ready," I assured her.

"Very well," she said. She turned Katy and guided her toward the door. Phil jumped to open it for them. I don't think Natalie even noticed. She and George's daughter stepped out into the cold. I hoped she would remember to put dry slippers on when she got back to the house but I doubted that she would, not until it came time to dress herself for the visitors.

For a long moment we all stood wordlessly where we were. It was all so sudden, so unexpected. He had been such a vital man. It left me with a hollow, empty feeling deep within me, and from their faces I believe the others felt the same. Jess and I the most, I guess. And Casey. We had known him the longest and the best. Jess and I had ridden stirrup to stirrup with him, dragged calves to George's irons back when he was still out doing a part of the riding, back before he became chained to ledgers and account books and endless correspondence with the stockyards and the railroads, to the marketing journals and the newsletters and the government publications.

It was that sort of thing that had occupied George these last years. That and spending time with his family. Lord knows he had earned that time. I was glad he had had it while he could, for many men will wait and think there is always a tomorrow when they can pack a lunch and drive the wife down along the creek or can find the time to sit and listen to the daughter as she shows off a new piece on the piano. At least George had had that for a time.

Still, I remembered him best as a grinning, sweat-streaked, beard-stubbled face on the other side of a high-country night fire and as the shadowy figure seen flitting dimly past through dense, hoof-churned dust. And, Lord God, how we would miss him.

"Time to saddle, boys," Jess said. His voice was low and none too steady. He would be remembering George as I was, I was sure.

"No, not yet," I told him. "Eat first. There's some hard, cold riding ahead. You'll all hold up better if you eat before you go."

Jess stood for a moment. He seemed to have to take the time to stop and consciously make an effort to evaluate what I had said before he could reach a decision and respond. "All right," he said finally. "Fill up, but make it quick."

The boys sat and bolted their food in silence, consuming beef and potatoes and bread and pie like so many machines designed to harvest plate-sized fields. They were done within minutes.

"All right," Jess said. "Phil, tell the line camps. They're to pull in right away. Someone can ride out from here each day to chop watering holes if they're needed. Anything else can wait.

"Pete, you go round to the neighbors. Hit all this end of the valley you can, but be back tomorrow, hear?" Chapman nodded.

"You head straight for Warcry, Casey. They can get the word out to the north part of the valley. Tell the TC&W agent. And ask Rev. Archer to come out tomorrow if he can. He can stay over for services, probably the day after. If the road is bad, you'd best stay overnight and come with him in case he needs help."

"Sure," Casey mumbled. He sighed.

That would leave Jess with the tasks at home to get ready for the people who would be coming. The lower pens had not been used for months. Paths would have to be cleared to them and hay hauled for all the driving horses that would be coming. Watering places would have to be cleared and chopped open. He would need help, but when the line crews got in they could dig the scraper out of the snow and build fires to thaw the bucket and the ratcheted trip levers. They would need it to clear snow from a big enough area to park the rigs that would be coming.

And someone would have to build the coffin.

The upper hay barn could be used for extra sleeping room if the men overflowed the bunkhouse. The women would put up in the big house. By tonight Natalie would need their company anyway.

The boys took off, and the kid and I got busy. We cleaned up from breakfast and kept going at top speed. I could have used some more ovens this day. I cut two roasts, as big as the one oven would hold, and filled in what space we had left with a coupla hams. The other oven we kept full with baking. Breads and pies, a fresh pan going in as soon as another was done.

The kid spent most of the morning either carrying wood or peeling potatoes, dropping the cleaned spuds into tubs of water to keep them from darkening before they were used. In this weather and with the distances people had to travel they would be bringing little with them, only what they might happen to have on hand that freezing would not hurt.

The first arrivals were there by dinner-time. The Abbots. The Tynells. Wayne was not with them. The Mays came soon after.

We carried a meal over to the main house, piling the table full so there would be plenty available as more people came.

Somehow Natalie and Katy had gotten through what they had to do. George was laid out in the front room, washed and the shaving finished. They had put his best suit on him. I noticed Natalie had put his best boots on him, too. He had worn shoes a good bit these last coupla years, but I remembered when he had gotten those boots. It was after our first really big shipment of three-year-olds on a high market. The boots were made of lizard skin, and he had always loved them. She had laid his spurs at his feet, his old using pair that he had had for as long as I'd known him. I had seen those spurs many and many a time before.

I stood and looked at him a long while and found that this yellow-fleshed, waxen figure was not my friend. The features were almost the same as his, but this was not George Senn. I could grieve for George but not for this body that once had been his.

But still, when I turned away from the draped door on which he had been laid, I was ready to believe that George was gone. It surprised me to realize that I had not believed it before. Until then I had only been doing what I was expected to do but without quite feeling why I was doing it.

I guess I was more shaken than I'd realized, for even through her own distress Natalie must have seen something of what I was feeling. She left the ladies who were trying to comfort her and stepped to my side to touch me on the arm and give me a smile of encouragement. She did not speak. She didn't need to. I got out of there as quickly as I could.

The Eason boys came in from the line camp that afternoon and got to work building the coffin. They did a fine job of it. Phil, Jim Fuller, and Earl Crane would not be in until morning as Phil had to ride first to the north camp, then turn and cross all the way down to the south line before he could even tell them.

More south-valley people came in the late afternoon and evening, and the kid and I were kept busy trying to provide for them all. Too busy to do much in the way of deep thinking, for which I was thankful.

They came to pay their respects to George Senn and stayed to offer comfort, to eat, to buzz with the talk of people who have not seen each other often enough, to tell their jokes and remember to keep the laughter respectfully soft the way folks tend to do at funeral gatherings.

By the third day all had come who would, or could, and we had burned fires the whole night through to soften the ground so the boys could chunk a grave open with pick-axes and hard work.

Wayne Tynell arrived that morning and took over the chore of comforting Katy when her father was put into the ground. It galled me some, more than some, to see him standing so straight and tall and handsome with an arm curved around her small shoulders and her sobbing into his chest, but it was not a time for me to be speaking to her about such things.

George was buried late in the morning of that day on the hill above the headquarters place, not far from where I had stopped that day to give the kid his first look. There were no trees here to shade his marker or draw fluttering birds to the site. What there was was a grand view of the headquarters buildings and the water and beyond that a sweep of grass and cows. And above it all the mountain that sheltered us from the really hard weather and gave us summer graze and year-round water for the making of more beef.

The Rev. Archer delivered the service, him so cold we could scarcely make out what he was trying to say but the words not mattering in any event. It was still a good service, because of the man George had been and the people who had come to honor him. The only things I regretted about it were Tynell standing so close to Katy at a time when she was in so much need . . . and that my gimpiness kept me from helping carry George those last few yards he would travel. I would've liked being able to do that for him.

The thing was quickly done and the older men took turns tumbling frozen clods back into the hole, and everyone hurried back down the hill toward warmth and the big dinner we had laid out there.

Now that the burying was over, people spoke louder and laughed more freely and drew Natalie into their jokes, persisting until they got her to laughing along with them, which was a good thing.

The kid and I stayed busy providing things for the women to distribute to the tables, all of them in the big house for this meal though the men finished their eating quickly and ducked out to the more comfortable surroundings of the cookhouse or the barns where they could smoke or spit or talk about beef without offending anyone.

The kid and I stayed as long as there was

feeding going on, and Wayne Tynell stayed, backed off into a corner with Katy huddled on a chair beside him. The kid kept giving the girl hidden glances, his face a study in mixed sympathy and anxiety, but I made sure he was too busy to interrupt them.

Not that I cared a damn how Wayne Tynell would come off if the good women of the valley saw him in an uproar, but neither Katy nor her mama needed that kind of unpleasantness just now.

I was glad when the women stepped in to do the cleaning up and I could snag the kid by the sleeve and take him back to the cook-house.

It was lonesome when everyone left the next day. But not nearly so lonesome as I imagine it was in the main house.

# CHAPTER 23

The big thaw came late in March, and the world soon seemed to be made of brown mud and rushing water. The ground underfoot was greasy with moisture and still-frozen crystals as the frost came out of it, and for a time you just had to wonder whatever had happened to the clean out-of-doors.

The boys rode out to comb the thickest of the breaks and returned driving every horse we owned — or all of them they could find, anyway. They drove them into the biggest of the pens, and we gathered on the rail to look them over.

They were not a very inspiring sight at this time of year. They were gaunted down from the winter, ribs and backbones prominent on the mares that had been feeding two bodies on the poor winter forage. They were still shaggy with thick fur, and it did not help any that those temporary coats were dull and lifeless in the weak spring sunshine. Some had already started to slip their dead hair; these looked patchy and positively ragged.

As usual we shook our heads and moaned and talked about the fine horses we had known in the past, but the fact was that if you had an eye that could look past that surface nastiness these were some pretty decent animals. The foal crop was started already, thanks to last year's early grass. If the later arrivals were as good, we would be in fine shape for horseflesh the next few years at the very least. The colts on the ground now were straight-legged and sturdy little creatures and none the worse off for having been dropped in a snowbank or maybe in a patch of freezing mud. They were bright-eyed and quick-footed and showed plenty of promise.

The stud horses had trailed the bands in. For the next few days they would hang around downwind of the pens, bugling cusswords at us for taking their harems away just when the sap was beginning to rise.

Unlike these modern youngsters who work for their livestock instead of holding that the livestock should work for you, George had always followed the old school when it came to handling his stallions. For all practical purposes, they weren't handled at all.

We had three well-bred stallions, and not a one of them'd had a halter or even a rope on them since the day they were brought onto the place. They were turned out and left alone to sort the mares out for themselves. Since they were all of quality blood, it didn't really matter which stud covered which mare — we weren't trying to raise purebred horses anyway — and we avoided unwanted blood by gelding our colts as yearlings.

Once the boys had brought all the horses in, they separated the mares from the crowd first, letting this-year foals stay with their mamas but turning back the tag-along yearlings that wanted to hang on to the mares even though they were long since weaned.

Last year's using horses were penned apart, too, and then the boys went through to cut in with the aged horses those that had just come three. The threes, of course, had never really been handled except for when they were branded and cut as yearlings. It was these that would make Casey's life interesting for the next month or so, the way they used to do for me.

The three-year-old fillies were put in with

the mares, as they would be old enough to breed now.

All the two-year-old geldings were put with the mares, too, to be turned out for another year of growing, but the filly twos were kept separate so they would not be exposed to the stallions until they had some more bone on them. They were old enough to stick but young enough that a foal this soon might stunt them. They would be held in pens until the breeding season was done with for this year.

When all that was done — and it took several days of hollering and the boys coming in covered with mud and their arms leaden from heaving ropes and lashing with rope ends — only the yearlings were left.

The mares and two-year-old geldings were turned out again. The mares would go with the stud horses, and the geldings would slink off in their own small bands, careful not to offend the stallions.

The yearlings were all branded then and the colts cut. And believe me, throwing a scared yearling and branding it can be some interesting work, especially when the footing is bad and the mud is flying.

The kid was happy as a dead pig in the sunshine, though. This was a short-handed time of year, so Jess let him take his rope

and get in there with them. All his practice
the year before had taught him to forefoot a
colt just fine, and he had himself one hell of
a good time doing some real cowhand work
with a rope.

For two nights there he came dragging in
looking like he'd spent the day in a hog wallow. He looked like a brown, lumpy pile of
something with a double row of teeth grinning out of it near the top. He must have
been dog tired as well, but he was enjoying
himself so much I don't think he ever realized it. He seemed to be operating on the
raw energy you can get out of real pleasure.

That work ended, though, and the yearlings were turned out to fend for themselves
another year. The boys went back to paying
attention to the cows, which would be dropping calves right and left by now. The
remaining horses were left in Casey's tender
care.

The kid did not mind, though. Casey,
knowing a good thing when he found it, was
kind enough to let the kid talk him into giving him a hand. And I guess I would have
to admit that I'd dropped a hint or planted
an idea here or there.

Anyway, while Casey broke the threes to
saddle use, the kid was allowed to take the
rough off last year's using horses. After a

293

winter of being on their own, some of those horses had some pretty fair kinks in their spines, and now the kid was showing up with bruises under his mud coating.

After the first week of it, though, it was getting so I could see more bruises than mud. It seemed he was using the seat of his britches more for sitting a saddle than for plowing. By the end of the work even the bruises had started to fade, and it was not entirely the dry-up that let him come to the table without much mud for decoration.

I guess he was about as happy then as I have ever seen a human being.

It was not that way with old Jess, though.

Since George died — or, thinking back on it, since before that, since December or so — Jess had not really been himself. He was quieter. Less given to exchanging insults. Of course, now he had the responsibility of keeping the ranch books, but that should not have been it. At this time of year there was practically no office work to be done, and anyway Jess has never been one to shy away from any kind of work. I couldn't figure it out, and he wouldn't talk about it, not even the few times he was willing to pull a late-night cork and share a small snort with me.

After a few times of asking and getting rebuffed, I got the distinct impression that I'd best shut my mouth and keep my questions to myself. He didn't want me messing into it. And he was entitled to that much, so I did shut up about it. I couldn't help fretting and wondering, but I could stay shut on the subject.

I found out something of it about the time of the green-up. The boys were off looking for cows that might need help with their birthing, keeping an eye on where the beeves were located at the same time so they could report back and the roundup work be planned soon. Casey was off teaching his threes some of the finer points of being obedient so they would not be so likely to try turning themselves inside-out when they met something new. The kid, back now to being a cook's helper, was cleaning up after breakfast.

I thought about loading my pipe and doing some contemplating but decided against it. There was a fresh pan of biscuits in the warming nook on the oven chimney, and I got to thinking that the womenfolk might like them. I got my coat and hat and a clean towel to wrap the warm pan in and carried it over to the big house.

I was about halfway across the yard when

I saw Katy on one of her mares cross the lowest bridge and head down the road at a brisk canter. That meant they'd have finished breakfast. I almost turned back but decided since I was this far I'd drop them off anyway. The biscuits should still be all right for lunch. I went on up to the back porch and let myself into their kitchen.

Natalie was sitting at the big, round kitchen table, looking small and alone there by herself. She was just sitting there, staring at nothing it seemed. A plate of bacon and another of potatoes were on the table and a loaf of bread with a cloth around it. Two places had been set at the table. Neither had been used.

"You've taken to eating awfully light," I said softly.

She jumped. She swept her hands down off the edge of the table and hid them in her apron. You'd have thought I'd caught her doing something shameful from the look on her face when she turned toward me. She managed a weak, apologetic smile.

"I didn't hear you come in," she said quickly. "You startled me."

"I thought I'd started a more interesting subject than that one." I crossed to the table and put the pan of biscuits in front of her. When I flipped the towel back a bit of steam rose. "The polite thing would be for you to eat some so you can tell me how good they are," I suggested.

"I really couldn't. . . ."

"You really can," I insisted. I pulled out the chair at Katy's place and lowered myself into it. I put a coupla pieces of bacon on her plate and a spoonful of the potatoes. She added a biscuit on her own.

She ate quickly, and I watched every mouthful go down even if it did seem to make her self-conscious. "Satisfied?" she asked when the plate was empty.

"It'll do for the moment." I looked her square in the eye. "What is it, Natalie?"

She looked down toward her hands. They were back in her lap, twisting and tugging at the folds of her apron. She didn't say anything.

"At least you haven't told me it's nothing," I said.

She looked up and gave me another of those weak smiles. "When was the last time you lied to me or . . . him?"

"It must have been awhile, I guess. I can't remember right off hand."

"I thought so. Well, I won't start fibbing to you now either. But I don't know that I want to talk about it yet. It's . . . so confusing."

297

"It gets that way sometimes. And some-times it helps to get a second opinion." I fumbled around in my coat pocket and remembered just in time that this was not the place to be hauling my pipe out. "Look, Nat . . . Mrs. Senn . . . if you'd rather not say anything to me about it, at least talk it over with Jess. I mean, he's your foreman. There isn't anything you can't tell him, you know."

She gave me a sudden, haunted look. "Oh no!" she said quickly. "I . . . couldn't."

I raised an eyebrow and stared at her until she became flushed and looked away again.

"What is it, Nat? Troubles with Katy?" What I was thinking was that maybe I was getting too pushy here. If this was some sort of mother-daughter thing, it was time for me to butt out.

Natalie Senn did not see what I'd been about to get at, though. Once I hit on that, she squeezed her eyes shut. Hard. She was not a crying kind of woman, but I sure thought her lashes looked moist now. She nodded, almost too little for it to be seen.

"Katy has been . . . very difficult lately," she said. "Since her father died. And I guess . . . before that too. But not so much. George could handle this so much better than I." She sighed heavily. "With me she argues. And they both know that I don't know *anything* about cattle. I just don't."

"They? What 'they' are you talking about, Nat?"

"Why, Katy and that Wayne Tynell she's been seeing, that's what they I mean. She thinks she wants to marry him. And turn the FR-Connected Bar over to Wayne to manage for us."

# CHAPTER 24

If she had picked up a chair and hit me in the face with it, she couldn't have surprised me more. Or hit me harder. Why, Katy was but a child yet. And of all the people in the valley, of all the people in the whole damn world, Wayne Tynell.

"I didn't even know she was seeing anybody," I said stupidly. I guess I needed time to let the worst of it sink in.

"Since last summer," Natalie said. She got up to pour coffee for both of us. For the first time she looked old to me. Her movements were slow, as if she was afraid she would lose her balance if she moved quickly. Even the hands supporting the coffeepot were seamed and wrinkled, the skin too large for the meager weight of bone and flesh beneath. All of a sudden it seemed like the whole world was getting old, a few parts of it not soon enough. Funny, though, inside I still felt the same as always and I'd have bet that Natalie and the fellas did too. I wondered if George had ever got around to feeling old — or if he would have had he known what that daughter of his was thinking now.

I sipped at my coffee without being able to think of a thing to say that would comfort Natalie or help her with this thing.

My God, the implications of it!

If ever there was a boy who could be counted on to destroy half a lifetime of work, Wayne Tynell had to be the lad for it. If he and his ill-mannered, ill-tempered, ill-informed ways ever got hold of the FR-Connected Bar, there was no way the outfit could survive.

Oh, I don't mean it would dry up and die off. Not really. The grass and the water, the carefully developed blood of the beeves and the horses, those would be hard to kill off. They were too solidly built to fall away in a year or two even of outright neglect. They could be destroyed, of course. Overgrazing could thin the grass. That, in turn, would change the water runoff to lessen the supply of water and, curling back in the same cycle, further deplete the grass, which would further lessen the supply of water, which would reduce the growth of grass, which would. . . . Yeah, and so on and so on and so forth. But it would take both time and stupidity for that to happen.

The same sort of thing holds true with blood lines in your livestock. Slough off your effort and your knowledge of selection and culling by sale or castration, and you are soon feeding animals that eat as much as another but put on a little less meat for that amount of feed. Pretty soon you are breeding yourself downhill, and the tendency then is to try to keep the profits up by carrying more animals in the place of better animals — which leads to overgrazing, which. . . . Anyway, that is the way it can work.

It goes both ways, up or down, that attention you have to give to your operation, and the man at the top is not the only fella responsible for it all. The thing that had made this outfit work so well over the years was that everyone in the crew cared about it. Not just George had. Not just him and Jess and maybe me neither, if I can set myself into their company, which they had always done themselves anyway.

Even the youngsters who hooked on with our crew knew they were with a top outfit. They busted their tails to learn what was wanted and to be worthy of the crew they worked with.

I could just imagine what would happen if Wayne took over as ramrod of the outfit. First off he would lose the people around here who knew how things should be done. Jess would be gone, and I would be. Casey would certainly leave, and probably Chapman and Crane would go, for they were old hands and would not take the insult of working for an idiot. The best of the youngsters would catch the spirit of the thing and would ride out with them. Boys like Jim Fuller and Billy Knowles.

And Wayne, he would likely encourage them to leave. He wasn't the kind who would heed advice or even want it given. He wouldn't want anyone around who could be comparing his ways with the old. What he'd end up with would be a raw, new crew that wouldn't know our beeves or their hidey-holes, who wouldn't know out of hand where to find the best grass and the best water at a given time of year. Our boys could, down on the winter range or up top either one. They knew how to shift the beeves so they would walk the least and gain the best, and that sort of thing can make a big difference in the shipping weights from which the sales checks are figured.

A few years under that incompetent yahoo and the place would not be anything like the FR-Connected Bar I'd known under George and under old Fred before him. It wouldn't die exactly, but it might as well. It would sure be mined.

Katy might not realize any of this, but I'll bet Natalie could at least guess at it. If it frightened her, it was no wonder. Her man had put himself into this place for years, and now she stood to see it all wasted.

"Is there no way to make her see what it would mean?" I asked.

As if she had followed every thought in my brain, the aging woman shook her head sadly. "None." There was an emptiness in her voice. A deep sadness.

"You could stop it," I suggested, though with scant hope.

"If she marries, her husband will have the right to decide her affairs," Natalie said. "The place will be hers when I go, anyway. The only way I could really stop it would be to sell and divide the money with her."

And what good would that do? It would leave the place in the uncertain hands of strangers. Worse, Natalie would be put off her man's place. For her that would be unthinkable, no matter the consequences of staying.

"Have you talked to her at all?" I asked. It was a poor question, even a hurtful one, as

I could read in her eyes as soon as I asked it. I was sorry I had.

Natalie sighed heavily. The sound fluttered in her throat. "I tried again at breakfast this morning." She motioned toward the unused plate and tableware in front of me. "You see what result I had."

"Might she listen to anyone else? Rev. Archer, maybe?"

"I don't think so. It can't do any harm to try, though I've been avoiding it. I suppose I must."

I stood and touched her on the shoulder. "If I can do anything . . ."

"Yes. I know. We. . . . Thank you."

She never looked up as I left I felt slow and old and awkward going back to my cookhouse.

That was nearly as black a day as the one when George died. Which, I suppose, just goes to show how damned selfish a man can be. For the thing that was fretting me the most I guess, was wondering where I could go and what I could do if I had to leave here.

I mean, this place was my *home,* for crying out loud. This wasn't just a place to work awhile and draw a wage and leave when the mood struck. If a man could ever be said to have roots after a lifetime spent nursing other people's cows and horses —

or meals — then mine were twined down into the soil of this valley. I'd been a part of it since those first heifers were pushed across the pass. I'd been on speaking terms with the great-great-great-great-granddaddy of every cow and every steer that wore the FR-Connected Bar today.

If I had to go somewhere else, why, there wasn't anywhere else to go, that was all.

What could I do? Look for some other outfit? One willing to hire on a gray-haired, cripped-up old devil as a cook? A fat chance I would have with that. I couldn't turn to any of the valley outfits. That would be the same thing as asking for out-and-out charity. I wouldn't have my friends see me do a thing like that. Not as long as I could scrounge the price of a train ticket out, I wouldn't.

I thought I had understood before about Fletcher Lewis heading straight for the depot when he took his time from the Slash WT. Why, hell, I hadn't known the half of it then.

And outside the valley. . . . Anymore I probably didn't know, really know, a round dozen men from outside the valley. Outside this valley I wouldn't be a rough-string rider who happened to've had a bad tumble. Anywhere else I'd be nothing but a gimp.

Someone who'd be expected to whine and stumble and get in the way. No one would be apt to hire a man like that.

I had a bit of savings put away. How long would that last? Not long. I could string it out for a year. Really tighten down and maybe stretch it as far as three years. And what would happen if I lived longer than my savings could be made to hold out? Swamp in saloons like some common drunk? Drag back to the valley with my tail between my legs looking for handouts from my friends? My leg being what it was, I couldn't even straddle a pony to ride up onto the mountain to die decently alone.

Oh, I was cram full of self-pity that day, I was. The kid had to do all the work. I wasn't the least use to myself or to the outfit the livelong day. And that just on the idea of what might, maybe, happen in the future. Not even with it known to be coming for sure, just on the basis of Natalie Senn's worries. That night there was enough to make a man think.

Anyway, I ate what the kid fixed for supper, and it was about as good as I would've made myself. Normally that should have made me tickled with the kid and all he'd learned. This night it only made me think how I was drawing my pay but wasn't really needed. Somebody else could feed the crew as well as I could.

After supper I dug a bottle out of the duffle cluttering the bottom of my wardrobe and carried it over to Jess's room. I knocked and went in and found him sprawled on his bunk with his boots still on, which was not at all like him. He didn't smile when he saw me.

Jess eyed the bottle in my hand. He said, "If you've come to pester me with more of your . . ." He got a look at my face. "No, I guess you didn't," he said wearily.

"No, I guess I didn't." I set the bottle down and helped myself to a seat. I pulled the cork and had a nip. It didn't taste as fine as it might have. But then I've never been much for the idea of drowning sorrows. "I had a talk with Natalie this morning."

"Oh?" There was a sharp edge honed onto that one word.

"Yeah. About Katy. And Wayne."

Jess breathed out a short, flat cussword. I handed him the bottle.

"I don't suppose you have any ideas on what to do about this?" I asked him.

"Sure I have." He paused to swallow, swallowed again, and handed the bottle back. "Shoot the son of a bitch," he said seriously.

"And short of that?"

He shrugged. "Nothing I can think of. Hurry up with that, will you?"

I gave him the jug, and he took a coupla more healthy snorts. That, too, was unlike Jess Barnes.

"What it comes down to," he said, "is that if George's baby girl insists on making a fool of herself, she makes a mess of all of us. It's that damned simple, old ugly."

"Well, apart from not knowing what Katy might see in the likes of him," I said, "I don't understand how she's had the chance to see much of him to form that much of an opinion. Neither one of them spends that much time socializing in town. Not at the same places, for sure."

"She'd have been better off is she *could* see him around other people," Jess said. "Maybe then she'd see what kind of bum he is. What they've been doing so far is meet for little talks and pic-nics and such down along the creek."

"With nobody around?" That thought made me kinda mad. "When have they had time for all this?"

"On all those brisk rides she was taking last summer and fall, I guess."

"Aw, she's always ridden. All over this place. Ever since she was big enough to crawl onto a horse without a mounting block, for cryin' out loud."

Jess pulled at the bottle again and made a face. "Maybe so, but more recent she's been riding down the creek to meet her neighbor. The boys kept coming onto tracks last fall, though they didn't know whose tracks they were, not Wayne's anyway. Well, now we know, damn the luck."

"Sheesh. What a fine mess children can make," I moaned. "It's just a shame she's too old to take a belt to."

"He isn't," Jess said. Looking into the dark anger that lay behind his eyes, I wondered if Jess was thinking about taking a small work detail from the crew and doing some thumping on Wayne Tynell.

I hoped not, for a thing like that would finish Jess in the valley regardless of what else might happen. A man in a responsible position like foreman of the valley's finest outfit just can't go around beating up on his neighbors.

Now I might get away with it. Except for one little thing. I can't quite see myself getting someone else to do that particular sort of nastiness if I am not man enough to do it myself. Which I am not. Not anymore, I'm not.

The biggest reason I was determined to

talk Jess out of such notions, though, was simple: If we went to beating on old Wayne-boy, it would make him that much more of a hero in Katy's eyes. We might as well buy them a marriage license and send a rush-order rig for the Rev. Archer as to do that.

We augered back and forth and up and down through half that night and all of that bottle. In the end we came up with the only thing that really seemed to be left open to us.

"Let it slide, old man," Jess said. "We'll just have to wait and see."

# CHAPTER 25

Hopeful waddies looking for work began to show up nearly as soon as the first blades of new grass. The regulars came to claim their places in the bunkhouse as quickly as they could get a nod from Jess. The others stayed for a few meals. Just long enough to let the ramrod look them over and maybe test them a bit by asking the favor of would they please top that old sorrel or dun or speckled horse and haze those pesky critters away from such and such a pond. Unlike the half-grown younguns who clung to the table like so many leeches while we were making up haying crews, these hands stayed long enough to get a wink or to know they shouldn't expect one. If they didn't get it, they got out of there and hit for another place.

Billy came back sporting a new mustache and a big sack of candy his mama had made for him to remember her by.

As always there were a few of the proven ones who didn't show. Someone said Hank Murphy was laid up somewhere with a broken leg and Bob Donner was doing a little time for a county sheriff down in New Mexico. No one asked why, but it was generally understood that he'd been in a fight and was overly vigorous in the way he tried to win it.

Anyway, Jess put his spring crew together, and the kid and I were back into a busy time of the year.

We butchered two beeves and made a fast trip into town to restock our winter-depleted storage rooms and listened to Clete Purty speculate on the oyster crop this year. To Clete there was no such thing as a calf crop, and it wouldn't bother him overmuch if there was never another heifer calf born in the valley. All he cared about was his volunteer fire department and the contribution us cow-smelling fellas made toward the fry each spring. I assured him our icehouse was freshly filled with cut blocks and if he'd send us a load of sawdust — which the department always did, free of charge, for anyone who would be contributing oysters — we would bring in our share like always.

Our spring work might have looked a little haphazard to those who have plenty of stout pens or who have few enough animals that they can work them in pens, but what matter to us is that it gets the job done.

Rather than aggravate our cows by trying to hold them in one big bunch for so long a period, we work them fairly loose in small gathers put together here and there across the ground we claim.

Most of our calves were on the ground and the most of the work was in catching, branding, earmarking, and cutting the little fellows. The two- and three-year-old steers and the coming heifers were left alone as much as possible. Too much pushing from men on horseback seems to peel the weight right off them, and there is no point in it so long as they stay healthy and don't need doctoring.

Then too, we've tried to keep a good deal of the old-timey blood in our cows. Those bony, slab-sided old longhorn cattle were not much for making meat, but they were the most independent, purely fearless and sometimes downright mean bovines ever to chew a blade of grass.

As many bad things as there are to say about those animals — and Lord knows there is a long list of their bad points — they had quite a string of good points too. For one thing, you don't have to mother them or their calves all the time. They could fend for themselves in almost any conditions and with so little good feed that another cow would lie down and admit starvation.

We had got away from raising those old beasts a long time back, like everyone else in the business who had a lick of sense, but we were careful to keep a good bit of their blood in the herd down through the years.

The boys who'd gone heavy with white-face blood found that they were getting big, beautiful, blocky-built calves on the ground. But their calves were so big, the cows too often had trouble with the birthing. Their crews spent an awful lot of time squatted down behind an ailing cow helping pull the calf. Most times it worked, but they lost a lot of cows and a lot of calves from it, too.

Our mixed-blood cows with more long-horn breeding in them gave us smaller calves, but few of the cows had trouble with them. The old cow would creep off by herself like some wild thing and spit her calf out like a youngster plopping water-melon seeds. Of course we lost some, too. You can't have animals without losing animals. But I believe we kept a sight more than we would have otherwise.

And once they were on the ground, our

crossbred calves made awful good use of the high-quality feed and water the FR-Connected Bar offered them. I've never seen any figures to prove it — I guess it would take one of those college experiments to work it out in numbers and such — but I would've been willing to bet that our calves put on more weight from each pound of grass than the purebreds did. Like I said, you'd play hell trying to prove it, for how do you count and weigh each blade of grass a free-ranging animal will eat, but when you've been around it awhile, you can judge your forage and graze fairly well just from looking at it. And that's what I do believe about it.

The first part of the spring work, the kid and I trundled along with them in the wagon while they worked the densely bunched areas. We'd go out in the morning to where they were gathering and cook a dinner. The boys would bunch the ones they wanted, eat, and then go to branding. Everything was turned loose at night, and they would start over somewhere else the next day.

When they worked the south and east lines, we stayed out for a week, as it would've been too far to try going back to headquarters just to sleep at night and would've been needlessly hard on the horses.

The kid loved that. He got downright good at cleaning up so he would have time after dinner to grab himself a horse and a rope and help with the calf-catching.

Jess — I suppose in the spirit of letting the kid get acquainted with some of the hard part too — put him to doing some flanking as well.

The first day he was flanking, the kid discovered what the term cow-kick means.

I'd guess he thought he was all checked out on this business of avoiding hooves. After working with the horses, he knew where he could safely venture behind an animal and where he couldn't. Yes sir, he did.

Well, about the fifth or sixth calf he got hold of was an uncommonly big bull calf that was thrashing around at the end of Billy Knowles' rope and walling its eyes and raising itself quite a dust

The calf being a hefty, long-legged devil, I guess the kid decided it wouldn't do to drape himself over the critter's back like the other fellows did. It would be easier to pick up the near foot and spill the beast away from him. Sure it would.

The kid bent over to grab that near foot

and made it handy for the calf by sticking his red head into the bull calf's flank. Mr. Calf was not buying such mistreatment on top of the manhandling he'd been getting from Billy. He gave a little hop and a lurch and came up with that foot. He popped the kid a good one smack in the jaw.

The calf bawled and the kid squawled, and the two of them separated right quick. Jim Fuller stepped in to drop the calf the right way and wrap him up, and pretty soon the bull calf was a steer and was sporting a new brand.

The kid wallowed around in the dirt some, hanging on to his jaw with both hands like he thought it had come loose and might fall off if he let go. He came up to his knees and shook his head and finally made it to his feet, wobbly but upright.

He looked around and, sure enough, everyone was watching. I grinned at him and gave him a little wave. He grinned back at me — more or less — and spat out some blood that seemed to have some white ivory chunks mixed in with it.

"Now you know why so many cowhands don't have to open wide when they spit 'tween their teeth," I hollered at him.

He found his hat where he'd been trompling it on the ground and slapped it against his leg a few times, though there was as much dirt on his jeans as on the hat, and spat a few times more. The last few blasts were almost free of blood, so I knew he was all right.

After that he remembered to go over the loins to that off leg when he wanted to drop a calf.

We spent the week out like that, enjoying the work, and a good thing that was, too, for there was plenty enough work to go around. But it was good work and satisfying. Other than being strenuous — and it wasn't even that for me — the only thing really difficult about that week was trying to keep our buckets of oysters cold. What we did was to shift them from place to place as we moved, keeping the buckets with hammered-tight lids in running water even if it meant storing them several miles from camp. Which it did on three of the eight nights we stayed out. Those buckets were filling nicely, though, which pleased me for a lot better reason than the firemen's fry. It was a proof of how well the outfit was running.

Once the easy gathering had been done and all the big, open bunches were worked, the boys had to start digging them out of the heavy brush and rougher coulees in ones and twos.

The boys had to scatter some themselves to do that and it would've served no purpose for us to try to operate a regular camp then with sit-down meals. So I dragged the kid away from his fun and hauled him back home. Those who could would show up there to eat and sleep. Those who couldn't would shift for themselves. It wouldn't be brand-new to them.

Since the kid was already feeling so full of himself from being allowed to do some real cow work, I decided he might as well step into responsibility with both feet. I turned the kitchen over to him, hitched the big team, and took myself into town.

I did some chuckling on the drive in and amused myself by wondering what I would find in Warcry this time. It was on this same, mid-work trip the last year that I'd found and fetched home the Keystone Kid.

One of the biggest reasons I made this trip each year was to check with Clete on the date for the fry, so as soon as I'd parked at Wiggins's loading dock, I drifted toward Clete's dry goods store.

Purty was busy measuring off white muslin from a tall stack of bolts, all of them the same stuff, piled at the end of his long counter. It was the time of year for curtain replacement. I stepped around to the shelving where he stocked a few books. I admired them while I waited, but he had nothing new there, nothing I couldn't get along without. And — it was the first time I'd had such a thought in nearly twenty years — if I was going to be moving along again, I wouldn't want any more dunnage than I already had.

That sort of shook me, thinking something like that, realizing what I was doing. I forgot all about what I'd come for and turned toward the door. Damn this whole thing anyway.

# CHAPTER 26

The kid unloaded the wagon, leaving four cases of canned milk in it. Those I took straight over to the shed, where they would be handy to the pen of orphaned calves the boys had been carrying in from time to time. I stacked the milk there, surprised to see there was still nearly two cases left from the last load. It was getting close to suppertime, and from the way the orphans were bawling I wondered if there might be some reason other than overbuying for all that milk to still be there.

I heard a clatter of hooves in the alleyway at the far end of the shed, where Katy's mares are stalled. It occurred to me that this year she hadn't been out to fuss over the new fillies when the horses were being worked. I weaved my way past the parked rigs and the haying equipment that we liked to keep out of the weather.

She'd been riding a delicate little white-footed blue roan that would have been no good as a brood mare — it had missed out on the sturdy build we like for our using horses — but the little mare was nice-mannered and made a decent saddle horse for pleasure riding. I didn't know how long she'd been gone or where she'd been, but there was no lather on the mare as there would have been after one of Katy's usual outings.

Katy had already pulled the pretty side-saddle George had had made up for her a year or two back. She slipped the English-style bridle and turned the mare into its stall without giving the horse a brush-down.

"Your calves sound hungry," I said as I came near, which really was not a very bright opening remark but was the first thing that came to mind. I guess I was a little upset with the girl.

Katy looked up and saw who it was. She started a welcoming smile, from habit I suppose, but never finished it. The pleasure that had flickered briefly in her eyes faded. "Don't tell me you're down on me too," she said. She set her chin and tossed her head a little. Her bonnet was unpinned on one side. It flopped a bit and landed slightly askew.

"Aw hell, child. I'm sorry. Can we start

over?" I gave her my best smile. "Hello."

She ducked her head. When she looked up again she was smiling too. "Okay. Hello to you, too." She fiddled with her bridle, wiped some partially chewed grass off the link of the snaffle pieces, and draped the bridle over the knee hook of the saddle.

"And of course you're right," she said. "They *are* my responsibility, and I've been neglecting them lately. I've been . . . sort of fussing with Mama lately. I guess I've been more anxious to get away from the house than to do what I should. I won't do it again. I promise. Okay?"

"You don't have to make me any promises. I'm just a hired hand, remember?" I grinned. "But I'll bet those calves would appreciate a promise from you."

"Just a hired hand? Pooh! Why you're . . . ," she paused, swallowed before she went on. ". . . the next best thing to Daddy." She ducked her head again.

I touched her on the shoulder and said, "Come on, child. I'll help you feed those babies."

She nodded but didn't look up right away. I led the way back through the maze of wagons and mowers. The place smelled of dust and grease and harness oil. It had the smell of an old barn. I could remember when it was built, although then, of course, I'd been a bronc buster and top hand and took no part in such work as building sheds.

We mixed up pails of canned milk and creek water, and I helped her pour them into the trough. Most of the orphans dipped their muzzles into it greedily, but one little fellow still had to be helped by a hand held under the surface so he would have a finger to suck on. Another day or two and he'd figure it out for himself. Katy knelt beside the trough with her hand in the milk while he ate.

She looked at the soft, liquid-brown eyes and long lashes of the tiny steer. "They're really beautiful, aren't they?"

"Uh-huh. Stupid beasts when they grow up, but they do make awfully cute babies."

Katy sighed. "Everything's nicer as babies. People too. Babies don't have any problems. Maybe that has something to do with it."

"Could be, child." I couldn't hunker down with that one leg the way it was, so I sat in the dirt beside her and leaned back against the sloping, rough wood side of the trough. "Look, maybe I can help. I'm always long on advice, you know." I smiled at her. "I can't handle my own problems, but I can sure-God give an answer to anyone else's."

"Can't we all?" Her hand rose to too shallow a depth, and the calf noisily sucked air. "Sorry, baby." The soft muzzle kept a firm, grasping hold on her finger and followed it deeper into the milk. She kept her attention on the calf, not speaking again.

"It comes free, you know," I said after a while.

"What does?"

"The advice."

"You're about as persistent as Mama."

"If you don't mind, I'll take that as a compliment. Your mama is a good woman. And we both do love you. You haven't forgotten that, I hope."

She looked at me. Her eyes began to fill. "I know you do. Mama too. I just . . . forget sometimes." She pulled her hand free and went to the creek. She rinsed the milk off and returned to sit beside me. She drew her knees up and wrapped her arms around them. She bent forward and laid her cheek on her knee. I waited.

"I don't suppose it's any secret," she said finally.

"Which?" I asked, playing it dumb. It should be up to her how much she wanted to discuss.

"That I've been keeping company with Wayne, of course." She was looking straight ahead, not at me, but I could see easily enough from the set of her jaw that she was ready to scrap if that was what I wanted.

"Uh-huh. I heard," was all I said.

"Well?" There was a definite, steely edge of defiance in her voice now.

"You don't need my permission to fall in love, little girl. And I didn't hear you ask for any opinions of the young man. So what's your problem?"

"Mama, of course. She doesn't understand about Wayne and me. And she thinks . . ." She spun her head toward me. The bonnet flopped again, and she reached up to remove the rest of the pins and drop the bonnet onto the ground beside her. "Wayne is a fine man. Really he is. And he has marvelous ideas about the cow business. Why, he's been in it all his life. Mama's really just afraid Wayne might want to change things from the old-fashioned way Daddy did things. That's what she's really afraid of."

I could not help saying, "Your dad was in the business all of his life too, child. And your mama loves *you*. More, even, than she loves this ranch. And it is all she has left of George. This place was his life's work, you know. It's understandable if she is kinda protective about it. But she loves you more."

She was weeping openly now. "I *know*

327

that!" she wailed. "But why does she have to make this so hard for us. This should b-b-be the happiest t-t-time of my *life*. And it *isn't*!" She leaped to her feet and went tearing off toward the big house. She left a string of fading sobs behind her.

I picked up her forgotten bonnet and trailed slowly along behind. I laid the bonnet on the rear stoop and went back to the security of my cookhouse.

The kid already had supper so well in hand that all I had to do was sit back and smoke my pipe and prepare to take credit for the work he'd done. He was even getting so he could bake a decent pie, though in a perverse way I was almost pleased that he couldn't yet bake a biscuit as light as mine. When he went to making the biscuit dough, I stepped in and took over.

The hands drifted in a few at a time. Or maybe that is the wrong way to put it. Some of them came larruping in with the lather off their horses staining their teeth. It was a standing rule that anyone not in by sundown got cold chow.

The boys, at least, were feeling pretty good. The hard part of the spring work was about over. Playtime was coming up. And they'd be drawing pay until the herd was up top and settled on summer pasture.

■ ■ ■ ■

We rambled into town for the big fry as a single group this year, even the newest hands keeping to the pace of the family gig as an escort for the women. The boys split off when we got to Warcry, and Jess took Natalie and Katy on to the hotel while I drove our oyster contribution around to Clete's icehouse. We had more this year than last. Not because we had a better calf crop but because Jess and I hadn't felt like dipping into them ahead of time with George not there to share in the crime.

It was a good-enough fry. Plenty of beer laid on by the Masons and plenty of oysters the next day. There was more equipment to admire, and a horse-trading firm out of St. Louis had sent a coupla cars of heavy drafters in matched teams that they were offering to sell or to trade for light stock suitable for harness. I spent a good bit of time with those big'uns, but our old boys were still in good shape and had all the heart in the world. If we were lucky it would be another four or five years before we had to think about replacing them.

The crew seemed to have a good time, too, judging from the limp and lanky way they set their horses going home afterward. Billy Knowles had a bright mouse under his left eye, and the kid looked like he'd been run through a potato ricer once or maybe even twice.

When I asked him about it later, he gave me a broad grin, exposing the gap way back on the right side of his mouth where that calf had left its mark. It didn't hardly show most of the time. Even less now that his lips were swollen.

"Aw, I had a bit of a snootful last night, and Billy and me got to wondering if he could still take me as easy as he did last year." He laughed and said, "It wasn't *quite* as easy this time. Or so they tell me, anyhow."

The scrap did not seem to have left any lasting ill feelings, if there had been any to start with. If anything, the kid and Billy seemed to be more sociable than ever.

About the only one in the crowd who didn't seem cheered by the trip to town was Jess. He was downright morose the whole way home.

# CHAPTER 27

"You're going to get nebby again, aren't you?" he accused belligerently.

"If that comes as a surprise to you after you've been knowing me this many years, Jess Barnes, then you are even more ignorant than I suspected. And I suspect plenty."

"Well, I still don't understand why you think your nose belongs in everybody's business," he said.

"It's a mixture of cussedness and curiosity," I told him. "And a natural lovableness that makes people want to tell me things. Why, if I hadn't decided to make my fortune in the cow business, I would've made a pretty fair reporter for some newspaper. In fact, if I ever decide to retire from this way of life, I might just write some letters and see if one of them would like a correspondent out here in the Wild West."

"I suppose you think those eastern readers would want you to tell them about the state of the grass on the public lands and whether Clark Doyle decided to buy some new mowing machines?"

I grinned. "Hell, no. I'd tell them about the shoot-'em-ups and the robberies and all the desperados hiding out in the hills, just like all the correspondents do." I paused. "Did he?"

"Huh?"

"Clark," I said. "Did he get new mowers?"

Jess shook his head in mock disgust, but he was smiling again. That was nice to see after so long a time. "Yeah," he said. "Three new Deere mowers and a half-dozen Percheron geldings. Blacks and steely grays."

"The ones at the upper end of that dealer's picket line? Those are some fine stock. I must've spent a half hour looking at each of them."

"The same," Jess said. "If they pull as good as they look, they should really do a job for him. But that's a lot of horseflesh to winter-feed, and you couldn't turn an investment like that out to rustle for loose forage."

"Mm-umph! Almost makes me jealous just the same."

The amenities done with, I filled my pipe and lighted it, and Jess pared a fresh chew off his plug. He sat contemplating his tobacco for a minute before he said, "I ran into the Slash WT foreman at the fry yesterday."

"Yes?" If Jess wasn't even willing to use the young idiot's name, then I had to figure that our foreman was almighty peeved with theirs.

"He informed me that the Slash WT will be taking their beeves up top starting two weeks from today, and they will require use of the gap for six days."

"He informed you of that, did he?"

"He did, indeed, old man. Right blunt about it too, he was. That's when they are going up, and we had best stay out of their way."

It was no damn wonder if Jess was having green and purple fits. I was commencing to boil some myself. "Won't that mess up Tom's plans?" was all I said, though.

Having the least valley grass of any of us, Tom Abbot was always the most anxious to get up to the high graze each year. This year in particular the new growth was not coming in nearly so fast as it had the year before. And after wintering on his smaller piece, Tom's cows would be in the most need of the first grass in and near the gap itself. We all had to use the same patch of ground, pretty much, for about two days or so as we went through, and if Tom had to follow the bigger Tynell herd without giving the new growth time to recover, his cows would be losing some of their milk production if nothing worse than that. At the best it would not do his calves any good, and a calf needs a strong start if it is going to make the most beef in the long run.

"Yeah, that's when Tom had wanted to move too," Jess said. "I . . . suggested he go a few days earlier than he'd figured. He can get clear before the little bastard moves their herd."

"My God, Jess," I exploded. "Do you mean you're going to sit there and let that low-life son of a bitch tell us all what to do? Close him off from the gap, dammit. Tell him if he cuts our wire, we call the law in. If that doesn't work, we can by God hand out rifles, and I'll take the first one. Let him find his own way up top if he wants to be that way about it." By the time I was done, I was snorting and bellowing and pacing around the room. I hadn't felt that kind of deep burn in a long while.

"You think I haven't thought of just that? Well, I have. I told Fletcher last fall it's what I would do if the decision was mine. But it ain't my land he intends to cross, and it ain't just you and me would have to carry the worst of it if we got our backs up, dammit. What kind of friends would we be to old George if we got his women involved in a war practically as soon as he was cold? And with the other party his girl's intended, at that?" There was a deep pain showing in the man's eyes.

I guess it was that kind of thinking that separated the foreman from the likes of me. And maybe Katy was right. Maybe there was still some old-fashioned thinking going on around here. She'd just been wrong about who was doing it. I sat down, though it was difficult to keep still.

"So what do we do?" I asked. I was feeling kind of helpless. It was no wonder that Jess was down in the mouth about this thing. It was like using a broomstraw to fight off a swarm of mosquitoes. Frantic and frustrating and getting no results.

"I sure wish I knew," he said. I'd never heard Jess Barnes sound so defeated. "For everything I want to do, everything I feel I should do, there's a good reason why I can't." He sighed. "What I keep coming back to is that about the only thing I can do to get out of it is to quit."

That was unthinkable. "You could always marry the Widow Ramsey and have a place of your own." I intended it as a bright and breezy little joke to lighten Jess's mood, but I guess it came out as more of a snarl. As a mood-lightener it was a flop.

"Oh, I ain't going to quit," he said. "That would be a fine way to repay George, wouldn't it? Cut and run the first time his women needed me. No, I ain't going to quit. But that boy's ways are sure hard for a man to swallow."

"What can we do, Jess?"

He shrugged again. "It sticks in my craw, old man, but I guess the FR-Connected Bar is the last onto the mountain this year. I just don't see anything else we can do. We can't make Daisy pay for it, and he'd figured on Tom and then us and then him going up, as usual."

It had been that way for years, dictated by the way we liked to do things but also by the elevations and therefore the growth of grass on the public lands where the four outfits ranged on the mountain. So, doing it this way, we would lose a little of the weight gains we should have been able to expect. And that stupid Tynell kid would not gain a thing. If he wasn't careful, he might even foul his own nest, put the Slash WT on summer graze too early and damage his own stand of grass. I kind of hoped he would, though I hate to see any man's beeves in poor condition. In his case I was willing to make an exception.

We sat and stared at the floor awhile and talked a bit about the state of our beeves, but we both had the other thing on our minds and so I wandered back to my own room early.

The kid was still awake when I came into the kitchen. He was seated at the worktable with a lamp in front of him and the latest batch of kittens squirming on the floor at his feet. He'd been reading a thick book that he'd bought or borrowed somewhere. When I came in, he laid a scrap of paper between the pages to mark his place and flipped it closed.

He gave me so searching a look that I wondered what he was seeing, what he might be thinking. "Got a minute?" he asked.

"Sure. A young fellow like you would find it hard to believe how much time us gray-heads have for squandering purposes." I dragged my stool over to the table and sat.

The kid's face had colored to a bright, multihued patchwork pattern after the fight with Billy. His features were a bit ragged and lumpy, but it didn't seem to be bothering him much. "Want some coffee?"

"That'd be nice, Kid. Thanks."

He got two cups and the pot he'd been keeping warm on the stove. It was thoughtful of him, for such a thing made extra work for him in keeping the woodbox full. He poured the coffee and sat, continuing to peer at me closely.

"Something is bothering you and Mr. Barnes both," he said, "and Mrs. Senn hasn't been humming or singing to herself when she hangs out her laundry."

Hell, that was something I hadn't noticed myself, but once he mentioned it I realized it was true. Natalie always used to hum little tunes or sing softly to herself when she was out at the clothesline. We could generally catch scraps of the sounds coming through the window that faced toward the house. I hadn't noticed that omission lately — maybe because I was some preoccupied myself — but the kid had. He was far from being a dummy. That was something to keep in mind.

"I don't suppose you'd accept a simple 'nothing' as a response to that?" I asked him.

"No, sir, I don't guess I would."

"How about: It's nothing for you to worry about?"

"Only if you can honestly say that it doesn't concern me. Or any of my friends," he said in a level tone of voice.

Well, I wasn't going to lie to him. That is not a thing I've ever been good at, and I have no desire to cultivate the talent at this late date. "I don't guess I could tell you that, Kid. But I can say there's not a damn thing you could do to help the situation. You didn't cause it, and you can't solve it, and you might say it is a family kind of thing that I'd really rather not talk about."

"I guess I pretty much have to accept that, then. I thank you for not lying to me, anyhow. I really appreciate that." His face softened, and he looked sort of pensive. "I guess . . . you're about the first person who's ever taken me serious. I appreciate that, too. And I guess I better shut up and go to bed." He left the table and crossed to his bunk.

This being his bedroom as well as my workroom, I left my coffee untouched on the table and went to bed myself.

Jess took the beeves up top so late that it was certain the first arrivals looking for haying jobs would have shown up at the door before the crew got back down.

I would've liked to have gone along. They weren't going into the Squawman this time, and the wagon could have made it along the whole route. But someone had to be at headquarters to take charge of the hay-crew applicants and cook for them and make sure the women were comfortable with so many strangers around. So again I had to stay down in the valley. The kid went along as camp cook again, but this time driving the wagon, which does make it easier by eliminating those annoying packs.

Sure enough, the first peach-fuzzed boys looking for haying work began to come in, and at least I had some work to do once they did. They were no trouble to keep in line, though, and several of them were downright eager for me to give them chores to do so they could prove their worth. I marked those boys in my mind to be pointed out to Jess when he got back.

Counting the time needed to finish pushing the herd together — they'd been loosely held in readiness for the move practically since the end of branding — it should have taken them no more than twelve days to get it done and get back. Say, two weeks at the absolute outside. By the sixteenth day I was seriously considering a tour through the bunkhouse looking for a boy who could ride a horse and had a sense of direction.

Of course, I couldn't have done a thing to help. Whatever was keeping them up there so long would be handled by Jess and the boys. Them taking time to handle it had to be the reason they were late. And not *all* of them could be in trouble up there.

Unless maybe they'd all come down with food poisoning.

Oh boy, the things a person can dream up when he's worried.

And that was all it was. Simple worry. I just wanted to know what was going on, that was all. So I could quit worrying about them. I swear I'd have been happy to know that half the herd was dead and half of the remaining half were dying, just so I could *know*.

They came back the seventeenth day about midafternoon. The whole crew, every man jack of them from Jess Barnes right down to the Keystone Kid, was tight-lipped and sitting ramrod stiff. Cutting through even the fatigue of long riding, there was something biting at each and every one of them. I got the story from the kid while we were washing up after supper that night; Jess was still so damn mad he didn't want to talk about it.

For a change the kid had allowed me to bully him into sitting while I did the washing. He was dog tired but wound up as tight as a fifty-cent watch. I had an idea, too, that he'd been putting himself on short rations. That wagon had been awfully lightly loaded when they got back.

"Do you know what they found when they got up there?" he asked angrily while I rinsed the plates.

I granted at him and waited for him to go on.

"You know that broad, open sweep under the big rock face," he said.

"Yes." It was one of the best pieces of high ground we had, watered across a nearly flat bottom where a series of old beaver dams had been. The beaver had been trapped out long ago, before we ever found the spot, but their work had taken its effect. The aspen that must have been there had been burned off or died out for some reason, leaving a wide, grassy area with a tufted marsh through the low ground.

"They took the herd up there," he said. His voice became bitter. "There were Slash WT cows there already. Chapman said from the look of the grass they'd been there for weeks already. Our stuff got mixed in with theirs, and they had to separate them. And they only had a coupla Slash WT boys up there holding them in place. Our crew had to drive their cows north to their own area to get them out of ours."

No wonder the boys were so upset.

Not the work of it My God, our boys would work until they dropped if someone needed help with his herd.

But now the son of a bitch was stealing beef from us. Oh, he wasn't stealing animals wearing our brand. He was stealing the beef off our animals' bones before it ever got there and was putting it onto Slash WT stock. For to a cowman grass is simply beef that hasn't yet been converted into final form.

It was clear enough what had happened. Wayne Tynell had bullied his way onto the mountain before his higher summer pastures were ready for use. And rather than admit he was wrong, he'd stolen grass from us until his own was ready.

Maybe he'd even planned all along to do it this way. I wouldn't put it past him to do such a thing. I'd never known him to give a thought to the needs of anyone but himself, and if little Wayne-boy could do some quiet stealing this way and show a better growth rate than Fletcher had done in the past — with his old-fashionedly honorable methods — why, wouldn't that prove to his daddy how much better his boy was than the foreman had been? That could well have been the way Wayne looked at it.

For all I knew — and he might have been bright enough to check — he might even have a legal argument on his side. None of us owned the mountain grazing areas. No one assigned rights to one outfit for one area. It was just the way we'd worked it out over the years, the first ones in taking up what they needed and later helping the other fellow reach and protect what he needed. Maybe what Wayne had done was perfectly within the law. It was certainly a question none of us had ever asked before. Or had need to.

"Jee-zus!" I breathed. "Do you have any idea what you just told me, Kid? What something like that means?"

He nodded glumly. "There was plenty of talk about it up there," he said. "Some of the boys wanted to take it out on the Slash WT punchers, but Jess wouldn't let them. They were awful close to it, though." Even speaking from days-old memory he seemed shaken by the thought. I could guess why. Maybe no one carried guns any more, but they all had ropes. Someone was sure to've remembered that fact. Billy possibly, though he was a little young to think in such terms. Casey was old enough to have seen it before and, once somebody stoked his fire, probably feisty enough too.

Some of the younger ones would've been carried along by the excitement of a suggestion like that. They would have grown up hearing tales of the wild days when their daddies were young. This would've been their chance to take part in the old ways without any blame being attached to them. There would have been enough of them ready to jump in and go through with it.

Those boys probably would never know how lucky they were that Jess Barnes was there to stop them, for such a thing could never be forgotten. I knew. I still carried a few memories of my own from back in Texas more than thirty years before. That might've been part of the reason I loved the valley so much.

"Who were the Slash WT punchers?" I asked to get my mind off that particular subject.

"There were two of them. Ned Fenster and Harold Winston they said their names were."

"I never heard of either of them."

"No one else had either," the kid said. "According to our boys, their whole crew must be new boys, or close to the whole bunch anyway."

That made sense. Fletcher'd had a pretty decent bunch of boys over there. The good ones wouldn't have liked the way Warren Tynell treated their ramrod. And Wayne might've had his own reasons for wanting a crew that didn't know the valley and its ways, especially the Slash WT summer range.

"Something's going to have to be done about this," the kid said. "Mr. Barnes acts like an engine building a head of steam. Nothing showing on the outside but a real explosion coming when it lets go." He sounded as if he'd given the subject considerable thought.

"Yeah. Something. But what?" I didn't have any answers either.

# CHAPTER 28

Jess didn't come over to breakfast the next morning, and as long as I've known him I'd never known him to miss that five o'clock turnout. Even the several broken arms and four or five broken collar-bones or mashed ribs he'd gotten during that time hadn't kept him away from being with his crew in the morning. A busted leg might have done it, but I wasn't even sure of that, and he hadn't had one anyway.

With both the waddies and the haying boys to feed, the kid and I were running like a pair of rats thrown into a room full of cats, but I turned the whole shebang over to the kid and let myself out the kitchen door.

The air was softly cool, the stars beginning to pale. There was a light showing in Jess's window. I used the outside door and went in without knocking. I was afraid if I was polite about it he'd tell me to go away.

He was sitting on the edge of his bunk,

still in his underwear though he had his hat and boots on. He needed a shave.

"What do you want, old man?" he asked without looking up. But then he didn't need to. Aside from there not being anyone else on the place who'd barge in uninvited, there wasn't much chance of him mistaking the step-and-thump of the way I walk. There was no welcome in his voice.

"I came to see if you wanted breakfast in bed." I guess there was as much bite in my voice as there'd been in his.

"Sure. Oysters and truffles and an iced bottle of champagne," he said.

"Sounds like a last meal for the condemned."

"Maybe it is," he said in a low voice.

"Like that, is it?"

"Uh-huh." He looked up. I did not like the pain that was in his eyes.

"Quitting?"

"Nope," he said firmly. "Getting fired. There's a difference."

"Yeah." I rubbed at the back of my neck. "Mind if I sit down?"

He shook his head, so I took a chair and fiddled some time away while I messed with my pipe. I didn't want a smoke but lit it anyway.

"You've got to do what's best for the

outfit," I told him, going slowly and trying to pick my words with care before they were spoken, not after. "George would've wanted you to put the outfit first, Jess. That's the only way to really protect his family. This place is all they have left. Of him and for the future, too. He gave you the job of protecting it. If you lay off on that, you'll have to shave without a mirror the rest of your life."

And even if he did lay off, it wouldn't help anything. Push it now and he would get himself fired now. Lay off of it and Wayne Tynell would fire him later. It was as simple as that. About all he could do, really, was to do what he thought had to be done and take what came of it. At least then he would not shame himself. He would be doing what George left him to do.

"They say Texas isn't bad," he said. "Warmer there. Will you be going back?"

I shrugged. "I hadn't thought all that much about it." I had. The night before. "California probably. They say a man can live cheap there. And I've never seen an ocean."

At least Jess wasn't trying to play a noble act with me and say stupid things about me and the rest of the boys hanging on. We both knew that if he went, that was the end of it.

Our loyalty was to the outfit, but it just wouldn't exist anymore. Wayne-boy would have to build his own.

"I'd best to be getting dressed," he said. He got reluctantly to his feet, the legs of his drawers hanging loose around pipestem legs. He was a scrawny old bastard, which I'd known but never thought much about. "Be right back." He went out and turned toward the backhouse.

While he was gone I hurried back to the cookhouse. I grabbed a pot of coffee — if the boys ran short this morning they would likely survive the ordeal — and a kettle of hot water. I had the coffee poured and the water in his bowl by the time he got back.

He looked from the mugs to the bowl and gave me a brief, warm smile, almost the kind of smile that used to come so easily to him. "I haven't had warm water to shave in since the last time I was in Cheyenne," he said. "Or was it Denver? I disremember now."

He wet his beard extra carefully and lathered it good with the brush, letting the whiskers soak while he stropped his razor. He made the first pull along his jaw and said, "It's a damn shame I didn't get you trained to do this earlier."

He finished shaving and used a towel to

wipe the last traces of lather. He even put water on his hair to slick it down when he combed it. When he dressed he ignored the jeans draped at the foot of his bed except to transfer his pocketknife into his suit trousers. From the shelf in the top of his wardrobe he reached down his best John B. He settled the hat gently over his combed hair and gave it a jaunty little tap on the high crown.

"I'm coming with you," I said.

"All right." No argument. He probably knew the only way to keep me out of that big house now would be to tie and gag me. And he'd have been some dusty and some rumpled before he got the job done.

It was coming light now. We skirted the cookhouse, ignoring both the mild interest of the boys who were there looking for haying work and the blank, knowing looks from those members of the crew who happened to be outside.

Jess stopped at the back door of the main house to rap formally. We waited for an answer before we went in.

Natalie and Katy were at breakfast, both of them wrapped in heavy housecoats although the heat of the stove in the closed room had it uncomfortably warm even for me.

Nat must have seen something in Jess's face or in the stiff, precise way he was holding himself. She didn't just give us a howdy or wave us to a seat. She got up from the table and drew two chairs back to seat us across from her and Katy. "Coffee?"

"No thank you, ma'am," Jess said. He removed his hat and laid it on the table before he sat. I did the same. Other times those hats had been tossed onto a handy counter or dropped on the floor. Katy gave Jess a worried look.

"Is there something you need to discuss?" Natalie asked. Her voice was soft and polite, even gracious, but there was a hint of strain beneath that.

"Yes, ma'am," Jess said. He cleared his throat.

Speaking with no emphasis on one word over another, with no emotion in his voice or in the words he used, he told them about the drive onto the mountain. What they had found there. What the consequences could be to us and to Tom Abbot and, to a lesser extent to D. Z. May if this sort of thing were to go on. Even then he spoke about rates of gain and of grazing rights determined by use and custom. He stated right out that it was probably legal.

"I see," Natalie said when he was done.

Her eyes started toward Katy but halted and shifted down toward her plate.

The girl said nothing, but her lips were drawn into a straight line and her jaw was firmly set.

"Mrs. Senn," Jess went on, he too avoiding looking at Katy, "as foreman of the FR-Connected Bar I intend to instruct our crew that, after all of the herds have cleared the gap this fall, the Slash WT will no longer have permission to breach our fences or to cross land deeded to this ranch."

Natalie closed her eyes and squeezed them shut. Hard. She was trembling.

"You can't do that," Katy gasped. "That isn't fair." Her face reddened. "You know it isn't fair. Wayne was just trying to protect the whole summer range by not overgrazing part of it. You can't penalize him for that. It was the right thing to do, and you know it was. He told me about it when he got back, and I gave him permission to stay there. He had my approval. . . ."

"After the fact, I take it," Jess injected.

"What difference does that make?" she responded hotly. "You *know* he'd have moved those cows if I'd wanted him to. Why, I think you just don't want him to succeed. You probably think if you can make Wayne fail, his father will beg your friend

Fletcher Lewis to come back. Well, that won't happen either. Not after all the nasty, ugly things he said about Wayne last fall. Mr. Tynell will never allow that man on his land again, and I don't blame him."

"I suppose you know all about last fall?" Jess asked quietly.

Tears had begun to creep out from under Natalie's eyelids.

"Of course I do," Katy said. "I do know all about it. Of course that crazy storm wasn't your fault. Wayne knows that too. He was just overwrought at the time. Because he takes his responsibilities so seriously. As you could plainly see if you would be fair with him, Jess Barnes. You just don't want to let him succeed. Why, if you knew him as well as I do, you'd know there is not a finer young man in this whole valley. Nor a finer cowman either. But you just don't *want* to see that." Her voice was pitching higher and growing louder. She chopped the words off and stared wide-eyed at Jess. There was both anger and pleading in her eyes. "Please," she said in a softer tone. "Promise you will not be so unfair with Wayne in the future."

Jess shook his head with finality. "You heard what my instructions will be, miss. They will stand as long as I am foreman of this ranch."

The pleading disappeared from Katy's eyes, leaving only the anger. "That can be changed too," she snapped.

"Yes," Jess said gently.

"Fine," she returned with a glare.

"I can be gone in an hour," Jess said. He reached toward his hat.

"No!" Natalie plucked a hanky from a pocket of her housecoat and wiped her cheeks. "I still decide such matters, Katryn, and I have not asked Mr. Barnes to leave. I . . . can't do that. Your father had as much faith in Mr. Barnes as he did in himself. I will not ask him to leave us now." Nat's voice was quavering. I think she was afraid of what Katy would say but felt she had to try.

Katy was caught up now more in the heat of her own anger than in the argument itself, I believe. Her eyes narrowed and she practically hissed when she said, "In that case, Mother dear, I will move in with the Tynells, and I will not set foot in this house again as long as this man is here. Do you understand that, Mother? Not until he is gone," she ended with a triumphant flourish.

Natalie uttered a half-audible groan. Her cheeks were streaked with shiny tear-tracks that she made no effort to wipe away. Her mouth gaped twice like a fish trying to breathe air. "Jess, I. . . . Please don't . . ."

"It's all right, Nat," he said.

Katy looked vindictively satisfied. But not at all pleased. If anything she looked a little scared by what she had done.

"Would you mind if I use the wagon to take my things into Warcry?" I asked. Neither Jess nor I had the right to say so now.

"You too?" Katy cried. She seemed genuinely surprised.

"Why of course, child. The others can ride, but . . ."

"You don't have to go," Katy said.

I shrugged. I couldn't think of any way to explain that she would understand. Or that she wouldn't take as an attack on Wayne.

"If you think this will make me change my mind . . . ?" She was both defiant and oddly hesitant at the same time.

"Have I ever lied to you, child?"

She shook her head.

"And I won't start now. I'm not trying to force you into or out of anything. It's just the way things are."

Katy bit her lip but didn't say anything. She did not look half so angry now as she had a few moments before.

"Jess?" Natalie asked. "How many will go

today?" I'm sure she knew they all would before the season was over.

Jess sat back in his chair and thought for a moment before he answered. It was a valid question and needed a good answer, for someone would have to shape the summer's work.

When he spoke, it was slowly and again without emphasis. "We will go, of course. And Casey. I would say also Chapman and Fuller and Knowles today. Probably the Eason boys and . . ." When he was done he had listed every hand but three. I'd been keeping track.

"And the kid," I said. "Don't forget him."

Jess gave me a quick smile of apology. "Sorry. You're right."

That pleased me for some reason. The kid hadn't had time to earn his spurs, but he'd gotten Jess Barnes to respect him. I wondered if he would understand what that meant if I were to tell him. Maybe so, though he would not have a year before.

Natalie glanced at her daughter before she said, "Jess, I have no right to ask it of you . . ."

"You know I'll do anything I can, Nat," he said.

"We need. . . . We need your help. Both of you. We . . ." She was crying again. Or still.

She got control of herself with a deep, shuddering sigh. "Katy plans to announce her engagement to Wayne at the Fourth of July pic-nic. Would you . . . please stay until after that? Give us time to sort things out? It would mean a great deal to me. And you could leave a week after that or so. Everyone would understand and . . . it would help the ranch. Please?"

Jess's face was impassive, although Natalie was asking one hell of a lot of him. He waited for a response from Katy.

The girl looked at her mother and then at us. She nodded. Just enough to declare the temporary truce.

"Until July, then," Jess said.

We took our hats from the table top and left. I don't know about Jess, but I was feeling a sick emptiness that had nothing to do with missing breakfast. For good or for bad, though, it had been done.

# CHAPTER 29

It was no secret from the boys. Even if it could have been, Jess would not have wanted to keep it so. As soon as we were back, he called the riding crew, and the kid, into the bunkhouse. None of them had gone down to the corrals yet. Not even Casey.

He laid it out for them. Not all the whys and wherefores but the fact of us going come the second week in July and how he hoped they would stick with it in the meantime. As for the summer crew, he said anyone not interested in staying the whole summer, including after July, could please let him know by leaving the room now, but he'd like everyone to stay at least that long. He wanted to make sure this place — every fence staple, every foot of wire, every shingle — was absolutely top shape when he left it.

He'd been almost right when he told Natalie who all would leave. Everyone filed quietly out except for two youngsters named

Randy Hidel and Dick Morrison. And they began to get embarrassed about being the only ones left. They looked at each other and began to sidle toward the door.

"It's okay, boys, and thanks," Jess told them. "Someone has to carry over who knows where our cows are using, and I appreciate your being willing to do it." He smiled. "No sense in you fellas turning down a good job over someone else's troubles."

They bobbed their heads uncertainly, and while they didn't look really at ease, they did quit edging toward the door. Jess beckoned them over to him.

He gave his voice a man-to-man pitch that just oozed his confidence in them. "Boys," he said, "I'm going to ask a hard thing of you. You'll be the only ones staying over, and whoever is running the place will need good information on where the cows are and where they've already been and how conditions are up top. So if you fellas are agreeable, I'd like you to take a pack horse loaded with all you'll need and go back up there. I'd like you to stay straight through until the Fourth. But come back in time that you don't miss the pic-nic. You wouldn't want to miss that, I know."

"No, sir," Morrison said. "We'll be glad to

do that for you, an' we'll be back about the second of July." He turned to Hidel. "Right?"

The other boy nodded, just as serious. They both seemed impressed by the amount of trust Jess was putting in them.

They could've waited another day, but both of them rolled their gear right away and went off to find the kid and draw some supplies from the storeroom.

When the room had been cleared except for the two of us, all the confidence drained from Jess's expression. "Sheesh," he said. Then he grinned and wiped imaginary sweat from his forehead. "Guess a man can get used to almost any idea if he sets his mind to it."

Hell, now he was trying it on me. "Dry it up, you phony old cowpuncher. I'm no greenhorn."

This time his grin was for real. "C'mon, help me pick a haying crew. You know 'em better than I do this time around, and there's no sense in keeping the culls away from paying jobs any longer than need be."

"Or feeding them," I muttered.

The haying boys were clustered at the end of the cookhouse. Low voices blended into a honking drone that reminded me of a flock of geese snuffling and talking at feeding time. They shut up when we came into sight, their expressions worried more than anxious. I doubted that anyone would've told them what was going on, but they had to have felt something in the air. Even town boys, which most of these were, would know that cow crews do not normally hang around headquarters so far into daylight.

"Will you be making up a crew now?" one of the bolder ones asked as we came near.

"Right this minute," Jess assured him.

I looked them over, picking out the faces and trying to recall the names of the ones who'd been the busiest and the most helpful while they'd been waiting. In the end I had to resort to some finger pointing, but at least I did make a cut of them for the foreman. There were eight or ten left over when I had enough for a crew.

"Thanks, boys," Jess told those. "Sorry we can't use you this year. Anyone who needs a poke of food to see you down the road can ask in the kitchen." That got him a few grins and seemed to take some of the sting out. He turned toward the ones who'd been hired.

"As for you fellas, I'm going to have to ask you to bed down in the wagon shed. You can pull the mowers and heavy wagons out to make more room. Hate to do that, but we're keeping a full riding crew on awhile longer, so there won't be a place for you in the bunkhouse. If anyone objects tell us now, before these other boys leave."

That stirred some hopeful head-turning among the rejects, but there wasn't anyone who'd turn down a job for lack of a bunk.

"All right, good. Get yourselves settled. We start mowing day after tomorrow." That wouldn't give Casey much time to pair his teams for the mowers and rakes and wagons, but he would have more help than usual. And the haying crew could spend the whole of the next day oiling harness and greasing the machinery. Jess sure was pushing, though. The place was by damn going to be in top shape when he turned it over.

He sighed heavily as he watched the boys drift away. "See you later, old man," he said. He walked slowly down toward the horse pens.

Me, I clumped into the kitchen and began assembling some things I could tuck into sacks for the youngsters who were leaving. Cold meat, jerky, leftover bread and biscuits, whatever I could find that wouldn't need cooking. Most youngsters like that would sit on a barrel of flour and quietly starve to death from not knowing what to do with it.

The kid was still cleaning up after breakfast. He didn't say anything until he was all done and the last of the hay crew rejects had been by to get his sack.

"It's all over then?" he asked when we were alone.

"Sure looks like it, Kid. Sorry." I smiled at him. "Another year and you would've made a hand, son." I told him that Jess Barnes had counted him in as a solid one, and I believe it really pleased him.

"But isn't there anything we can do to fight those people? It isn't like they should have any say about this outfit."

"It isn't them that's the problem, Kid."

And maybe I should not have done it but I told him what had been going on. I guess I was just in a mood to be talking to somebody, and in a way I sort of felt I had let the kid down. Given a little more time, we could've made a hand of him. He was already plenty changed from the scrawny, ignorant big-eyed boy who'd gotten off of that train a year ago. There just hadn't been quite enough time.

"So that's what it comes down to, Kid," I said finally. "Your old friend Wayne Tynell and a little girl who doesn't know enough to see how badly he's playing her false."

"He really is a son of a bitch," the kid said

thoughtfully. "Somebody ought to tell her that."

"Sure. Just like that. Walk up to her and say, 'Little lady, your intended, the boy you think the grandest in this whole, wide world, is a spoiled braggart, bully, and liar, and if you'll just take my word for that, you can save us all a lot of grief.' Sure, Kid. But *you* tell her. Not me."

"Why not? I don't mean me. She doesn't hardly know me. But she'd believe you, wouldn't she? You said you've known her since she was yea high to a tree stump. Surely you could explain it to her."

"Hell, Kid, she'd just close her ears and set her jaw and claim I was just trying to save my job and my friends. There's nothing blinder than a female with visions of a wedding veil over her eyes, Kid. She won't listen to me or her mama or anyone else but that bastard Wayne now. Even if her daddy was alive, she wouldn't listen to him. He could've laid the law down to her, but even he couldn't've convinced her that the sun rises in the East if that boy told her to expect it in the West."

"Yeah, maybe," he said softly. I might have expected some indignation or anger, but he sounded more thoughtful than mad. I didn't think much about it at the time.

# CHAPTER 30

The FR-Connected Bar made quite a procession going in for the annual Fourth of July pic-nic. There were so many of us we practically made an army. The women in their gig leading, the cow crew bunched behind them like a troop of cavalry, the hay crew packed into wagons next like a platoon of infantry in train, and the kid and me coming along last with the light wagon loaded to the point of groaning. We were carrying the food.

The boys had earned themselves some fun in town, both crews of them. Behind us the haying was well under way, with the second barn nearly full. Every fence post and staple of the miles and miles of bob wire had been grabbed hold of and shaken to check for hidden looseness. There was no way to count how many new posts had been cut and trimmed and set deep into the ground where an old one had shown the least sign of rot or breakage — and there is something about a fence post that seems to make your average cow believe it was put there for scratching-against purposes, so that they get knocked down all too frequently.

At headquarters the whole place looked practically brand-new. Boys who normally wouldn't think of turning a hand at work that wasn't done from a saddle had rigged ladders and platforms and taught themselves how to use a hammer.

Pete Chapman had admitted to a hidden talent for splitting shake shingles. He said it was the main reason he'd left home those years before, but he scrounged a froe from somewhere — I didn't think we'd had one stashed anywhere on the place, but maybe I was wrong — and the boys kept him hopping to meet their demand for the roof work they were doing.

It took two trips to town with the big wagon, badly needed though it was for hauling hay, to carry all the paint Jess demanded, but as soon as it was on hand, the boys slurped it up and slopped it on so that the buildings looked fresh and neat and new.

Even the pens had been gone over to straighten out the sags and breaks. And normally there is nothing with a more ramshackle look about it than a working corral, for they do take a pounding.

A remount service buyer with his tag-along collection of experts and advisers and horse handlers had come by with a thick wad of currency and a special detail of four soldiers to guard his satchel, and Jess had told him to go away. To come back in another month or so when there'd be time to talk to him and show the horses. Right then Jess couldn't spare the man-power to do the sorting and showing. From the way the fellow — a civilian veterinarian, he was — was admiring our stout three-year-olds, I was guessing he'd be back.

If there was much of anything that hadn't yet been done around the place, it was because Jess hadn't yet thought of it. And I sure could not think of what it might have been either. He had been some kind of thorough.

We hit town with a whoop and a holler from the haying boys, and everyone scattered there.

This was another of the yearly occasions when everybody but just everybody made it his business to be in Warcry. It didn't matter if the Fourth *was* smack in the middle of our haying season; it was the Fourth and we were going to by damn celebrate it.

Whatever else might need doing was

dropped where it was, and for the next few days our places could get along without us.

The merchants in town had strung banners and brightly colored streamers across the streets from one roof peak to another. Small boys ran around with cigars in their hands — as useful as punk for lighting firecrackers and also handy for taking a puff on a dare. Sluttish horses were definitely out of place here, for not many of those boys could resist the temptations such a crowd of people and animals put before them.

There were no merchandise displays this time, but some wagons had been chained together and covered with planking to make a speaking stand for county officials and any other politicians who could be persuaded to come. Our own county crowd, of course, couldn't have been kept away by a tribe of wild Indians, but sometimes it was hard to get outsiders to come lend some class to the festivities. One year we'd had a United States senator for the main speaker, but this year all we'd been able to get was Judge Leo T. Hacker. At least he was a circuit judge and had once been a state senator.

The fire department provided a drum and bugle corps, and the school had a brass and percussion band — which would have been called a drum and bugle corps too, I guess,

if that title hadn't already been taken —
and the Masons wore their aprons, while
the Knights turned out in full regalia.

It was considered traditional that everyone
come into town on the Fourth itself rather
than coming in early and sleeping over. It
made for an early start by those of us who
lived further out, but there was good reason
for it. It let us stick with the haying that
much longer. And it put all the speechmaking in the evening after the small fry had
been stuffed with food and were worn down
enough that they'd not wiggle and squawl
so much — and so it wouldn't be so damned
hot. One year we'd had the speeches first
and quickly realized our mistake. There
wasn't enough brush around Warcry to
build arbors for shade, and the crowd came
close to melting into one huge grease
puddle before it was over.

Out beyond the speaking stand the town
people had cobbled together long benches
to hold all the food people brought in with
them. There was no way to find enough
chairs for everyone, so the eating would be
done on blankets or tarps spread on the
ground or in wagon boxes for the more
fastidious. Or those of us who couldn't get
up and down so easily anymore.

I drove the wagon out to the benches so

the food could be laid out. I passed Ransom Biedecker on the way. The old devil was wearing his G.A.R. cap again though we had asked and asked him not to. Every time he did, he ended up in a fistfight with Wallace Hart, and neither of those old gentlemen was of an age for such rowdy activity. Wallace had been a courier under J. E. B. Stuart's command and still did not appreciate any damnyankee — which was one word, he insisted — reminders.

Natalie directed the kid where and how to put our stuff, most of which she had cooked herself. For this affair I supplied only the pies, and this year especially I appreciated that. With double the usual crew to feed, the kid and I had been kept at it pretty good.

Katy had already dropped off of their rig in town. I could well imagine who she'd be looking for. I noticed that she was always the one who had to go do the looking, too, and he still hadn't had the decency to come do his courting in her home the way a gentleman ought. I hadn't seen him out at the place once, which may have been just as well. If he'd come around out there, he might've been awful sore on the ride home. At this point there wouldn't have been a hell of a lot to lose.

When the tables were loaded, I parked the

wagon, and the kid and I walked over to the open field where the school kids were having sack races and such. The men had been matching horse races out beyond there since morning, but all the really good races would've already been run, and anyway I didn't want to get into any wagering this time. I didn't figure I could afford any losses now, and there isn't a man alive who can find the fastest horse every time. Not until the race has been run.

We watched the children burn off energy until someone in town decided that all the tables were full and everyone'd had enough time to mill and chatter. The announcement of chow time was made by having the fire engine drive up and down the streets and out onto the play field, the bell clanging wildly and some partially drunk volunteer fire fighters hollering.

"If we don't get there soon, Kid, it'll all be gone," I said.

The kid gave me a skeptical look and raised an eyebrow. And no wonder. He'd seen how those benches were loaded. Every woman in the valley felt duty-bound to bring enough for her own people and twice that many more. We probably could've invited the flatland county to the north of us and not asked them to bring a thing.

Our boys had already found the wagon and were getting tin plates and utensils from the boxes. We got in there to grab ours too.

There wasn't any order to the serving. It was all a matter of jumping at the nearest table and loading up on whatever was handy. I pitched in there with them and when I got clear of the crowd again found I had a plateload of ham and corned beef and boiled eggs and potato salad and pickled onions. I went back to the wagon so I could sit while I got rid of it.

The kid was already there, and either he was becoming a mighty fast eater or he hadn't taken hardly a thing. He said he just wasn't very hungry right then, and he did look a little pale. It couldn't have been too serious, I figured, because he'd packed down a breakfast that I hadn't hardly believed a skinny fellow could hold.

I finished my mountain of stuff as quickly as the kid picked his way through the little bit he had taken. He offered to bring me a refill, so I took him up on it and proceeded to stuff myself that much more while he ran over to the Bull Shooter and brought back a beer. I'd offered him one too when he suggested going, but he refused. I didn't know who had fixed all the stuff I ate, but there were some pretty fine cooks in that group whoever they were.

People would be drifting to and from the tables the rest of the afternoon, but after a while the edge was well off everyone's appetites. The children flocked back toward the play field, and the grown-ups began to drift around visiting.

We stashed our plates under the wagon seat and took a tour around the pic-nic area. I saw Natalie in an arm-waving, hand-fluttering conversation with Dorothea Gibson and Alice Sidlow and a coupla other ladies. She looked happier and more relaxed than I'd seen her in months.

I howdied people here and there and stopped to talk with Jess and Handy and Burton Vechter. Burton had a place east of town. He ran heavy on stock cows and sold his calves as yearlings for feeding-out back in corn country.

"What's this I hear about you maybe leaving the Senns?" he was asking Jess as we came up to them.

Jess looked uncomfortable, but with all the boys knowing about it, there was no way to keep it out of all the conversations that would be taking place this day. "It's true enough," he said.

Burton was not wanting to push him for all the gory details, though. Instead he said,

"I'm about in a position to be needing a good man to help run my place, Jess, and I can't think of a better one. If you'd consider it, I would be real proud to have you as foreman of the Double Y."

Jess's eyes widened a little in surprise. "Why, I thank you, Burton. I surely do. But . . . I'll have to turn you down. The truth is that I won't be looking for anything in the valley here. You can understand that, I s'pect."

"Sure. I was afraid you'd feel that way about it. If you change your mind before next spring, let me know."

The talk shifted to horses, whose horse had beat whose horse in the matches that morning and what each losing rider had done wrong. Funny how the winning jockey never seemed to've made any mistakes, but the more money a fellow had placed on a losing mount, the poorer his rider had done.

Handy and Burton were arguing about the merits of a colt by Sam Jasson's running stud when Jess stiffened like a bird dog coming on point. The color drained out of his face, and there was sheer contempt in his eyes and pulling at his lips. I knew right away what it was and reached out to take him by the arm before I turned to look. Wayne was strolling near, with Katy on his arm. It was obvious neither of them had noticed us. They stopped to talk with Mrs. Purty and Mrs. Archer, the Rev. Archer's wife.

" 'Scuse me," the kid mumbled. I looked at him in time to see his Adam's apple bob once nervously before he started toward the happy couple. He was moving in a casual saunter that didn't look quite real.

A sudden, powerful curiosity drew me along behind him.

# CHAPTER 31

The Keystone Kid stopped beside the little group. He nodded politely to the ladies and to Wayne. He took his hat off and held it in both hands before his stomach.

"Miss Senn," he asked softly, "may I bring you and the ladies a glass of iced lemonade from the tables?" The way he said it and the way he was holding himself, he came across not so much as polite but as a meek little flunky trying to ingratiate himself with his betters.

For a moment I wondered if I'd been mistaken about the kid all this time. I wondered if maybe he was fixing to do some bowing and scraping in the hope Wayne might let him hang on to his job.

You could practically see the hackles rising on Wayne Tynell's neck. He sucked in air and puffed his chest, and he began to show purple from the collar up.

"Thank you, Kid, but . . . ," Katy began.

She never got a chance to finish.

Wayne's hand lashed out. He grabbed the kid by the shirt front and rattled his teeth. "Why, you miserable, creeping little toady," he snarled. "You wouldn't work on my place if you crawled on your belly to beg for the job."

I was behind the kid and couldn't see his expression. The women were staring at Wayne with shocked, almost horrified looks on them. I still don't know what the kid could have done just then, but something sure-God happened. Wayne's eyes popped wide and then narrowed down to tiny slits.

"You little bastard," Wayne hissed. He transferred the kid's bunched shirt front to his left hand, clamped his right into a fist, and buried it in the kid's unprotected belly. The kid doubled over so violently the front of his shirt ripped, leaving Wayne with a handful of cloth and the kid writhing on the ground.

Wayne was absolutely furious. He was breathing so hard he was panting, and it would not have been from exertion. He'd only thrown the one punch.

The kid was on his feet in no time and standing face to face with Wayne. "I didn't ask to fight you," he said. The pain must have been fierce, but it never entered his voice. His tone was mild and completely calm.

Wayne's left hand shot forward again. Almost before he moved — maybe it *was* before he moved — the kid's face registered shock and surprise. This time the kid ducked. He flailed weakly toward Wayne's nose as he moved, but the punch, if that was what it was, didn't even come close to landing.

Tynell batted the kid's arm away like a man shooing a gnat and stepped forward. Again that big right fist came forward. Again the kid was doubled over and was dumped to the ground.

He came back to his feet, but not quite so quickly. He staggered as he came upright, but he grinned and stepped toward Tynell.

Wayne seemed to measure him as the kid moved forward. The big, tough cowman sneered at his younger, slimmer opponent. He drew his fist back with slow deliberation. When the kid was just where he wanted him, Wayne shifted forward onto his left leg and drove his fist into the kid's face. His full weight was behind the blow.

The kid's head snapped back. Blood streamed from his nose and a split upper lip. The power of it sent him reeling backward on rubber legs, but somehow he kept his feet. He caught his balance, shook his head like a hound caught by skunk scent, but when he moved again it was forward. Tynell waited for him. The bigger man's fury was barely controlled and seemed to be growing.

The women had been staring in shocked silence, but now Katy began to scream at Wayne, telling him to stop, telling him that was enough. I don't believe her words registered on Wayne. They did on others. The words and the shrill, frightened way she was yelling them.

So far only those people immediately around us had realized what was going on, but now others heard and saw and began to rush toward us.

Jess came up behind me and tried to shoulder past. He looked every bit as furious as Wayne was. I grabbed his arm and pulled him back. Stopped him, anyway. I was jerked forward as much as he came back. I hauled Jess's ear down close and hissed, "Leave 'em be, dammit."

"You're crazy," Jess whispered.

"The kid walked right into it. He had to know what Wayne would do. If he had reason enough to ask for this kind of beating, we oughta leave him to it."

Jess gave me an odd look, but he held still

when I let go of him.

When I looked back, the kid was down again. I couldn't tell if he was cut more on the face. There was so much blood it just wasn't possible to see where it was all coming from. He rolled belly down, got his hands under him, and shoved. He made it to his knees, looked up at Wayne . . . and if it wasn't so silly to think such a thing, I would've sworn then and there that he winked at Tynell.

As the kid came to his feet again, Wayne stepped in close and ripped a low, hard right into the body. The kid grunted as the air was driven from him. Wayne shifted his weight and had time to let fly with a left as well before the kid went down.

Wayne stood over him, triumphant pleasure written across his face. He seemed to be feeling somewhat calmer now. He stepped back and looked with satisfaction at the kid lying bloody on the ground.

Again the kid rolled, shoved. He came swaying to his knees though he had already taken a fearsome pounding without once returning any of the punishment.

The kid shook his head. Droplets of blood fell into the dust. He looked around to make sure none of the women were in a position to see him too clearly.

He did his best to grin and soundlessly mouthed an exceedingly vulgar word toward Tynell. It was about as deliberately provoking as anything could ever be.

I might have been surprised, but Wayne seemed to be purely astounded. For a moment he stood over the kid and stared at him as if he could not believe what he had seen.

If Tynell was wondering if he might have been mistaken, the kid clarified it for him. Damned if the kid didn't do it again.

Wayne was livid. Blood rushed to his head, turning his face purple. He trembled violently and clenched his fists until they were white with the strain. A sound was torn from him that was close to a growl.

Katy could not have known what he was going to do, but it was clear he was about to explode. She darted forward. She shouted his name and tried to step in front of him.

I don't think Wayne had any idea who it was or ever really saw her there. Something was between him and the kid, and he swept it aside.

Katy was flung to the side. She fell in a heap. The other ladies dropped protectively but too late to their knees beside her. The glares they sent toward Wayne were filled with sheer loathing.

Wayne never saw the looks they gave him. He groaned aloud in his anger and shifted slightly to his left. A tiny backward movement of his right foot gave scant warning.

The pointed toe of his right boot slashed in a rising arc toward the kid's face.

There was no time now for anyone else to help, and the kid must have been too battered to be able to duck aside. He barely had time enough to begin bringing his hands up in a futile attempt to block the vicious kick.

The kid's left hand moved far enough but he hadn't the strength to stop the force of the kick. The power of it smashed into his face. At least his hand was between his face and the wickedly pointed boot toe. It was the back of his own hand that was driven into him.

He was thrown onto his back, unconscious before he hit the ground. His face looked like so much raw meat.

Tynell raised his boot high and would have stomped the defenseless kid. There could have been no question about that from anyone who saw him.

Jess had already launched himself into the air, and Billy — undoubtedly drawn to the fun of watching a fight — tackled Wayne from the other side. They were not alone, though they were the first to reach him. Wayne was knocked off his feet, and a dozen or more grasping hands dragged him away from the kid. Inside the melee you could see the rise and fall of fists as some of the boys expressed their disapproval before they hustled Wayne away.

Jess joined me on the ground beside the kid. Someone, I didn't see who, handed us a wet towel and a cloth-wrapped bundle of the ice that had been packed around a lemonade tub.

Behind us I could hear Katy crying and the still quavering voices of the frightened, angry women who were trying to comfort her. Natalie rushed up and began crying too.

It seemed an awfully long time before we could bring the kid around to any awareness of the world around him. When we did, he tried to grin past what few teeth he had left.

# CHAPTER 32

None of our crew got to hear any of the political speeches that Fourth of July. We herded everybody together and headed for home, not even taking time to load our platters and bowls and such from the tables. Mrs. Archer stepped forward and assured Natalie she would find it all and send it out by way of Mrs. Abbot or with the Rev. Archer if need be.

We wouldn't have waited anyway. We wanted to get the kid — and Katy — the hell out of there.

Natalie insisted on riding in the back of the wagon, where we had laid the kid on some blankets, and she wanted Katy to ride there with her. The light driving team hitched to their gig was tied on a lead behind the wagon. From the way Nat insisted on Katy's presence and from the firm, unmotherly set of her jaw I was wondering if Natalie wanted to make sure her daughter had plenty of time to admire Wayne's handiwork. Natalie Senn and the good ladies of Warcry seemed to have about the same opinion of Wayne Tynell now as I'd held for a longer period.

The kid was sleeping in spite of the jostling of the wagon.

We drove out of town in the soft, summer twilight. The first sprinkle of stars was showing. Behind us we could hear the dull thud of fireworks. Roman candles and exploding rockets were outshining the stars back there. It was going to be a long ride home, time to start breakfast when we got there.

When we were clear of the town, Katy shifted closer to the kid. She bent close so she could see in the little light remaining in the sky. The sun itself had long since disappeared behind the western wall of mountain peaks.

Katy looked at him for a time, snuffling and shaking her head. She smoothed his hair and turned toward the front of the wagon.

"Would you . . . please ask Mr. Barnes to come here?" she asked. She sounded rather stiff.

"Sure, child." I gave a holler, and Jess bumped his horse forward to join us.

"Yeah?"

"Katryn Elizabeth would like to have a word with you." I turned to Katy. "Should I leave?"

She giggled. "To where? No. I want you to hear it too." She grew more serious again.

Jess caught the mood. He nudged his gelding alongside the wagon and stepped into the box. He sat and let the horse trail beside at the end of the reins.

"I want to ask you something," Katy said. She ducked her head. "Has . . . has Wayne always been . . . like that?"

Natalie looked at Jess, and he looked at me. Hell, I wasn't afraid to say it. "You can just bet your sweet . . . whatever you want to bet he has, little girl. For as long as I've known him, he's been a son of bitch, and I do *not* beg your pardon for using the term."

"Oh." She looked at the kid and then back to me. "He did that on purpose, didn't he?"

"Yes."

She sat without speaking for several slow miles. No one else seemed to be in a chatty mood either.

She became restless after a while. She fidgeted, checked the kid's pulse, and smoothed his hair again. She turned back to the rest of us and said, "I will not be getting married, of course. Do you think . . . would you consider staying on, continue to run the ranch? There wouldn't be any . . . interference from the house. Not from me, anyway. And you never had any trouble with Mama. It was all my doing."

"I'd still close the gap," Jess said. "I wouldn't change my mind about that. There'd be trouble with your neighbors for the first time ever in this valley. It might not die away easily."

"I know," she said. "That's what I've been thinking about. More than the rest of it, even. I'll have plenty of time to think about the rest of it later. So will you?"

"I . . . *we* will do some thinking on it," Jess said. "No need to decide now."

The big horses plodded on toward home.

Two months later the Keystone Kid left his bunk in the kitchen and moved into the bunkhouse with the other riding hands. Of course, he never will make a top hand. For one thing he just naturally is not strong enough to do the heavy wrestling when a steer is bogged or an old cow needs to be doctored.

For another thing, the little snot never had enough practice at it to be really good. He hadn't been at it more than two workings before he decided he'd turn to the book-keeping and marketing side of the business.

Even if he had to marry the boss's daughter to do it. Personally, I think he just wanted to have me referring to *him* as the old man.

At least he does have a good mind. And a world full of guts. Why, with a combination like that, the kid could end up governor or maybe a senator or something. Just you wait and see. Me, I wouldn't be at all surprised.

# ABOUT THE AUTHOR

**Frank Roderus** wrote his first story at the age of five. A newspaper reporter for nine years, he now lives in Florida, where he raises American quarter horses and pursues his favorite hobby, researching history of the American West. His previous books were *Journey to Utah* and *The 33 Brand*.

The employees of Thorndike Press hope you have enjoyed this Large Print book. All our Thorndike, Wheeler, and Kennebec Large Print titles are designed for easy reading, and all our books are made to last. Other Thorndike Press Large Print books are available at your library, through selected bookstores, or directly from us.

For information about titles, please call:
(800) 223-1244

or visit our Web site at:
http://gale.cengage.com/thorndike

To share your comments, please write:
Publisher
Thorndike Press
10 Water St., Suite 310
Waterville, ME 04901

CPSIA information can be obtained
at www.ICGtesting.com
Printed in the USA
FFOW05n0238050514